THE JOURNEY OF LOVE

Book of Love, Book Twelve

Meara Platt

ARE YOU SIGNED UP FOR DRAGONBLADE'S BLOG?

You'll get the latest news and information on exclusive giveaways, exclusive excerpts, coming releases, sales, free books, cover reveals and more.

Check out our complete list of authors, too!

No spam, no junk. That's a promise!

Sign Up Here

www.dragonbladepublishing.com

Dearest Reader;

Thank you for your support of a small press. At Dragonblade Publishing, we strive to bring you the highest quality Historical Romance from some of the best authors in the business. Without your support, there is no 'us', so we sincerely hope you adore these stories and find some new favorite authors along the way.

Happy Reading!

CEO, Dragonblade Publishing

Additional Dragonblade books by Author Meara Platt

The Moonstone Landing Series
Moonstone Landing (novella)
Moonstone Angel (novella)
The Moonstone Duke
The Moonstone Marquess
The Moonstone Major

The Book of Love Series
The Look of Love
The Touch of Love
The Taste of Love
The Song of Love
The Scent of Love
The Kiss of Love
The Chance of Love
The Gift of Love
The Heart of Love
The Hope of Love (novella)
The Promise of Love
The Wonder of Love
The Journey of Love
The Dream of Love (novella)
The Treasure of Love
The Dance of Love
The Miracle of Love
The Remembrance of Love (novella)

Dark Gardens Series
Garden of Shadows
Garden of Light
Garden of Dragons

Garden of Destiny
Garden of Angels

The Farthingale Series
If You Wished For Me (A Novella)

The Lyon's Den Series
Kiss of the Lyon
The Lyon's Surprise
Lyon in the Rough

Pirates of Britannia Series
Pearls of Fire

De Wolfe Pack: The Series
Nobody's Angel
Kiss an Angel
Bhrodi's Angel

Also from Meara Platt
Aislin
All I Want for Christmas

CHAPTER ONE

Devonshire, England
July 1821

"WELL, IF IT isn't Lorcan Brayden!"

Cammy Farthingale groaned as she heard the mail coach driver call out with irritating joviality to the rider whose horse was keeping stride beside them while their conveyance jostled along the well-traveled road to Barnstaple.

"What are you doing here, Lor? Is it official business?" The driver brought his team to an abrupt halt, sending Cammy toppling out of her seat inside the coach. She landed atop Mrs. Dalrimple's crate of chickens, which happened to be perched on the opposite bench.

"Yes, Matthias," Lorcan said in his deep, resonant voice that could melt a woman's heart. "I'm afraid it is official."

Cammy leaped up as the chickens began to peck at her bottom.

"Ouch!" she cried, bumping her head on the coach's roof.

Nasty creatures.

They hadn't shut up the entire ride, and they stank like old socks.

The other two passengers, old Mrs. Dalrimple and a smarmy looking gentleman by the name of Mr. Pryne, who had leered at her the entire ride, did not smell any better.

Lorcan had a lopsided grin on his face as he peered inside and cast his gaze on her much-maligned backside. "You have feathers stuck to your…"

Gad, had he seen her tumble onto those indignant chickens?

She hastily brushed the feathers off. "I am not going anywhere with you, Lorcan."

"I am afraid you have no choice." He dug into his breast pocket and removed a billfold that contained a shiny object resembling a badge with an impressive crown embossed in the center of it. "I am taking you into custody."

The driver leaned over to speak to the other passengers. "Nothing to worry about, folks. Everyone remain calm. He is an agent of the Crown."

"I knew she was a criminal," muttered Mrs. Dalrimple.

"I am not a criminal!" Cammy scowled at the unkempt, old woman and retained her scowl to now cast it on Lorcan, who did not appear in the least remorseful.

He tossed her another lopsided grin.

She refused to find it devastatingly appealing, even though—unfortunately—it was. He so rarely smiled or grinned or showed any expression other than seriousness. But when he did, his entire face lightened, bringing out the handsome lines of his jaw and high cheekbones, not to mention the seductive curve of his lips. "You cannot do this to me. We must be no more than an hour or two from Barnstaple. Please, Lorcan. Let me go home."

"I'm sorry. Can't do that. You will have to come with me."

"Did she murder someone?" Mr. Pryne asked.

"No, I did not murder anyone!" Cammy cast the odious man a glower that warned she would do him bodily harm if he opened his mouth again.

"She's a Cyprian," Mrs. Dalrimple intoned.

"I knew it," Mr. Pryne muttered.

She gasped. "I am no such thing!"

How could they believe she was a common trollop? Wishful thinking on Mr. Pryne's part, no doubt. He was now openly leering at her chest.

"Toss down her travel pouch, Matthias. I'll take it with us," Lorcan said in a deep, commanding voice of authority, completely overlooking that she was not sought after by the Crown, and he had no right to take her anywhere.

The driver scampered to the baggage boot and handed it to him without a moment's hesitation. Lorcan checked inside, no doubt to make certain it contained her precious book, then nodded to confirm it was there as he secured the pouch to the back of his saddle. "Cammy, please."

He opened the coach door and reached out his hand to her.

She might have put up more of a fuss had he not been so polite about abducting her. Besides, the ride to Barnstaple would now be impossible with Mr. Pryne propositioning her, Mrs. Dalrimple convinced she was a murderess, and those chickens lurking in wait for a chance to peck at her bottom again.

Their coach driver was now chattering about Lorcan and his feats of valor. "Saved my life, he did. More than once. Remember those times, Lor?"

"I do, Matthias."

"We were plagued by a band of ruthless highwaymen who wouldn't think twice about shooting their own grandmothers. Lorcan singlehandedly took them down. I heard you were knighted for your deeds. Were you, Lor?"

"Yes, Matthias."

Cammy stared at him, utterly stunned. "You are *Sir* Lorcan? And you did not once think to mention it to me?"

He did not bother to respond, just continued to wait her out with infuriating patience.

Typical of the wretched man.

He was known for his fierce gaze, his silver eyes turning cold and expressionless as they bored into you.

Except, his gorgeous eyes had never felt cold to her.

Others found him frightening, but she liked the look of him. Dark hair. Big, hard body. A fierce expression that somehow always softened when he glanced at her.

"Ready, Cammy?" He still had his hand out to help her onto his horse.

Her eyes widened. "I cannot ride on your lap!"

"Then walk, if you like. I'll ride alongside you."

"I am not walking all the way to Taunton. It will take days to reach it on foot."

He shrugged. "Then ride with me."

"I cannot ride on your lap!"

He arched an eyebrow. "Shall we waste more time talking in circles?" He scooped her up by the waist and hauled her onto his muscled thighs, seated sideways. "Safe trip, Matthias."

The man grinned at Lorcan. "You as well, Lor. Lucky man. That's some official duty. What do I get? Chickens."

The coach rolled off in a cloud of dust.

Cammy closed her eyes and pressed her face to Lorcan's chest as the wind swirled the dust around them. She felt his arms protectively close about her body, then he whirled his horse in the opposite direction to ride clear of the ball of dust.

"Are you all right?" he asked, stopping a moment later beside a bend in the road where the air was clear.

"No, I am not fine. Why did you come after me?"

"Your Aunt Charlotte sent me. Your sister is worried about you, as well. Since my brother is besotted with your sister, it means he is worried, too. You should not have run off like that."

Her sister, Willow, had just married Lorcan's brother, Shayne. In truth, she felt bad about deceiving them and probably ruining their newly wedded bliss. "What did you expect me to do? I've been telling everyone I have no desire to go to London, but no one will listen. I'll run away from you the first chance I get if you insist on behaving like their hired assassin."

"A little theatrical, aren't you?" He spurred his horse along the road back to Taunton.

Cammy was jounced with each loping stride, so she shifted position to avoid pressing into his chest and obscenely rubbing against it. The man had a solid chest and muscled arms that circled around her like steel bands.

He was the size of a granite mountain and just as hard.

"There, that's better," she muttered even though facing outward was little improvement. Lorcan's arms were still pinned around her and positioned within inches of her bosom. To his credit, he was doing his best to avoid touching her *there*.

But she had a full-sized bosom.

Not to mention her bottom was rubbing against his thighs. "Stop your horse. I am going to walk."

He did not appear amused. "No."

She had not expected him to refuse. "I'll jump off."

"Go ahead."

His mount was going too fast.

She would break her neck if she tried now.

She gave up and eased back against his chest. "You are a beast."

"You are not the first to call me that." Those muscled bands, also known as Lorcan's arms, remained protectively around her. Well, at least he did not smell like those foul chickens.

Actually, he smelled quite nice.

Leather and musk.

His breath held a trace of mint.

Yes, much nicer than those chickens.

They rode eastward for what felt like an hour until Lorcan drew back on the reins, dismounted, and led his horse to drink at a nearby stream. Since he had not bothered to help her down, she remained seated in the saddle and now scowled at him.

"Don't think to steal my horse. She only responds to me."

"As all women do, I'm sure," she said with open sarcasm.

He sighed. "Are you thirsty, Cammy?"

She folded her arms across her chest and tossed him a stubborn look.

"As you wish. You are only depriving yourself." He lifted her from the saddle without warning, set her down on a patch of grass, then left her side to kneel by the water and scoop some into the cup of his hand. "Are you sure you don't want to drink?"

She turned her back to him.

"Stubborn," he muttered and took it himself. She heard him slurp…perhaps it was his horse now slurping that cool liquid from the stream.

Cammy was hot, dusty, and thirsty.

"Fine," she said in surrender. Yes, she was stubborn but not completely stupid. She knelt on a rock by the bank of the stream and moistened her handkerchief to rub the cool, damp cloth over her face and neck.

Lorcan cleared his throat. "I'd move off that rock if I were you."

She ignored him, rinsed off her hands, and then cupped them to draw water from the swiftly moving current.

She swallowed the cool liquid, smiling, for it felt so refreshing sliding down her throat.

She leaned over to draw a little more, then yelped as the rock suddenly tipped forward, and she fell into the water. "Lorcan!"

It wasn't deep, but she'd tumbled in head first, and now all of her was soaked.

"What is it with you Farthingales and water?" He reached over and lifted her out, picking her up as though she weighed no more than a feather, even though she was sopping wet.

She shoved several wet tendrils of hair off her face. "You might have warned me!"

He cast her another of those ever-suffering glances that she was growing to detest. "I told you to get off that rock."

"You *suggested* I move off it. A mere suggestion is not a warning." Her gown made a sucking sound as she started to walk away. She stopped and instead tried to wring the water out of it.

The wind had cooled only slightly and had barely picked up force as sundown approached, but the water had been cold. It now turned the breeze frigid as it blew straight through her gown and into her bones.

She began to shiver.

"You'll have to take off your clothes." Lorcan walked to her travel pouch tied to the back of his saddle. He began to search through her belongings, then turned to her and groaned. "All you have in here is that book, a hairbrush, and a nightrail that is so scanty, it wouldn't cover a mouse's arse. Did you not think to bring even a change of undergarments?"

"It is not at all scanty. How dare you suggest I…" She snorted. "I wanted to travel light. I did not expect to be hauled off the mail coach by a big Brayden ape."

"Thank you for that flattering description of me," he said dryly.

She tipped her head up in indignation, refusing to feel sorry for insulting him. "Why would I bother to take anything but essentials when I knew I would be home within a day? What I did not expect was to be mauled by—"

"Got it. Big ape. You have to get out of those clothes," he said, cutting her off before she hurled another insult. "You'll fall ill if you keep them on. That water was cold. Your lips are already turning purple. And I am mentioning only your lips to be polite."

"What do you mean?"

"Really, Cammy? Must I say it? Your body is displaying other signs of cold."

She looked down at her herself and gasped. "Don't you dare stare at my chest. I am not taking off my clothes. Do you think I am so stupid as to prance around naked in front of you?"

She was being harsh with him, but it was his fault for coming after her. He was taking far too much delight in interfering with her plans. Nor did she appreciate his smirking at her discomfort. "I wouldn't be in this predicament if not for you, Lorcan. I think you ought to give me your clothes."

"Yes, that's an idea."

Her eyes popped wide as he drew the shirt off his back in one magnificent, rippling motion and handed it to her. "We'll camp here tonight. We couldn't have traveled much farther anyway. This is as good a spot as any to stop. Take off those wet things and put this on."

The shirt slipped out of her hands.

She couldn't move.

She couldn't breathe.

Were his muscles real?

His body was a bronze, sculpted wonder.

He sighed and picked up his shirt. "Must I undress you?"

She nodded.

He made a choking sound.

Then she realized what he had just said. "No! I mean, I'll do it myself."

He let out the breath he must have been holding. "Call me once you are decent," he grumbled, stuffing his shirt back in her hands. "I'll hang up your gown and undergarments to dry."

"All right, but wait. The lacings are knotted. I can't..." She looked up at him. "Will you help? No, I take it back. I *demand* you help. This is all your fault."

"Raise your arms." He moved to stand behind her. His touch shot tingles through her body. "All right. Done."

He strode off into the nearby woods.

She hastily removed her clothes and put on his shirt, which was far too big. What served as an opening at his collar plunged down almost to her navel. Thankfully, it had laces she could pull tight. She did them up. But his shirt only reached to her knees, baring the rest of her legs.

She would hit him with a stick if he ogled her.

Since her hair was also a wet, tangled mess, she took out her hairbrush from her travel pouch and began to brush her hair.

Lorcan made no comment when he returned.

Instead, he started a warming fire and then took her wet clothes and neatly placed them on a nearby tree branch. Once done, he took out his knife, grabbed a long, thin fallen branch, and began to whittle it into a spear.

He held that knife as though he was quite expert at using it. "What are you doing?"

"Going fishing. You want to eat tonight?"

She nodded and settled beside the fire. "You berated me for failing to pack clothes, but you did not bring any either."

"I was mad with worry about you," he said with a surprising depth of feeling. "Besides, I did not expect to have to give you the shirt off my back. Are you all right? Warmer now?"

"Yes." She sighed. "Can I do anything to help?"

He cast her another of his heart-melting grins. "Just keep away from the water."

As night fell, she was comfortably settled beside the fire and had eaten the most delicious trout anyone had ever prepared for her. She was sated and tired, but where was she to sleep?

Lorcan must have understood what she was thinking.

He rose, and working by firelight, began to build a makeshift shelter. "I'll give you my blanket, and you can sleep in there," he said once he was done. "I'll leave you my oilcloth as well. Put it on if it starts raining."

"What about you?"

He arched an eyebrow. "What about me?"

She cleared her throat, and her heart began to race. "Where will you sleep?"

"Here, beside the fire. I'll use my jacket for a blanket and my saddle for a pillow." He studied her expression. "Don't fret about me, Cammy. I'm used to camping out. This is a jaunt in the park. It is far less pleasant in winter."

"I've never camped out before."

He cast her yet another heart-melting grin. "I know. It is obvious."

The kindling crackled as he tossed on some more wood to keep the fire going. She was seated close to the fire and now inhaled the scent of burning bark, fresh country air, and the lingering trace of smoked fish.

She didn't mind at all.

In truth, there was something quite exhilarating about being outdoors on a starry night, a full moon glowing overhead, and the gentle rush of the stream only a few steps away. She heard the whirr of crickets and the occasional croak of a bullfrog.

Of course, she found all this pleasant because Lorcan was with her.

He looked quite handsome by firelight, his dark hair slightly too long and the ends curling at his neck. His body was big and sleek, his movements graceful, and his muscles rippling as he went about his tasks.

He had a warrior's build and fierceness.

Would he kiss her goodnight?

She was trying to figure out a way to casually ask him when he suddenly moved close and drew her behind him. "Don't say a word and keep down."

She saw the glint of his pistol barrel as he withdrew it from his boot.

"Lorcan," she whispered, suddenly frightened out of her wits as two unsavory-looking men stepped forward.

"Well, what do we have here?" one of them said, emitting a raspy chortle as he edged closer. "Will ye look at that beauty. Keepin' her all to yerself?"

"Touch her, and you're a dead man." The ice in Lorcan's voice sent a shiver through Cammy.

The other man spit on the ground. "Ye look like a clever fellow. No one needs to get hurt here. Just let us take her, and ye'll come to no harm."

"Put your weapons down, walk away, and I will not kill you." Lorcan's tone was lethal and steady. "Is there something about my warning you do not understand?"

The first man shook his head and sighed. "Stubborn, are ye? Perhaps a shot to the gut will change your mind."

Cammy desperately scanned the ground for a weapon to use, but before she had the chance to move, shots were fired. The next thing she knew, Lorcan had pulled her into his arms and was trying to turn her head away from the two villains who had dropped their rifles and were now screaming in fear as they tore back into the woods. One would think demons were on their tails. "They won't be back. I shot them each in the leg."

They had looked as though they were limping. But she had heard them fire first and was more worried about Lorcan. "Did they hit you? Are you all right? Oh, Lor! Tell me."

"I'm fine. Not even a graze."

"Are you certain? Please don't lie to me."

"I never would."

She threw her arms around him and held onto him fiercely. "Thank you for saving my life." Tears began to roll down her cheeks, and her body began to tremble with relief. "This is why I dare not go to London. This always happens." She emitted a racking sob. "Men see me, and they want to have me. They think it is all right to leer and ogle and paw. They think I have no brain or feelings and say the rudest things to me."

"Cammy, I'm so sorry." He stroked her hair, no doubt hoping to calm her. "It's over, sweetheart. You're safe now."

"I'll never be safe. The same will happen in London, only worse because those peers can say or do anything to me, and they will be untouchable."

"No, Cammy. You don't understand."

She looked up at him through her tears. "What don't I understand?"

"Those men…they never saw you. I had you hidden behind me before they entered the clearing." He used his thumb to gently wipe the tears from her eyes.

"But they said they wanted you to turn over the beauty. What were they talking about if not me?"

He groaned lightly. "My horse."

Her cheeks turned fiery with embarrassment. "Your horse?"

"But I can see where the confusion might arise."

"Are you comparing me to your horse? Oh, my heavens! You must think me the most vain, self-absorbed, useless, most frivolous—"

"Cammy, stop. You are none of those things."

She drew away and buried her hands in her face. "And here I was trying to think of a way to get you to kiss me."

She heard his intake of breath. "You wanted me to kiss you?"

"What?" Her stomach sank into her toes, realizing she had just spoken the thought aloud. "No…I…what?"

She stared up at him, her mouth agape.

"Hell of a time to do it," he muttered, crushing his mouth to hers.

CHAPTER TWO

Kissing the luscious Camellia Farthingale was something Lorcan had yearned to do from the moment he had set eyes on her. But this moment of gratification had to be the biggest mistake he had ever made in his twenty-five years of life.

Still, he did not regret it.

Nor did she appear to be regretting it.

He felt the soft give of her lips as his mouth closed over hers with a possessive hunger that surprised even himself. But her lips were sweet and lovely, and so was she. Indeed, she was the prettiest young woman he had ever beheld. "Cammy...sweet heaven..."

The thought of her running off in her state of distress had left him mad with worry. For this reason, he'd wasted no time in leaving the Ashcott Inn to go after her. He was the best man for the task anyway, a professional tracker in his line of work for the Crown. He readily accepted to help when her sister and aunt pleaded for him to find her, for they were desperate to have her safely returned to Taunton.

He was not about to trust anyone else with Cammy anyway. Within minutes of starting his search, he'd learned she had climbed into the wrong mail coach and been riding north toward Gloucester for much of the day. Thank goodness he had thought to do a little questioning before taking off after her. If not, he would have wasted hours riding west to Barnstaple and never finding her.

Of course, he would not have taken her off the coach had it been the one to Barnstaple, for she would have been safe enough once reaching her home. She had grown up in the town, and this is where her parents would be waiting for her. Her father might have been angry to see her return, for both he and her mother had wanted Cammy to have her London season. But they were loving parents and would never have turned her away.

"Lor," she whispered against his lips.

He deepened the kiss, drawing Cammy's exquisite body up against him as he moved his mouth over hers, savoring her warmth and sweetness.

She ought to have smelled like the chickens old Matthias had been carrying on the mail coach. But instead, his nostrils filled with the delightful scent of cinnamon and apples. Well, this explained why he simply wanted to eat her up.

She was delicious.

This girl.

He also realized this was likely her first romantic kiss.

In truth, it was obvious in the way she was responding, startled and yet eager to explore.

"I had better let you up for air," he said with a raspy moan.

"You needn't." Her eyes were still closed, and she was leaning into him. She licked her fleshly lower lip as though to savor his touch, to memorize the soft press of his lips and the light lick of his tongue. "Please don't pull away."

He loved that she trusted him enough to take her guidance from him and wanted more. He drew her up against him, circling his arms around her and lowering his mouth to hers once again. She responded to everything, the touch of his hand, the pressure of his lips, the intimacy of their positions.

She was quite enjoying these new sensations.

All the more reason, he should never have kissed her.

All the more reason, he was glad that he had.

But having done all these things, including now spending the night alone with her, he knew there was no getting around the obvious. She had taken the wrong coach, and that would not remain a secret very long.

He would have to marry her. It did not matter that he was not going to touch her beyond this kiss.

He'd purposely kept it gentle because this was her first experience. There would be no roaming hands or bodies grinding together with ardent urgency.

Torrid haste and hunger would have to wait.

He would teach her all that love between them could be once they were married.

Despite knowing he ought to draw away before things became more complicated than they already were, he buried his hands in her hair and cupped the back of her head to gently draw her into another kiss. He was never good with words, had no romantic phrases to spout to convey how strongly he felt about her.

What could he say?

He was no more prepared for marriage than she was.

"Lor," she whispered, the sound of her sweet voice rippling through him like a summer wind on water, "I never knew it could be like this."

Nor had he.

Until now, he'd been with women simply to satisfy his physical urges whenever they arose. Taking a wife would bring vast changes to his life and the work he loved. "Cammy," he said, nibbling her neck, "we have to talk about this."

"I know. Oh…heavens, that's nice. Not yet."

"I have to, before it goes too far." He was not used to losing control, but this luscious innocent had him almost mindless. He was not prepared for the impact she was having on his senses. "Or do you not care? We'll have to marry anyway."

"Marry?" She pushed out of his arms and stared up at him in confusion.

"Yes. What did you think this was about?" For several years

now, he had been one of the Crown's best agents, taking on the toughest assignments and never failing to successfully complete them because his instincts and cold calculation had never failed him.

He had stayed alive through some of the most dangerous assignments because he never made mistakes.

But as he noted the rising panic in Cammy's eyes...had he been wrong? Had he misread the big-eyed looks and breathless smiles she had been casting him from the moment they'd met?

Had he been so caught up in those ocean-blue eyes and glorious, dark gold tresses, not to mention that body so beautiful it could stop a man's heart, that he never considered what she actually wanted?

He blew out a breath and took her hand. "Cammy, I know this situation is bad."

"Then why even mention marriage?" Her eyes rounded in alarm. "You hated the kiss?"

"What? No. I thoroughly enjoyed it."

A rosy flush swept across her face to mark her embarrassment. "I...I felt out of my depth. Even after reading *The Book of Love*, I did not know what to expect. The kiss caught me up in a flood of sensations, some I had never experienced before. I'm glad we kissed, Lor. In truth, I wanted this first time to be special, and I knew it could only happen with you. But you needn't be polite about it. I know I must have disappointed you."

"No, Cammy. How could you possibly?"

"But surely you've had better kisses."

"No, nothing to compare. Your innocence is refreshing."

"It is?"

"Yes. It was delightful kissing you."

Her blush deepened. "That is very kind of you to say. But I did not know what I was doing. And how does a stolen kiss make anything all right?"

He had earlier set out his blanket under the makeshift shelter but took it now and spread it beside the fire. "Sit down, Cammy.

We need to talk."

She helped him lay it out neatly and then curled her legs under her as she sat beside him. "Yes, we have to figure out how to avoid my ruination and your forced marriage to me." But in the next moment, she inhaled sharply. "Lor, how can you not hate me for this? I am so sorry."

"Don't apologize to me. You are not forcing anything upon me. I am offering."

She eased beside him and nodded. "Because you are a Brayden, after all. And Braydens always do the honorable thing, don't they?"

"Yes, we do."

"That does not ease my mind. And it does not make me happy."

He nodded. "Nor I. This is not how I expected to marry."

"It is terrible, isn't it?"

"Don't say that, Cammy. It doesn't have to be. We like each other, don't we?"

She cast him a look of surprise, then laughed softly. "I wasn't sure what you thought of me. You give nothing away with your expression, and until you pulled me off the mail coach, you had done little more than grunt at me. I did not think you liked me all that much."

He shook his head and laughed. "I like you."

"You needn't pretend that you do."

"I just kissed you."

"To satisfy your curiosity, perhaps. Kissing me does not mean you like me and certainly does not mean you are in love with me. You must think I am a helpless, hopeless rustic with nothing to offer but an attractive face and a pair of large breasts."

"Cammy!"

"I'm sorry if I've shocked you. But will you deny this is what I am to you?"

He cleared his throat. "Blessed saints."

"Now you look appalled. Don't be. This is what men do. *The*

Book of Love explains it all. You needn't fret, Lor. Your wanting to kiss me is scientifically required for our survival."

What the hell?

"Cammy, that is ridiculous."

"No, it isn't. If you'd read the book, it would make perfect sense. You see, men have two brains. A low and a high."

He rolled his eyes.

"This low brain is the male's lustful urge that seeks out women with which to...you know, do those things young ladies are always warned against doing before marriage. This interest in women is innate in men. It is how they determine whether a woman can bear his children. That's why, when looking at a woman for the first time, a man's eyes will always stray to her body. Breasts primarily because they provide the sustenance for their offspring, hips next because they must be wide enough to properly deliver their offspring into the world."

"Stop," he said, groaning. "What in heavens name are you spouting?"

"I've told you, *The Book of Love*. It is why Juniper fell in love with Augustus MacLauren, and Willow fell in love with your brother, Shayne."

"Neither of those men fell in love because of a book."

"It's all true. It is scientific fact. I could see it unfold before my very eyes. Men are drawn to the shape of a woman's body first. Do you deny that you do this? If they find her body pleasing, only then will they move on to look at her face. If that is also pleasing, the man will once again move on to explore the five senses— touch, taste, sight, hearing, and scent. I understand the process now that I've read the book. There's more, of course. These are merely the first steps."

Lorcan wasn't sure he understood what she was telling him. He certainly recognized himself in that rather unflattering description of men. Scientific, she called it. He had never heard lust described that way.

Yet, seeing Cammy for the first time had been like a hammer

blow to his skull. All his senses had exploded at once. Yes, he had taken all of her in. Gaped at those parts of her body she had just mentioned, stared far longer than appropriate.

And another rousing yes for his response to the beautiful shape of her.

But he had also been enraptured by her smile and her loving nature. Perhaps it had taken too long before he stopped gawking at her body, for she was lush where she ought to be and slender everywhere else.

Still, he had moved on to take in her face, which was exquisite because it was genuinely warm and inviting.

She was no ice princess but a truly nice person. Polite and thoughtful to the maids and attendants serving her at the Ashcott Inn where she had been staying. He'd noticed. He'd been watching her.

She was also compassionate and caring toward her aunt and sisters. Indeed, not afraid to risk her life to protect and defend them.

His stomach twisted in a knot recalling her valor firsthand, for she had been taken hostage by a deranged guard. If not for her poise, even with a pistol to her head...he'd come so close to losing her.

"Lor, we must come up with a plan to avoid our having to marry."

"Why? Who's to say we cannot fall in love?"

Her eyes widened, then she pursed her lips and regarded him thoughtfully. "Love isn't something we can force on each other."

"Perhaps not, but we had better give it a try. What does your book have to say about successful marriages? There is no getting around our being alone tonight. We are not going to avoid scandal, so what choice do we have other than to try to make it work?"

"You would do this for me?"

"For us. But you would be the one doing me the favor. You are the one settling for someone lesser."

She inhaled sharply. "How can you think of yourself that way? You are exceptionally handsome. You are a knight of the realm. You do important work for the Crown. And since you also have a share of your brother's business interests, I expect you are not lacking financially. Therefore, you can aim higher for yourself. Aren't you the one who is settling?"

The notion was laughable, and he told her so. "Had you continued to London with your aunt for your come-out, you would have had a swarm of titled suitors desperate for your hand in marriage."

In truth, he did not understand her reluctance to go to London and enter society. She was a diamond of the first water, to use their parlance. "You could have snared a duke for yourself."

She clasped her hands together and lowered her head, but he'd noticed pain shoot into her eyes before she had turned away. "Cammy, why is the notion so odious to you?"

"I don't want to talk about it."

"Very well." He had no intention of letting the matter drop, but he would not pursue it now. She had been through enough for one day. He leaned back and looked up at the stars and the silvery moon that was almost full. "I love the night sky."

She relaxed when she realized he was not going to press her on the topic. Leaning back, she nestled beside him. "So do I. We rarely see it this clearly in Barnstaple because we are so close to the water. Clouds roll in from the sea to obscure the view. But sometimes, when the night is crystal clear as it is tonight, my father and I take his telescope onto the hill behind our home and gaze at the stars for hours. I don't see how a glittering ballroom can ever match the splendor of the sky."

"They each offer a different kind of sparkle."

"London is a false sparkle. None of it is real. The men are there to impress their peers and find an heiress to marry them. The ladies are there to grab the highest title they can attract. I understand it is the way of things. I just don't wish to be caught up in it."

She sat up and clasped her hands again. "Why won't anyone understand? I don't wish to be put on display, trotted out like a filly at auction at Tattersall's. I've had my fill of overindulged lords who think they can take what they want or hurt others with impunity."

Lorcan sighed. "Lord Belfy and his friends are the scum of the earth, but he is now dead, and his friends are now safely behind the sturdy walls of Exeter's prison. Most lords are nothing like that rabble. Many are loyal, brave, and valiant."

She gave a dismissive snort. "Well, they've never made their way to Barnstaple, if that is so."

This bitter distrust was quite out of character for Cammy. He did not like to think something had happened to her to skew her opinion. He needed to puzzle it out, for she did not fear men in general. Not even after that hostage incident last week in Taunton. Thankfully, it had been brief, and he had been able to quickly take down her captor.

But this desperation to avoid London and the marriage mart had happened long before that unfortunate occurrence.

"Cammy…" He reached for her hand, but she rolled to her feet and scampered to the edge of the stream.

She wrapped her arms around herself. "I don't want to talk about it."

He rose and came to her side. "You would be surprised how talking—"

"No." She turned toward the woods at the opposite end of the clearing. "Do you think those awful men will return?"

"They're wounded and will be too busy seeking help to come back to bother us. I merely grazed them, since I wasn't trying to hurt them too badly. They are just petty poachers and thieves and not very adept at their chosen trade."

She cast him a reluctant smile. "Their mistake was in tangling with you."

He shrugged. "Those fools are not going to say anything about where they've been or what they've done. Stealing a horse is a hanging offense. They'll cook up some story no one will believe, and that will be the end of it."

"Are you sure?"

"Yes, Cammy. I've been dealing with men like these for years now. You can ask me more questions about that while on the ride to Taunton. But we have a full day's ride ahead of us, and we both ought to get some sleep."

She nodded. "Are you sure those men won't return?"

"I'm sure." He moved the blanket back to the shelter he had built for her.

"Lor," she said, about to scramble into it, "we have to talk about this marriage business, too."

"We will. Tomorrow."

"All right. I'll bid you goodnight then."

He waited for her to bundle herself up in the blanket before quietly reloading his weapons and settling beside the stream. The fire was still burning, but he preferred to remain in the shadows, out of sight, on the chance those thieves returned.

He did not expect them to, but others might be lurking about.

Those fools had been so intent on stealing his horse, they hadn't noticed Cammy. Others might not be so easily distracted.

Hopefully, his shots had scared away anyone else with similar designs.

"Cammy," he whispered, wondering what her response would be when he told her she had gotten on the wrong mail coach and hadn't been heading home at all. But he would leave that discussion for tomorrow as well.

He settled against a sturdy tree trunk and fell into a light sleep.

As soon as the sun broke over the horizon, Lorcan rose and quickly looked around. The air was thick and humid. He glanced up and noted thin streaks of gray beginning to obscure the blue sky. However, all appeared quiet in the morning haze. But when he went to the makeshift shelter to look in on Cammy, all he found was his blanket.

His heart shot into his throat. "Cammy!"

"Over here," she cheerfully called to him from behind a copse just downstream from their campsite.

He rushed toward her. "Why didn't you wake me?"

"Good morning, Lor," she continued from behind the shrubbery. "I didn't have the heart to disturb you. I hope you slept well. Oh, but don't come close. I'm washing up."

Too late.

Fireworks exploded through his body as she came into his line of sight.

Blessed saints.

He silently backed away before she realized he had seen her through the foliage. Blast the girl! She wasn't simply washing up. Washing up meant keeping your clothes on and merely rolling up your sleeves. It meant sticking your hands in the water and splashing some on your face.

Bathing was an altogether different matter.

Bathing meant taking off your clothes and stepping naked into the water. Well, she had only been wearing his shirt to begin with, but it was off her luscious body now. He might have been spared a full-on view had she turned away while lathering her body with the soap she'd brought along with her, one of the few things she'd thought to toss into her travel pouch.

But no, she was facing him while chirping away, asking him how he'd slept.

He'd been fine until now.

One look at her, and his loins had lit up like a torch. He groaned and closed his eyes, for his eyeballs were throbbing. Was there any part of his body that was not?

Hell of a way to wake up.

She was too busy concentrating on keeping her footing in the stream to notice he was standing there like a baboon with his mouth agape.

A light breeze carried the scent of cinnamon and apples toward him. He recognized these were essences infused into the soap she was using.

No wonder she always roused his hunger.

Her skin, were he to lick it, would taste like a warm apple pie.

He took another step back from his vantage point, for she wasn't even partially hidden amid the overhanging branches.

She was still facing him, gleefully chattering at him about how restful her night had been and thanking him for the blanket. All the while, she was lathering soap all over her soft skin, languidly rubbing it along her limbs and up and down the front of her.

Blessed saints.

He was going to die if he didn't start breathing.

He stared as she set the soap aside and cupped water into her hands to rinse herself off.

But he found no relief in knowing she was almost done. He struggled to catch his breath as beads of water slid down her neck and shoulders to pearl at her breasts.

He turned away before his body burst into flames.

Or his heart gave out.

He returned to the campfire and busied himself by dousing the last of the burning embers. He then began to gather their belongings, for her clothes were still hanging on the branch where he had set them out last night. He checked them, but some were still damp.

Another hour under the sun would have dried them off.

However, the sun was quickly disappearing behind gathering clouds. They had no time to linger if they wanted to make it back to Taunton by nightfall.

He gathered her clothes.

Her chemise and corset had sufficiently dried. He'd hoped they would be since they were made of light fabrics. The chemise, especially, was delightfully sheer. But this was no time for fantasies that he had no intention of acting upon unless she agreed to marry him.

He felt along the remaining garments. Unfortunately, her stockings and gown were still wet. So were her shoes.

He cleared his throat and called to her. "Cammy, are you done yet?"

She walked back into the clearing, her hair freshly washed and cheeks scrubbed pink. Since she had not taken the time to dry her body, his shirt was clinging to her skin. "Yes. Here I am."

He handed her the undergarments and gown. "We have to get back on the road. Can you put these on? The gown is still damp, but there's no help for it. Forget the shoes and stockings for now. They've hardly dried. They're still too wet."

"All right." She held out the soap to him. "From the Oxfordshire Farthingales. They make perfumes, soaps, colognes, and lotions. My cousin Belle is the genius behind these scents. Honey is the financial brain."

He grinned and took it.

Well, why not?

He needed to wash up and did not mind smelling like cinnamon and apple pie. Quickly undressing, he dove in, then grabbed the soap off the rock he'd stuck it on and began to lather himself up.

He briefly wondered whether Cammy was watching him but gave it no more thought. He did not need the distraction. They were in enough of a mess.

Once finished bathing, he dressed and returned to her side to help her lace up her gown. Now that she had taken off his shirt, he grabbed it and put it on. She had slept in it, and the delicious scent of her filled his nostrils.

"Let's go. Hopefully, we'll stay ahead of the rain." He saddled his horse, then lifted Cammy onto the saddle and mounted behind her, circling one arm around her waist to draw her securely against his body. He gave the site a final inspection, making sure the fire he had earlier doused was truly out and that neither he nor Cammy had left anything behind.

Not that they had brought much with them.

Satisfied, he spurred Berengaria, his sturdy chestnut. She was feeling frisky and immediately took off at a gallop, terrifying Cammy, who had nothing to hold onto but him.

Lorcan quickly reined in his mount, keeping her to a more manageable canter.

However, at this pace, they would not reach Taunton until tomorrow. He glanced up at the sky, noting how swiftly it was growing overcast. The wind blew in ever-increasing gusts and had turned unbearably humid.

Tendrils of ominous black clouds now threaded through the graying sky.

"What's wrong?" Cammy followed his frowning gaze as he looked up. "Oh, that doesn't look good. How bad a storm do you think it will be?"

"Bad. A torrential downpour if the strengthening breeze and darkening sky is any indication. Do you hear that rumble of thunder in the distance? We'll manage a couple of hours riding if fortune is on our side. But we had better find shelter soon. This storm isn't going to pass quickly, and I'd much rather wait it out in comfortable lodgings."

She nodded. "Another delay."

"Seems there's no escaping the inevitable."

She looked up at him. "The rain or the marriage?"

"Both. We're not going to make it to Taunton tonight. There's a respectable coaching inn a couple of hours away. I hope we can reach it before the skies burst open."

"All right, but you'll have to stop before we get there to let me put on my stockings and shoes."

Lorcan arched an eyebrow. "Why? They're still wet."

"Lor! I am not going to walk into a respectable inn with my toes peeking out from beneath the hem of my gown. I look wretched enough as it is."

"Fine." They rode south for several hours without speaking, each lost to their own thoughts. As they approached the outskirts of Clifton, he pulled up on the reins and helped her down. He tried not to gawk as she scurried to a nearby rock, sat on it, and slid the stockings over her gorgeous, long legs.

But it was an impossibility.

Fire tore through his body.

What was wrong with him? Were they not in enough of a bad situation?

Not that it was anyone's fault, of course. She had run off because she was overset and scared. Going after her was not a mistake either. They had all been frantic with worry about her being on her own. Rightly so, since she had gotten on the wrong coach. "Cammy, there's something you ought to know."

She looked up at him. "Oh, dear. Is it more unpleasant news?"

He sighed. "I would not have taken you off the mail coach if you were actually headed to Barnstaple. I know Matthias would have delivered you safely home."

She frowned. "What are you talking about? I *was* going to Barnstaple. You *did* pull me off."

"You were riding to Gloucester."

Her eyes widened. "What?"

"Matthias was taking you to Gloucester. That is his mail run, Exeter to Gloucester and all towns in between…including Taunton."

"Where I accidentally got on?"

"Had he been headed to Barnstaple, I would have simply followed the coach to make made certain you reached your home without incident." Of course, he would then have met with her parents to determine the next step, perhaps taking her side in arguing for postponement of her London season.

But there would have been no scandal attached.

And no need for them to marry.

However, her mistake in taking the wrong coach had worked in his favor. Those hours of riding with her tucked against him had firmed his resolve.

He wanted to marry Cammy.

Now, the outcome was assured.

She would be his because even without his cold, purposeful calculation, they would be spending another night together, and there was no way to get around that.

He was pleased for himself, but forcing her to wed him left a bitter taste in his mouth. This was not the same as hunting down a rebel or criminal. This was about winning her heart.

Nor had he ever envisioned finding himself a bride in this manner.

But did it matter?

He had no wish to give her up.

"Bloody fool," he muttered, knowing he had to make things right for Cammy's sake.

She inhaled sharply and buried her face in her hands. "You're right. I am so stupid. How could I get on the wrong coach? What you must think of me, not only vain but an idiot."

"No, Cammy. I was calling myself the fool, not you. This is not at all what I think of you."

Was she crying?

Bollocks.

She was.

Being around men was a whole lot easier. It seemed he could not open his stupid mouth without insulting her. "I only mentioned your taking the mail coach in the wrong direction because—"

She wailed into her hands.

He sighed. "I only mentioned it because I did not want you to be surprised when we reached a town, and you did not recognize it."

She gave a bitter laugh. "Oh, you needn't have worried. I would have remained blithely unaware. I know nothing of the world outside of Barnstaple. I could have been on my way to the moon and not realized it. You were not wrong in calling me foolish."

He knelt beside her. "Cammy, will you please stop beating yourself up? Your mistake is understandable. You were overset and not paying close attention. That hardly qualifies you as dumb."

She groaned and shook her head, once more burying it between her hands. "Dumb! Yes, that is precisely what I am."

He growled as he drew her hands away and then tipped her chin up so that she had to look him in the eyes. "I did not say that. Stop putting words in my mouth. Believe me, I do not tolerate fools. You would know if I thought you were a peahen and did not like you."

"How? Until yesterday, all you did was grunt at me. And if you were not grunting, you were berating me."

He cast her a wry smile. "See? Obviously a man in love."

After a moment, she shook her head and laughed.

"Come on," he said, taking her hand. "We'd better get going before the storm hits."

Their destination was a coaching inn known as the Belvoir Inn. It was a lofty name for a simple place, but he had stopped there a time or two over the years and found it comfortable. It was well maintained and had an excellent kitchen. Once they were settled in, he was determined to get his hands on that book she had been spouting at him last night. *The Book of Love*. Despite everything, he wanted Cammy to marry him out of love and not because of any twist of fate.

He had kissed her, and she'd liked it. That was a good start.

But marriage was built on more than kisses.

He tried to think back to his parents, for theirs was a love marriage. But who the hell remembered the how or why of it? They had died years ago, and as a boy growing up, he never gave thought to their affection for each other. There was food on the table and a roof over his head. What more did a boy need?

He wrapped his hands around Cammy's waist and lifted her up in the saddle. But he kept hold of her as he momentarily lost himself in thought.

"Lor, is something wrong? You are frowning again."

"Sorry. No, just thinking." He swung onto the saddle and

settled her against his chest, then circled one arm around her waist to hold her securely.

"Thinking about what?"

"Not important." But he was a man used to following logic and reason, never his heart…until now. Would it lead him astray?

And what of Cammy?

He could not ignore the fact that his actions had now sealed both their fates.

"Nothing," he muttered, spurring his mount as the first raindrops began to fall.

The approaching storm was going to be bad. He expected it would rage all day and into the night. However, seeking shelter at the coaching inn posed another problem.

He could not pass Cammy off as his sister. No one would believe it.

Nor could he pass her off as a friend.

She was too beautiful, and no one would believe he was keeping his hands off his *friend*.

There was no help for it—she had to be introduced as his wife. How else was he to protect her reputation? Their marriage was inevitable. What harm would there be in signing the inn's register in this manner?

With that problem solved, he moved on to the next. Taking separate rooms was out of the question. He could not risk having her run off again or some scoundrel sneaking into her room to have his way with her.

He'd kill any man who tried.

But the point was to avoid the problem altogether.

A beautiful woman alone was too much temptation.

He would pass them off as married and share a room.

He glanced at her.

Cammy was a terrible liar.

Could she pull off the deception?

CHAPTER THREE

C AMMY TRIED NOT to look appalled when Lorcan led her to a surprisingly pleasant inn called the Belvoir Inn on the outskirts of a town called Clifton and signed them in as husband and wife. Not only signed them in, but under the name of Brayden, not even trying to hide his identity.

Well, she was not a good liar and probably would have botched a made-up name, but that was beside the point.

They were to spend the night *together*.

Sharing a room.

He cast her a warning glance, which she heeded since she had no desire to be declared a woman of immoral character and tossed out into the storm that was about to unleash in all its fury. The town was situated halfway between Gloucester and Taunton, or so Lorcan had mentioned when removing her travel pouch from his saddle and bringing it in with them.

Since her travel pouch was light as a feather, Cammy offered to take it upstairs to their chamber while he went to the stable to make certain the ostler was taking good care of his precious Berengaria.

"Our common room is open if you'd like a midday meal," the friendly maid attending her said. "Or would you prefer to have it delivered upstairs, Lady Camellia?"

Cammy blushed. "I will let my husband decide. He'll be back in a moment."

The maid giggled. "He's awfully nice looking."

She set aside her travel pouch and grinned. "He is, isn't he?

The maid said nothing more as Lorcan strode in, looking every bit the conquering warrior. Big. Rugged. The size of a Roman gladiator. Cammy could see him with shield and mace in hand, his body muscled and oiled, his silver eyes sharp and assessing as he methodically took down his opponents.

Indeed, there was something fierce and brutal in his aspect and yet incredibly appealing. He had a broad mouth, firm jaw, and a nose that appeared to have been broken a time or two. But that slight bend to his otherwise perfect nose enhanced his good looks.

He paused to regard her with deep, sensual eyes.

She blinked, struggling to regain her senses.

He had only to look at her, and she came undone. "Dearest," she said, trying not to melt at the handsome sight of him, "would you care to dine in the common room or share a meal in the privacy of our guest chamber?"

He arched an eyebrow. "Which would you prefer?"

"Our chamber." Obviously, they could not afford to be seen in public and discovered to be unmarried. The innkeeper would boot them out faster than a hummingbird could flap its wings.

Lorcan turned to the maid and put a coin in her hand. "The best for my wife. And see that we are not disturbed."

Cammy sank onto the bed with a groan the moment the maid shut the door behind her. "This is awful. She called me Lady Camellia."

He shrugged. "Because you are the wife of a knight. Could be worse. We could be out in the storm with no food or shelter. The inn is packed to the rafters because of this bad weather. I'm going to light the hearth fire myself. We'll be waiting an hour before it is otherwise done."

She watched as he set about the chore, pleased by how quickly the fire chased all dampness from the room. It also provided a soft illumination, bathing them in a golden light. She did not think it was possible for Lorcan to look handsomer than he did, but there was something magical about seeing him in this intimate light.

The hour was still early, but one could not tell by the darkening sky. "Lor, how are we to find a way out of this coil?"

"There is no way out," he said with brutal honesty. "You ran off. I chased after you. We've registered here as husband and wife. There is nothing to do now but plan the wedding."

"Why are you not overset about this?"

"Who says I'm not? But I am willing to make the best of it. We'll have all night with nothing to do. Let's read that book together. I've already told you I will marry you. All we have to do is figure out how to make our marriage work."

"And you think this book will provide the solution?"

He glanced at her. "Don't you? Why else would you be toting it around?"

"I wish you hadn't come after me." But he was right, she had grabbed it, somehow hoping beyond hope that it could help her through the pain she had kept hidden from everyone, even her own parents.

He sighed. "And I wish you had not run off."

She cast him an anguished look.

Could he not see how badly she ached?

"Why did you, Cammy?" he asked, his voice surprisingly gentle. "You cannot avoid this conversation. I know you are beautiful, and men constantly ogle you. I know it upsets you. But there is something more going on with you than mere displeasure."

She pinched her lips and turned away.

"Fine, don't look at me. But ignoring the issue solves nothing. You would have had Braydens, Farthingales, and their spouses to protect you in London. What scares you so badly about your debut season?"

He came to her side, sat on the bed beside her, and took her hand in his. "You cannot avoid the question."

"Yes, I can." She rose and crossed to the fireplace for no reason other than to move away from him and that piercing gaze of his that missed nothing.

To her relief, he did not follow. Instead, he stretched out on the bed and propped his hands behind his head while staring at her. "You may think you've succeeded in avoiding me, but I will get to the truth."

"It is none of your business, Lor."

He said nothing for a long moment. "If we are to be married, then it is my responsibility to protect you. I will never shirk in that duty. Help me protect you, Cammy. What are you afraid of?"

A knock at their door saved her from responding. "They've brought up our food."

She rushed to open it and stepped aside to allow the maid who had settled them in a few moments earlier to pass. She was carrying a large tray that, judging by the divine aroma, contained their meal. "Oh, thank you. Smells wonderful."

As soon as the maid had set the tray down on the small table, she raised the lid off one of the salvers and inhaled. "Is that venison? In an apple and plum sauce?"

"Yes, m'lady. Leeks and potatoes, too," the girl said with a nod, lightly waving away the steam that rose off the tempting dishes. "And cider to wash it down."

The girl now turned to Lorcan as he rolled off the bed and strode toward them to join Cammy in perusing the food. "Would you care for something stronger, sir? An ale, perhaps?"

"No, cider's good for me."

"Very good, sir." She followed his every movement, obviously enraptured by him.

Who wouldn't be? He was incredibly rugged and handsome in a manly way. He had only to look at a woman, and she would melt.

The maid finished setting out their plates and table linens and bobbed a curtsy. "I hope you find all to your satisfaction."

"I'm sure we will." Lorcan strode to the door and held it open for the girl, a not-so-subtle hint for her to leave. "Thank you, Miss."

She stared at him and smiled inanely. "Just place the tray outside your door when you've finished," she said with a giggle. "Someone will come by to pick it up. My name's Effie. Call for me if you need anything."

"Thank you, Effie." He shut the door as soon as she left and bolted it.

The room was nicely appointed, containing a bed, a bureau, two chairs, and a small table where the maid had set out their meal. Lorcan now drew out one of the chairs for her and took his own beside her. "I'm famished. Let's eat."

Cammy had just picked up a serving spoon to ladle some of the venison onto his plate when lightning split the air. She dropped the spoon and cried out as it crackled overhead with startling force.

Lorcan took her hand in his. "That was close. You all right, Cammy?"

She nodded.

Another bolt of lightning struck overhead, and rain began to fall in earnest a moment later. First, it was a steady pitter-patter, then a torrential gush, pouring down on them like a swiftly moving river current. The roof began to rattle ominously, and a howling wind pushed the rain aslant so that it pelted the windowpanes with enough force to break glass. "The world has split open."

"Sounds like it," he agreed, still holding onto her hand.

She shivered, for shattered windows and a roof falling atop their heads seemed the likely outcome of this storm.

She had never experienced anything so fierce, not even the Barnstaple storms that swept in off the sea.

Lorcan had yet to remove his hand from hers. "We're safe, Cammy. This place is sturdy. Can you not see it is built of stone and has probably withstood the elements in this very spot for a thousand years?"

Another bolt of lightning lit up the sky simultaneously with an ear-shattering clap of thunder. "Are you sure, Lor?" She glanced up at the ceiling, expecting the wooden rafters to start splintering atop them. But Lorcan was right. As the deluge continued, nothing leaked in from the ceiling, and the windows held firm.

"We may as well die with our stomachs full," she joked and resumed ladling the venison, leeks, and potatoes onto their plates.

He poured cider into mugs for them.

Since it was hard to talk above the storm, they ate in silence.

This suited her just fine since Lorcan would have been interrogating her otherwise.

She glanced at him, hoping he was not getting too comfortable with the notion of marrying her.

Of course, she could do a lot worse than this magnificent man. More to the point, she doubted there was anyone she would have liked better as a husband. But she had no intention of trapping any man into marriage. If he wished to court her at a later time, she would gladly accept his suit.

She felt his unrelenting gaze on her, so she kept her head down and busied herself eating. He grinned when she piled a second portion on her plate, knowing she was not hungry but had taken more because it was easier to avoid any discussion while her mouth was full.

As for him, he inhaled his food and spent the rest of the time watching her as he toyed with the mug of cider in his hand.

When they finished eating, he piled their plates back on the tray and placed it outside their door.

She said nothing as he bolted the door again to close them in, but her heart was in a rampant beat because she did not think she could put him off from asking questions any longer. He cast her an irritating smirk, then settled back in his chair and casually lifted the mug of cider to his lips.

Yes, he knew she had been cramming food in her face to

avoid talking to him. She had gotten away with it because he had allowed it. But the arch of his eyebrow and his fixed stare warned he was done with her delaying tactics.

She tried not to appear unnerved as they sat in silence for several minutes longer. He had not taken his eyes off her the entire time, and she was studiously avoiding his gaze.

The wind howled, its whistle eerie and frighteningly shrill.

However, the worst of the thunder and lightning seemed to have passed. Those flashes of light and turbulent rumbles were distant now. The rain had also tapered off, but she knew the damage to the roads had been done.

The road to Taunton would surely be flooded, and many trees uprooted.

But tomorrow's journey was not her immediate problem.

She was sharing a room with Lorcan.

They would be trapped here all night.

How was she to avoid talking to him?

She clasped her hands and rested them on the table. Should she move away from him? Pretend she was tired and settle on the bed?

No, that would be worse.

Lorcan sighed and eased his big body off his chair to kneel by her side.

"What are you doing?" she asked, her eyes rounding in alarm.

Was he on bended knee to propose to her?

"Your stockings and shoes are still wet. I'm going to take them off you before you catch your death of cold."

She breathed a sigh of relief. "Thank goodness. I thought…"

He eyed her curiously. "What did you think I was going to do?"

"Nothing." However, in the next moment, she sighed for a completely different reason. The touch of his hands as he slowly slid her stocking down one leg and then moved to the other to achingly slide that one down, as well, had her gasping and melting and shivering all at once.

Tingles shot through her body.

Mercy.

She did not know a man's touch could affect her this way. The rough heat of his hands felt so good upon her skin.

Was she a fool to fight the inevitable?

He rose and set her shoes by the hearth, then placed her stockings on pegs atop the mantel. "Thank you, Lor."

He turned back to her and studied her quietly for another long moment, his expression unreadable.

The room suddenly felt stifling, but it had nothing to do with the heat of the hearth fire. Those flames still burned brightly and cast Lorcan's features in flickering light, somehow drawing out the beauty of the brutish angles of his face and the hard contours of his body.

She ached to touch him but banished the thought immediately.

"Well, we could posture all night," he said with a trace of mirth in his voice, "me staring at you, and you pretending you are not sneaking glances at me. Or…"

She rose and clasped her hands together. "Or what?"

"We could get comfortable and read *The Book of Love*." He strode to her travel pouch and dug it out to show her.

"I've read it." She cleared her throat, wondering what he was doing. Was he not going to question her about her reasons for running away? Or was this a sly trick on his part to get her to open up? "Why don't you read it yourself? Stretch out on the bed and make yourself comfortable."

He shrugged. "Let me help you out of your gown first. It's still wet and needs to be placed near the fire to dry."

"I cannot traipse about in my undergarments."

"I am not suggesting you do. I'll give you my shirt. I won't need it while we are locked away here. I have no intention of going downstairs tonight."

"Not at all?"

He grinned. "No. I've stayed here before and would rather

not run into people who might know me."

"Oh, I see."

He moved to the bed, placed the book beside him, and then bent to take off his boots. "My shirt will do the trick. You don't even have to take off your corset or chemise. Multiple layers. Will that make you feel more comfortable?"

She nodded, then realized it would leave his chest bare. Not to mention those broad shoulders and gloriously muscled arms. "No."

He laughed. "Then why did you nod?"

"Did I?"

He cast her that know-it-all grin because he noticed everything, and she could hide nothing. "Naughty girl, you did."

She blushed furiously. "Keep your shirt on. I'll wrap the blanket around myself. Do you mind?"

"Not at all." He rose to help her out of her gown and then turned away.

"Here, Lor." She placed the garment in his hand. "But don't turn around yet."

"Wouldn't think of it." He smoothed out the delicate fabric and placed it over a chair back, then moved the chair closer to the hearth.

In the meanwhile, she scampered to the bed and grabbed the blanket.

"Are you decent yet, Cammy?"

"Yes."

She had covered herself from her chin to her toes.

He studied her and laughed again. "Afraid I'm going to ravage you? You needn't worry. If you hold it any tighter against your throat, you'll choke."

"I am perfectly fine."

"If you say so." He stretched out on the bed and took the book in hand.

She sat by the footboard, stealing glances at him as he began to read. To her dismay, tingles shot through her body. He was just lying there, the pillows propped at his back and one leg slightly bent as he balanced the faded red leather tome on it while perusing the chapters.

Of course, he looked magnificent.

And dangerous.

She was still tingling, and now her heart was skipping beats. Why was she responding to him this way? He was fully clothed. She had the blanket around her, and he had kept his shirt on.

Would he mind if she nestled beside him while he read?

Her body began to warm.

More than warm.

It really was too hot wrapped up in this itchy blanket while the fire blazed.

She quietly eased it off her shoulders.

Lorcan glanced up but paid her no more attention as he resumed reading. What page was he on? Was he concentrating on the page about a man's arousal responses?

It was still too hot in here.

She lowered the blanket to her waist.

After all, her chemise and corset hid most of her bosom. The little swell that peeked out was nothing more than she revealed when wearing a modest gown...well, perhaps a little more. But not much more.

Her feet were getting hot, too.

She kicked aside the lower part of the blanket and swung her legs out. She wasn't showing Lorcan anything he had not seen before. Hadn't she been wearing his shirt last night? And hadn't it fallen short, failing to cover her legs below her knees?

How was this any different?

With the blanket now hiding her only from her waist to her knees, she dragged it along the floor and crossed to her travel bag to take out her brush. She returned to Lorcan's side, settling closer so that she could more easily reach the nightstand to place her pins on it as she unbound her hair.

She felt the heat of his gaze on her.

Was he going to kiss her again?

Being closed in with him in this cozy room while a storm raged outside was rather intimate and gave one ideas.

Would she resist if he attempted another kiss?

He cleared his throat.

She turned to him with a smile and leaned toward him because…heavens, she wanted to kiss this man again. "Yes, Lor?"

"Would you mind moving? I'm trying to read, and you are blocking my firelight."

She was mortified.

Had he realized she was practically throwing herself at him? She dropped the pins and hairbrush and scrambled off the bed with an *eep*. But in her haste, the blanket wound around her legs like thick cords and tripped her.

She crashed to the floor.

Thankfully a carpeted floor and the blanket padded much of her fall.

Lorcan shot off the bed and knelt at her side. "Cammy! Blessed saints, are you hurt?"

She looked up at him, still aghast for wanting to kiss him when he had no such thing in mind. She lay flat on her back, her heart in a thunderous roar so that his words seemed muffled.

She could not move but quickly realized it was only because some of her long hair was trapped beneath her bottom, and her legs were trapped within the folds of the blanket.

She took several deep breaths to calm her rampaging heart. "I think I am all right. I'm sorry, Lor. I did not mean to interrupt you."

He ran his hands along her neck and shoulders, then carefully along her arms and torso. Did the room just catch fire? Because her blood was molten, and her body was burning.

"Wait, don't move yet," he said with a deep murmur when she squirmed and tried to roll to her knees. "Let me check your legs."

She closed her eyes.

Her lungs felt as though they were about to burst.

Mercy.

His touch.

Those calloused hands of his, rough and hot, slid up from her ankles, cupped her calves, skimmed over her knees, and up her thighs.

"Oh, heavens." She let her breath out in a moan.

He frowned. "Did that hurt?"

Did wild ecstasy count as hurt? She did not think so. He was referring to sprains and bruises. "No. I just…no."

"I'll move to a chair and read. You can take the bed. Put your arms around my neck." He lifted her into his arms and rose. "All right?"

She nodded.

Her hair spilled over his arm in an unruly tumble.

Since he did not seem to mind, she made no move to gather it neatly to one side. Instead, she buried her face against his shoulder. "I'm so embarrassed."

How many more stupid things did she need to do before he decided she was the silliest peahen ever born, and he wanted nothing to do with her? "You won't have to be burdened with marriage to me. I will not insist on it. I don't care if I am considered ruined. I will return to Barnstaple and live with my parents for the rest of my days, a recluse with a dozen cats to keep me company since no decent person will ever want to have anything more to do with me."

His chest rumbled.

"And my sisters will not abandon me. They'll provide for me, of course. So I can live out my days in comfort eating kippers and cakes at tea time with my cats in that big, rambling house in Barnstaple. They'll hire a companion for me…I hope she likes cats…I hope she likes kippers."

He burst out laughing.

"It isn't funny, Lor." She looked up and frowned at him. "I am serious. I won't saddle you with an idiot for a wife."

"Then it is a good thing I am marrying you, isn't it?"

"Are you not listening? I just told you—"

He kissed her on the lips to cut her off, a short, deep kiss that he ended swiftly. "You weren't wrong. I did want to kiss you."

"You read my thoughts?"

"I read your eyes. Cammy, your expression hides nothing. I'm sorry I startled you. I was just trying to think of a way to politely get you out of my reach before I hauled you atop me and... Well, what I wished to do with you went beyond kisses and does not bear mentioning. I did not expect you to leap off the bed and dive onto the floor."

She smiled sheepishly at him. "I thought I did it quite gracefully. It's all those years of lessons in becoming a lady, you see. I'm sure I would have dazzled the *ton* when taking to the dance floor to show them that move."

"I, for one, would have found you charming and immediately claimed two dances."

"Oh, Lor. I am such a fumbling fool around you. Why are you so nice to me?"

He sat her down on the bed, took the book back in his hands, and settled beside her. "I managed to read two chapters before you took your dramatic plunge. How about we read the rest of it together? You might have your answer to that question once we're done."

She gave an unladylike snort. "I have read the book several times over with my sisters. What makes you think I'll learn anything more reading it with you?"

He leaned ever so close. She felt his breath upon her lips and saw the silvery smolder in his eyes as he said, "I am not your sisters."

Merciful heavens.

Indeed, he was not.

"When do we start?"

CHAPTER FOUR

LORCAN SETTLED CAMMY in one of the chairs by the table and took the other one beside her. "I think we ought to remain upright. It is safer than reading in bed together," he said by way of explanation when he noticed the confusion in her bright blue eyes.

But he also noted an assessing gleam in them and knew she was eager to test the love recipes contained in this book on him. *Test frog* was the term he'd heard Shayne mention when grumbling about Willow and the helpless way he seemed to be falling for Cammy's sister. It was uncannily as predicted in these chapters.

That he was about to fall next was a humbling realization.

Brayden men were protective by nature. They were also natural leaders and always liked to be in charge. Brayden men believed they were in control of their destiny and in control of any situation.

To be taken down by a slip of a girl was something none of them were prepared for. Not only taken down, but brains turned to soft-boiled gruel because it seemed that falling in love meant putting her needs above your own, and that meant never, ever winning an argument again.

"Shall we start?" Cammy looked up at him and cast him a smile that pierced his heart, at once tender and hopeful and hesitant.

He found her irresistible and returned the smile with a wry one of his own. "Sure."

She laughed. "You make it sound as though you are on a death march."

He grinned. "Perhaps I am a little wary. Can you blame me?"

"No. I still find this business of love quite puzzling. Where shall we start, Lor? Do you want to discuss the chapters you've read, or shall we pick up where you left off?"

"Let's pick up where I left off."

"Oh…I thought perhaps we ought to…"

He shifted uncomfortably, knowing he was about to lose his first argument. "What, Cammy?"

"I think we ought to be thorough. We should start at the beginning. I don't want us to overlook anything."

"Rest assured, I have overlooked no part of your body. Is this not what the first chapter is all about? A man's lustful urges?"

She blushed as she folded her hands in front of her and rested them on the table. "The discussion of low brain and high brain is a thoughtful, scientific analysis. It is about our survival instincts more than anything else. But did your low-brain response happen just as the author claimed it would? First noticing my…" She glanced at her bosom. "Then noticing my hips, then my face."

"Not quite."

She was obviously waiting for him to say more, but how was he to talk scientifically about her breasts, which seemed to be the female weapon that brought down all males? Or her hips? Or any other spectacular part of her? Yes, his eyes had immediately gone to those body parts when first meeting her, filling him with a savage need to claim her for himself. It was a completely instinctive response and not anything he could control, just as the author had claimed.

He understood it now, for this was his low brain springing to life and deciding Cammy was a desirable bedmate. This is what the discussion in the first chapter had been about, the man's two brains—the high and the low—and most importantly, the animal urges associated with the lustful low brain.

Scientifically, that overwhelming need to mate with a desirable female was deemed a necessity for the survival of mankind.

Ah, yes. His eyeballs had almost imploded from the raw ache to see her body and the subsequent strain of filling in whatever was not readily available to his view. This is what the author had written in the opening chapter, the arousal of the male when coming upon a fertile female, the unthinking need to spawn and spread his seed.

The need to see her healthy breasts.

Right, that would never have happened had he not accidentally come across Cammy bathing in the stream. His heart had yet to recover from that magnificent sight.

"What would you like to tell me about your low brain, Lor?"

"Nothing." He was not about to admit he'd seen her or how powerful his feelings were for her. A man's low brain dealt with lust. A man could bed many women without thought of commitment to them.

A man's high brain dealt with love, finding that one woman he would care for and protect to the end of his days.

Cammy was that high-brain girl for him.

She cast him a gentle look of chastisement. "Nothing at all?"

"Does it require mentioning? You claimed top honors as far as my low brain was concerned."

"But you said it did not happen quite as the book explained it would. How was it different for you? Did you not like me at first?"

He leaned forward, wanting to cover her hands with his but deciding against it. They needed to talk. Merely touching her, no matter how innocently, would set off his low brain even worse than it already was. "Not only did I like you right away, but you immediately went from 'healthy female, want to bed her' to the high-brain female of my choice. Within a minute's time, I had assessed you and moved you from my unthinking, lustful low brain to my high brain."

She cast him a look of doubt. "The one capable of feeling love?"

He nodded. "You were a woman I wanted to keep."

She pursed her lips. "I don't see how you could have made that assessment in under a minute. I would not have had time to appeal to all your senses. Sight, touch, taste, hearing, and scent. Not to mention the other qualities necessary for a happy marriage."

"Why not? We were standing close enough to each other, so I could easily see you. Obviously, I liked what I saw. You put your hand on my arm to gain my attention, and that was all the touch I needed. It was pleasant." To be precise, fire had surged through his body the moment she'd placed her delicate hand on his forearm. "I heard your voice and liked it, too. When I bent my head toward yours, I caught the scent of your body and found it appealing." Ha! Another understatement. She had roused every wild beast urge in him. If he were less civilized, he would have been sniffing her and licking her warm skin...not to mention other things he would have liked to do to her.

Or other places he would have liked to lick.

He tamped down those thoughts.

No Brayden male would ever take advantage of a lady.

"But you did not know about taste."

"Everything else about you was perfect. I figured...rather, my brain filled in that missing part and decided the taste of you would probably be perfect, too. Which it was. Our first kiss merely confirmed what I already believed. And now, let's talk about you."

She cleared her throat. "What about me?"

"The book also spoke of the woman's brain." He chuckled. "Obviously, yours is better developed than ours since we require two brains to figure out our lives, and you manage it on only the one."

Her snort was dismissive. "Obviously, mine is lacking."

He frowned. "Why do you say that? Inexperience is not the

same as lack of intelligence. You now know that you passed all my 'suitable female' tests. Where do I stand with you?"

"The book speaks of the woman's need to find the strong male to protect her because she and her newborns are so vulnerable, especially when she has just given birth."

"Right, I read that. They need to be protected, so they are not eaten by wolves."

She nodded. "It is a scientific necessity. Not real wolves, of course. Any predator, whether four-legged or two-legged, is a danger. This is why the woman must find the mate who can keep that danger away and give her and their offspring the best chance of survival." She studied him a long moment. "I know the author did not mean merely seeking a male with physical strength, although you certainly are strong. It also means a combination of power, intelligence, compassion, wealth to some extent, and the will to protect."

"And?"

"You have all those qualities. It was obvious from the first. Of course, I did not know the extent of your wealth, nor do I now. I truly do not care."

He arched an eyebrow.

Oddly, he believed her.

"Every woman has different requirements in the level of comfort she expects her mate to provide." She began to wring her hands. "I don't care if I have new gowns for every season or keep a carriage in town. I don't care about having the most enormous house or servants to attend to my every need."

He folded his arms across his chest and leaned back casually. "Then what is it you want, Cammy?"

She appeared surprised.

"What's wrong? Isn't it important for me to know what matters most to you? What are your hopes and dreams?"

"Yes, it is important."

"Then what is the problem? Why are you looking at me so oddly?"

"Do you know that you are the first person ever to ask me that question? What do I want? What do I hope for and dream about?" She gave a mirthless laugh. "All my life, people have been telling me what I *should* want. All my life, they've assumed to know what is important to me. Not once have I been given the chance to voice my opinion."

"You have it now."

"And I appreciate it so much, Lor. You have no idea how much it means to me that you bothered to ask, that you are bothering to listen. What do I want? Most of all, a love marriage. I want a husband who will be considerate of my happiness, just as I will be considerate of his. I want his friendship, too. And his support. I also want the freedom to indulge in pursuits outside the home."

He tensed. What sort of pursuits was she talking about? "Such as?"

"I love to paint. Did you know this?"

"No, Cammy." He eased back and silently chided himself. He ought to have known she was not talking about indulging in other men. "Why did you not mention it until now?"

She shrugged. "I just got used to people ignoring who I am on the inside. My talents, all the little things that make me who I am. They see my looks and stop right there. They never bother to peer into my heart. I'm quite a good painter, perhaps as good as my cousin, Rose. She and her viscount husband own one of the largest porcelain and glassworks companies in England. I've sent her a few of my designs, and she has incorporated them into her line of dinner plates."

He smiled, for her excitement was palpable. "That is remarkable."

"Before being packed off to London for the season, I was working with a naturalist, a Fellow in the Royal Society, who was compiling a journal of all the birds in our area. He studied their life cycles, the food they hunted, their mating habits, and nesting habits. He wrote scientific monographs, and I provided the drawings for him. I sketched the birds in their natural surroundings. His work will be compiled in a book shortly. I wanted to provide him more sketches but cannot now that my parents have decided to send me to London. I was not happy about their decision at all."

He gave her hand a light squeeze. "It must have been a disappointment for you."

"It was, but my parents were adamant. I was so unhappy about it, Lor. But I did not put up much of a fuss because I would rather be tossed onto the marriage mart with Juniper and Willow than face a season on my own."

He groaned. "And now they are both married."

"And here I am alone, facing what I had hoped to avoid."

"But you would not have been alone in London. You have your Aunt Charlotte as your chaperone. Not to mention all your London relatives who would have kept a watchful eye on you. You mentioned your cousin Rose a few moments ago. But I know that many of your cousins married well. I'm sure most of them would have gladly taken you under their protection."

He cast her a wry grin. "I have it on good authority that several of your Farthingale cousins fell in love with Brayden men. Namely, my cousins. Incredible, isn't it? Seems our Brayden brains are designed to fall for Farthingale women."

She nodded. "And ours are designed to fall for you. Although I think any woman would feel the same if courted by a Brayden. I find it all quite fascinating, especially after watching Willow and your brother fall in love."

Lorcan grinned. "He didn't stand a chance."

"We seem to like MacLauren men, as well," she teased. "Juniper instantly fell in love with Augustus MacLauren."

He shook his head and laughed. "Seems we face stiff competition from those Scots. Should I be jealous?"

"I hardly think so. But there is something to these attractions. It is discussed in later chapters about connections and expectations. First impressions are just that, merely impressions. How can we look at someone and immediately know they are meant for us? I don't believe it can happen."

"Then how do you explain Willow and my brother? Or Juniper and Augustus MacLauren?"

"I don't have an answer for it," she admitted. "*The Book of Love* says we must always look beyond the initial low-brain attraction and beyond the five senses as well. We have to be honest about what traits or quirks in another we simply cannot accept. Because even if the low brain approves and even if we find the other person pleasing to our five senses and even if we find threads in our lives that connect us and bind us to each other, there may be something that will ultimately pull us apart."

She paused a moment to look at him. "I don't mean *us* specifically. This would apply to any couple. But I think I am getting too far ahead of this discussion."

"Yes, we diverted from our course. Let's go back to the original question about your hopes and dreams. What do you desire in a husband? Obviously, it must be someone who will not only protect you and your children financially but support your love of painting and the work you do regarding the local birds."

She nodded. "Lor, it is obvious only to you because you are taking the time to get to know me. As I've said, no one has ever bothered before. I noticed your brother is an accomplished artist himself. Shayne drew an excellent portrait of the man Willow saw running from the scene of the carriage house fire. It turned out exactly as Willow described him. Do you draw as well?"

"No, absolutely no talent for it. But I do admire those who can. Shayne isn't like you, though. Drawing is simply something he can do well. He does not need it like one needs air to breathe or food to eat. However, you do. I see your passion when you talk about it. Tell me more, Cammy."

Who could overlook the pride and excitement on her face, especially in the brilliance of her eyes?

She cast him a beaming smile.

One would think he had just admitted he loved her and had

ardently proposed to her. But no, her heart was captured by her love of painting. This is why she was so reluctant to enter the marriage mart. She did not view finding a husband as a means to secure her future but rather as a sure way to impede it.

But was there more to her reluctance?

"I thought about bringing a few of my sketches to London, but my parents did not think it was a good idea. They wanted me to find a husband and stop thinking about my birds."

Her eyes were still aglow as she smiled at him. "Now, back to our discussion about the perfect man. Yes, he must be strong enough to protect me and our children. But it isn't merely brute force that would attract me to him. It is strength of character, something you Braydens have by the bucketful."

He laughed. "Also known as being prideful, possessive arses. But do go on. I like your description better."

"You have reason to be proud. You are quite accomplished. I also admire the way you and your brothers look out for each other. You and Donal came to Taunton to spend time with Shayne, take in some fishing, and riding at his estate. Instead, you've spent the past few weeks chasing down criminals, and now you were sent off to find me. I am truly sorry about that."

"Don't be."

"How can I not be? Is this not what our discussion is about? My trapping you in an unwanted marriage."

"I never said it was unwanted."

"Untimely, then. Inconvenient. Are you not afraid this is all a big mistake?"

He had earlier cleared off their plates and left them outside their door but had kept the jug of cider and their mugs. He now offered to fill Cammy's mug.

She shook her head to decline.

He poured himself a mug and drank the cider down, for his throat felt parched. "It does not have to be a mistake, Cammy. Let's turn the discussion around. Never mind about what makes us right for each other. Tell me what you think makes us wrong.

What do you not like about me?"

She stared at him. "You want me to list your faults?"

He nodded.

"Oh, Lor. I don't think you have any."

He laughed heartily. "Shall I help you out? Stubborn. Loner. Impatient. Unforgiving."

"What would you not forgive?"

"Many things. Betrayal. Breaking a promise. Greed. Laziness. Lies. Being unfaithful."

"Most people would feel the same. The book explains it, too. The important thing to take from its teaching is that for any marriage to work, there must be honesty and trust. Even if I found you divinely handsome, I would never be happy if you were faithless and lied to me."

He took her hand. "Then let's be honest. What do you think of me, Cammy?" What he really wanted to ask was what she feared most because there was a haunted look in her eyes that never quite went away.

He wanted to keep her talking in the hope a clue might emerge.

A young woman from an idyllic village and raised by a loving family should not have the shadow of fear in her eyes, nor should she be running away from London and the marriage mart.

"Lor, you will puff up and be impossible to tolerate after I tell you what I think of you. Have I not made your head swell already with my remarks?"

"Then you like me?"

She met his gaze, her expression soft and her cheeks now pink with embarrassment. "You know I do."

"Actually, I do not. I still have not heard what precisely you like about me."

"Everything. How is that for an answer? I first saw you as you were hauling Lord Belfy and his miscreant friends from the Ashcott Inn to the magistrate's prison after they had attacked my sister and Augustus. You were a beast. Fierce and stronger than anyone I had ever seen before."

He arched an eyebrow. "A beast?"

"But in a good way. We had been reading that book, and the first thing I thought of was how protective you would be of me and my children. Of course, you immediately leaped to the next level for me, which were the five senses." Her cheeks turned a brighter pink as she continued. "I certainly loved the look of you. And the scent. Touch, too. As for the sense of hearing, that was a lot harder. You never talked to me. You just grunted."

He laughed. "When did I do that?"

"You naturally do it. You don't like to talk."

"That's true." He shook his head and sighed. "I think I've done more talking with you today than I've ever done with anyone in my life. My mouth hurts from the effort. So does my brain."

"Poor, Lor." But she wasn't in the least remorseful. Her eyes now sparkling with mirth. "Obviously, you have not lived with sisters. This is nothing. We can chatter for hours without pause."

He gave a playful wince. "Has it not been that long?"

"No." She laughed and lightly nudged his shoulder. "Not even an hour. But I think I shall take pity on you. We needn't discuss the book any longer. Read it on your own, or just set it aside. Sometimes it helps to sleep on the matter and allow the information to be absorbed."

He nodded, but this was not his intention.

He wanted to keep her talking.

"We can also make lists," she suggested. "That is, if you find those helpful. Sometimes writing a thing down helps clear a problem in your mind."

"What sort of lists are you talking about?"

"Oh, it can be anything. A list of what we like about each other. Another list of what irritates us about each other. Another list about the qualities of an ideal mate. Or—"

He laughed. "Got it. You can add 'hates to write' to that list of things I hate to do."

"You are a very difficult test frog."

"Was this a test?"

"No, but I had hoped we could get to testing some things out on each other."

He poured a little more cider in his mug and drank it down. "What sort of things would you like to test?"

"Well, I am still curious about kisses. That's the sense of taste. You are the only man I've ever kissed."

He growled. "You are not thinking of kissing someone else."

He hadn't posed it as a question so much as a possessive remark. Blast it, he did not want her kissing anyone but him. Not ever.

He did not care if he was behaving like an arse about it.

"No, I am not inclined to experiment beyond you. Just you. Because I trust you. I don't trust anyone else."

"Nor should you. There is no way to know what another man might do. I would never hurt you."

"I know. This is why I trust you. It is remarkable and wonderful to feel this way. Those others...I am merely something to ogle and possess, like one possesses a vase or painting. They think to impress me with their riches. They think they can buy me. They've never once thought to ask about my feelings."

"Cammy, men don't like to speak of feelings. To be honest, I detest it."

"So, you will not talk to me about your hopes and dreams? Or mine?"

He groaned and shook his head. "I will talk to you about them because it is important to you."

She gasped. "Lor, thank you."

Why was she thanking him? For hearing her out? For caring to know what she valued?

He was surprised when tears brimmed in her eyes. "Cammy?"

"That is the nicest thing you could possibly have said to me." She wiped at a stray tear that had fallen onto her cheek. "You are not a man who conveys his feelings through words. You are a man of action. That you would do a thing you detest because it would please me...is this not the purest act of love?"

"Cammy, do not put me up on a pedestal." He ran a hand across the nape of his neck. "It is not much of a sacrifice on my part. I am genuinely interested in you and want to know more about you."

She cast him a wry smile. "I think you will break out in hives if we speak any more about love today."

She rose, her body still wrapped in the blanket that had tripped her up earlier, and shuffled over to her gown to run her hands along the fabric. "I think it is dry."

She knelt and felt along her shoes. "Those are still damp. My stockings, too."

"Do you want to put on your gown?"

"No, it will get wrinkled if I sleep in it."

The rain had been falling while they spoke about *The Book of Love*. But the skies appeared to be clearing, and the torrent had tapered off. Lorcan thought the worst of the storm might have passed, but he was proved wrong moments later when a bolt of lightning struck so close to the rooftop, they felt its sizzle.

Then another bolt struck, and the skies opened up again in a renewed deluge.

Cammy raced into his arms, her heart hammering.

He took her into his embrace, immediately responding to the press of her body against his. "I felt that in my toes," she said in a shaky whisper.

"Yes, it hit very close."

"Perhaps I ought to sleep in my gown."

"I wouldn't bother."

She looked up at him. "Why not?"

"Because it is raining too hard for the inn to catch fire even with a direct strike. And if it actually hits us, then we'll be dead, our bodies burned beyond recognition, and it won't matter what we're wearing."

He was worried he had been too blunt and frightened her, for she was now trembling. But in the next moment, he realized she wasn't scared.

She was laughing.

He cupped her face in his hands to make certain she was not becoming hysterical.

But her smile was broad, and she was still laughing. "Lorcan Brayden, I think you are the most wonderfully romantic man I have ever met."

Her eyes were once again sparkling as she gazed at him.

She did not look hysterical.

In truth, she looked incredibly beautiful.

But was she serious?

What the hell had he said that was anywhere near romantic?

CHAPTER FIVE

CAMMY CREPT OUT of bed in the wee hours of the morning to peer out the window of their guest chamber. To her dismay, the rain had not let up since it had started yesterday. The inn's courtyard was now flooded, and she expected the roads would be in even worse condition.

She glanced at Lorcan, who was stretched out on a makeshift pallet on the floor beside the hearth. The fire had burned itself out hours ago, and the only source of light came from the thin, gray rays of approaching dawn.

She sighed and was about to make her way back to the bed Lorcan had entirely given over to her when she heard him softly call her name. "Cammy?"

"Oh, I did not mean to wake you. I was just curious about the weather."

He yawned and stretched his magnificent body. "Still raining. I can hear it pattering against the roof. Wind has died down, though. That's a good sign."

She crossed to the bed but merely sat at the foot of it while they spoke, trying not to gawk at him since he had removed his shirt before settling down to sleep, and she could make out the perfect contours of his toned body. "I don't know if we will be able to leave the inn today. The courtyard is flooded."

He growled softly. "Another day lost? I suppose it doesn't matter."

She inhaled lightly. "Why not?"

"Because you are compromised no matter how we look at it. I need to marry you. Which means I have to get you to Barnstaple to obtain your father's consent. Forget about returning to Taunton."

"But what about my sister and aunt? They're waiting for me at the Ashcott Inn, probably frantic with worry."

"We'll have to pass by Shayne's estate. It is directly on our route to Barnstaple. I'll grab his coach and driver. We'll save at least half a day by taking his coach. It works out well since I can leave him a note assuring him that I've found you and all is well. One of his footmen will deliver it to him in Taunton."

"That makes sense." She moaned and rubbed her face. "How could I have been so cruel to my sister and Charlotte? They must be worried to death."

"They won't be angry. They just want to know you are safe. Add whatever you like to my note. Shayne will read it to them."

She nodded, her mind now turning to the next worry. "What are you planning to tell my father?"

"What do you think? We have been together three days now, and easily four or five by the time we reach Barnstaple. There is no gentle way of describing our situation. Your father has to consent to our marriage."

She flopped back on the bed. "I know. I'll try my best to be a good wife to you, Lor."

"I haven't a doubt."

"Really? You trust me?"

"Yes. I would not have gone after you on my own unless I was willing to accept the consequences. There is no way in hell I would have allowed myself to get into this position otherwise."

"Are you saying that all along, you were willing to marry me?"

"Yes, Cammy. I'm surprised you did not immediately understand this."

The admission should have relieved her, and it did to some

extent. But it also burdened her heart with the knowledge that he had more faith in her becoming a good wife to him than she had in herself. "Out of curiosity, how can you be sure I am trustworthy?"

He scrubbed his hands against his face and sat up, now fully awake. "Easy, you cannot tell a lie. Your expression shows everything. Blushes and nervous giggles. Not that you have ever outright lied, but even when you try to soften the truth in order not to hurt someone's feelings, you cannot do it smoothly."

She groaned. "I know. This is another reason why I would make a terrible duchess. I would likely bite a hole through my tongue to keep myself from giving the pompous elites a piece of my mind."

"You know there are many good men with titles."

"You've said so before. But I'm afraid my cousins have married the best ones. I doubt I'll find another. I am quite satisfied with a knight for myself...Sir Lorcan. If we married, I would be a lady." She chuckled. "Is it not ridiculous? Lady Camellia Brayden. Effie addressed me as that earlier."

"Sounds nice." He rose and went to stand beside the window.

Cammy's breath caught.

He was so beautifully shaped, even down to the sculpted muscles of his back and broad shoulders.

"I hear people stirring," he said after a moment, turning to face her. "It must be later than we think, perhaps about five or six in the morning. Are you hungry?"

"A little."

"Me, too. I'm famished." He reached for his shirt and tossed it on, then grabbed the pillow and blanket he'd used for a pallet and tossed those back on the bed. Since she had moved to the hearth to see if her stockings were dry, he settled on the bed and burrowed under the covers.

"Did you wish to sleep longer? I can wait to eat."

"No, as I said. I'm famished. But the bed needs to look slept in by both of us. You know, husband and wife."

Heat shot into her cheeks.

He laughed and rolled back off it. "You are blushing again. And I'm sure you are also wondering how you will take care of the necessities while I am in here with you."

She nodded. "The thought had crossed my mind."

"I'll head downstairs to order our breakfast and secure this chamber for another night. But I would still rather we kept away from the common room. I dare not risk even their private dining rooms. We'll eat up here. Do you mind?"

"Not at all. As you say, it is safest."

"Good. I'll help you lace your gown once I return. Latch the door and do not allow anyone in but me. This is a respectable place, but you never know the vermin who may be lurking."

Cammy tended to her morning needs. She was washed, her hair properly done up, and her stockings, shoes, and gown donned by the time Lorcan returned. He had only to help her tighten the laces of her gown, which he did once he strode back in.

But he was frowning as he walked in, obviously having encountered something worrisome between the time he left their chamber and returned. "What's wrong, Lor?"

"I ran into someone I know. Apparently, Effie had been talking to him about me and my *wife*."

"Oh, no."

"He insists on meeting you."

She turned to face him, eyeing him curiously because Lorcan was not the sort of person to be forced to do anything he did not wish to do. "Who is he?"

"His name is George Maplethorpe. He happens to be one of the Duke of Wooton's aides. You may have heard of the duke because he is the lord minister who runs the Foreign Office. I report directly to him. Bit of bad luck that his clerk should be here. But he got caught in the same deluge on his way from Exeter to Coventry. Fortunately, he is continuing north while we are on our way south."

"You do not seem to like this man very much. Can we make up an excuse to avoid him?"

"I told him you were indisposed, a megrim brought on by the inclement weather. But the damage has already been done. I cannot blame Effie, that silly girl. Apparently, he noticed us when we first arrived at the inn and immediately began to pry information out of her. He will now report my marriage to the duke."

"Seems I've trapped you, indeed." She nibbled her lip. "Can you not later pretend we were meeting here for an assignation? You know, wink, wink. Wanted to protect the lady's reputation. Don't men indulge in such trysts all the time?"

"He's seen you, Cammy. Having done so, he will never forget your face."

"Is he that sharp to remember me so clearly even from a distance?"

"He is a dimwit. But you are too beautiful for any man ever to forget. And stop trying to look for a way out of our marriage. It isn't going to happen."

She met his gaze. "Then what are we to do?"

"I'll join him downstairs for a cup of coffee. But I would like you to stay up here. Effie will bring breakfast up to you shortly. Just be aware Maplethorpe may have bribed her to ask questions. He's a little ferret for the duke, poking his snoopy nose wherever it does not belong. Remember to act like you have a megrim and use it as an excuse not to talk to her."

"Lor, you know I am a terrible liar."

"I know. Just do your best." He placed his hands lightly on her shoulders. "This does not change our plans. As I said, there's no question of our marrying. However, I would have liked to control the timing of when the news broke out."

"We ought to get our stories straight since we are to continue with this subterfuge. What are you going to tell him if he asks how we met and insists on learning details?"

"Simple. We married in Taunton a few days ago. Basically, we'll steal Shayne and Willow's romance and their steps to the altar. All right? But you and I will quietly exchange vows in Barnstaple as soon as we talk to your father and obtain his consent."

She placed her hand across her stomach as it churned. "Starting off our married life with a lie."

"A necessary expediency. I will never lie to you, Cammy. But I won't think twice about doing whatever I must to protect your reputation." He kissed her on the forehead. "I'll be back as soon as I can."

Cammy latched the door after he strode out.

The Book of Love was perched atop her night table. She quickly tucked it back in her travel pouch. Effie might notice it and report back to that Maplethorpe fellow. All they needed was rumor to spread about them using a lewd book to enhance their sexual activities. Of course, it was nothing of the sort.

But truth mattered little when it came to gossip.

She drew a chair by the window and watched the rain continue to pour down. Within the hour, she expected the inn's courtyard to be a pond. No one was getting out today. This meant the duke's aide would also be here and watching their every move.

She shook her head, hating the lies that would be necessary.

Lorcan had said he would never lie to her. Nor would she ever lie to him. But he did not seem to hold the same qualms about prevaricating to others. He could pull it off, for there was steel in him. That fierce look he'd mastered could strike fear in any man.

She had nothing but pudding inside of her.

"Lady Camellia," said Effie, knocking at her door.

Cammy startled and shot out of her chair.

"Calm yourself," she whispered, setting the chair beside the table and hastily smoothing out her gown. She knew it was ridiculous to be in dread fear of the inn's young maid.

She took a deep breath and opened the door with a smile. But it quickly faded when she saw the stranger standing behind the girl. This had to be Maplethorpe, the duke's ferret. Wasn't he supposed to be waiting for Lorcan downstairs?

Or had this little ferret lured Lorcan away so he could steal a moment with her?

She tried to slam the door in their faces, but the man already had his foot in the door.

"Remove it, sir. Or I shall crush it."

But he was stronger and shoved past Effie as she stood in the open door.

She tossed the girl her fiercest frown. Of course, it wasn't very effective. "Fetch my husband immediately. Go now, Effie. Or shall I report your part in this underhanded ploy to the innkeeper?"

The girl's eyes widened.

"Oh, my lady! I had no part...I..." She deposited the breakfast tray on a hall table and ran off, hopefully to fetch Lorcan.

Her husband.

She was compounding lie upon lie.

And by sending the girl away, she had stupidly left herself to face Mr. Maplethorpe on her own.

Oh, clever move, Cammy.

She closed her eyes and swallowed hard, for these lies did not easily flow off her tongue. "This megrim has the better of me. Shooting pains through my skull. Kindly remove yourself from my chamber and allow me to shut the door. My husband will not be pleased to find you here."

The man refused to budge.

Instead, he cast her a treacly smile and confirmed his identity by introducing himself with a flourish. "His Grace will be delighted to know of Sir Lorcan's good fortune. He thinks most highly of him. Indeed, he is convinced there is no finer man than your husband."

He spoke with such disdain, his words sounded like insults rather than compliments.

"His Grace is obviously a man of intelligence. He is right.

There is not a better man than my husband."

Her disgust began to mount as his smile turned into a leering grin. "And no finer woman than you, I dare say." He licked his lips and leaned into her, his breath hot and panting. "Sir Lorcan always did have an excellent eye for the ladies."

"But I severely question your intelligence, Mr. Maplethorpe. Lying to my husband. Being rude to me. I asked you to remove yourself from my chamber." She wanted to shove him into the hall, but he was so oily looking and disgusting to her senses in every way.

This man had no manners at all. "Is there something wrong with you?"

He reached out to stroke her cheek. "Of course not."

She slapped his hand away. "Sir! I suggest you crawl back into your ferret hole as fast as you can and keep hidden from my husband until his temper calms. Oh, and never dare cross my path again, or it will be my husband having to hold me back from stuffing you so far up your little hole that—"

She stopped in mid-sentence as Lorcan suddenly loomed behind the man. "Is this officious toady bothering you?"

She smiled at Lorcan. "Yes, dearest. He is. I asked him to leave, and he refused."

Maplethorpe scrambled back a few steps. "I meant no harm. It's all been a misunderstanding. Perfectly simple to explain. I was coming down to meet you when—"

Lorcan shoved him against the wall. "Do not compound your lies. The duke shall hear of this."

"Oh, yes. Indeed! I shall report—"

"What? That you attempted to make your way into my wife's chamber after purposely luring me out of the way? I want you gone from this inn within the hour."

"But we're in the midst of a drenching downpour. The roads are flooded."

"You should have thought of that before accosting my wife. Fifty-nine minutes, Maplethorpe."

"Who do you think you are? I am the duke's man," he said, sounding quite indignant.

"You are his little toad, and I ought to squish you with my boot. Which I will do if you do not leave this inn at once. Fifty-eight minutes."

"I never liked you, Brayden."

Lorcan grinned. "I know. Don't care. Fifty-seven."

"The duke will hear of this!"

"I am cowering in fear. Fifty-six."

Maplethorpe retreated to his chamber and began to pack his belongings. He'd left his door open so Cammy could see into it and hear him ranting as he rang for a maid to assist him in packing. He growled at Effie when she appeared in response to his summons. "Stupid girl! Is there another decent place to stay anywhere nearby?"

"The Reaper's Tavern is just across the way. It also serves as an inn. The rooms aren't as nice, and the guests are of lesser quality, but it will provide a roof over your head."

Lorcan stood beside Cammy, casually resting his shoulder against the corridor wall as he watched the fellow scurry about his chamber. "Lor," she said quietly, "will he cause you any problems?"

"No. He's just a clerk with an elevated sense of his own importance." He spared her a glance and frowned. "Did he frighten you?"

"He irritated me. Angered me. But Lor, the work you do is dangerous. What if he goes out of his way to subvert it?"

"There is little he can do to me. He is just the duke's pet ferret. He fills the duke in on whatever information he gathers, but it only goes one way. The duke never trusts him with any information regarding our Crown activities. Those remain confidential. Only those in the highest echelons ever know what missions we are assigned. All sensitive documents are locked away from the eyes of officious prigs like him."

She placed a hand on his arm. "Don't be so quick to dismiss

him. He managed to lure you out of the way with a simple trick. Who is to say he has not done the same to the duke? It would take only a moment's distraction for him to sneak a glimpse of whatever documents are strewn on his desk or hidden in a drawer."

Her stomach tightened in knots as she thought back to their brief encounter. "And I might have said some unkind words to him."

Lorcan grinned. "I heard. Well done, Cammy."

She moaned. "No, it was not well done of me at all. Now he hates us both. How am I an asset to you when I mouth off at the slightest provocation?"

He shrugged. "I like your mouth."

"Lor, I'm serious."

"So am I." He glanced down the hall. "Forty-five minutes, Maplethorpe."

"Ugh, Lor. You are enjoying this far too much."

"Maybe, but I'm mostly angry with myself for falling for that stupid diversion. I saw him ogling you, reaching out his hand to touch you. I should have broken his damn hand."

"I'm glad you didn't. Tossing him out in the rain is punishment enough."

He growled low in his throat. "He's only going across the courtyard."

"That is excruciating punishment to a man with his elevated sense of self-worth."

"I suppose." He winked at her, then turned his gaze across the hall. "Forty minutes."

"Lor," she said in an urgent whisper. "Stop. You are goading him."

"He knows he is getting off easy. He tried to touch you."

"I slapped his hand away."

"He would not have respected your wishes and tried again had I not come up just then. No man gets to touch my wife."

"Which I am not yet."

He turned to look at her, his eyes that beautiful silver and filled with tenderness. "You are, Cammy." He tapped his knuckles against his heart. "Right here. Where it counts. Thirty minutes, Maplethorpe."

He kept his gaze on her. "I'm going to kick his bony arse down those stairs if he doesn't hurry up. Does he really think I'll change my mind and allow him to stay if he stalls long enough? He's lucky I don't walk in there and punch him unconscious."

"I don't know how I can find you lovable and insufferable at the same time. You do this all the time, saying something utterly charming and in the same breath behaving like an oaf."

He crossed his arms over his chest and smirked. "It's a gift."

She meant to admonish him but emitted a mirthful laugh instead. "I don't think *The Book of Love* has a category for you, Lor."

"Yes, it does. I'm a simple man when stripped to my bare essence. Loyal. Faithful. Protective of those I love. Twenty-five minutes, Maplethorpe! For pity's sake, how long does it take a man to pack?"

"As you said, he isn't packing. He's stalling."

"He should have thought about the consequences before he misbehaved. I'm truly sorry, Cammy."

"It isn't your fault."

"Yes, it is."

"Men have been doing this to me since I was fourteen," she said, hoping to assuage him. But her words only riled him further. "We can discuss it after breakfast when we return to reading the book."

"Fine. Go back inside our chamber now."

"Why?"

"Because I am going to grab that cur by the scruff of his neck and kick him out of the inn."

She regarded him in confusion. "But he still has twenty minutes left."

He cast her a steely-eyed look. "You can't seriously think I am going to give him more time. Maplethorpe! I'm coming for you."

The man darted out of his chamber, travel bags in hand, and scrambled down the back stairs used by the staff.

Lorcan strode down the steps after him.

With the men gone, Effie poked her head into the hall.

After a moment, she walked to Cammy, all the while wringing her hands. "Lady Camellia, please forgive me. I did not realize your husband had remained downstairs when I brought the breakfast tray up. That Mr. Maplethorpe tricked me into thinking he was to meet him at your door."

"I understand, Effie. I'm sorry I spoke harshly to you. He rattled all of us, didn't he? You needn't worry." She glanced at the tray still on the side table in the hall. "I had better eat my breakfast before it turns cold."

Effie quickly brought it into her chamber and set it on the table. "Is there anything else you need, m'lady?"

She wished she could say something to the girl. Would she ever get used to being referred to as a lady? "No, this is perfect."

She reached out and took Effie's hands in hers. "You're trembling. Please do not be overset. We know it was not your fault. You will not get into any trouble."

They were about the same age.

But in this moment, Cammy suddenly felt older and wiser, which was laughable because she was utterly clueless about the true harshness of life. She had been raised in a sheltered existence in Barnstaple by loving parents.

The worst that could be said was that men ogled her.

And sometimes, they fought over her.

There was also the one horrible time…that wretched lord had tried to take things farther. He would have succeeded, too, if not for Mr. Ogilvie's dog coming to her rescue.

She shook her head.

The incident had occurred over a year ago and still haunted her.

The scar on her back would be permanent.

She gave Effie's hand another squeeze and muttered another assurance that all would be well.

"Thank you, m'lady. That tavern is a dismal place. Anyone sent there is going to the Grim Reaper. It is no less than he deserves." The girl cast a shaky smile and hurried out.

Now alone, Cammy began to nibble her lip.

She hadn't wanted to tell Lorcan about her scar or that incident. But once they were husband and wife, he would have the right to undress her. He would notice the cruel, red slash across her back and start asking questions.

This is why she never wore low-cut gowns and often wore her hair down to purposely obscure it. But the odious mark could be felt through the fabric of her gown. Lorcan had only to touch in just the right spot, and he would feel it.

He would ask about it.

She was still fretting and had yet to eat a bite of her breakfast when Lorcan came striding in and immediately dominated the room with his presence. His hair was wet, as were his clothes. But he had a broad grin on his face. "One rat disposed of," he said with a laugh.

She feigned a cheerful smile.

Of course, he saw through it immediately.

"Cammy," he said, taking her hand in his. "Did he frighten you?"

"No, not at all. What an annoying fellow he is."

He nodded. "Why are you so overset? I didn't hurt Maplethorpe if that's what has you concerned. I merely walked him across to the other inn. It is truly a rundown place. Just what he deserves."

"I am not overset. I just…Effie was shaken up and…it was just an unpleasant situation." Which might have convinced him if her hands were not visibly trembling. Her stomach was in knots, and she truly felt ill. "I'll be all right in a moment."

He closed the door, bolted it, and then nudged her into a chair.

"Here, let me pour you a cup of tea," he said, taking the chair beside hers. "Drink to warm your insides."

Did he think tea would fix the scar on her back? Or the memory of that horrid encounter?

Her expression must have revealed her thoughts. He stopped pouring and set the pot down. "This isn't entirely about Maplethorpe, is it?"

"What do you mean?" She was so bad at hiding her feelings, he saw right through her.

"I am a fool. Ten times over. I didn't press you before, but I will now. And don't think of using a megrim as an excuse to avoid this discussion."

She rubbed her temples, dreading the question he was now going to ask. "But my head does hurt."

"Cammy, I think it is your heart that is in pain."

She nodded.

She hadn't meant to nod, but all of her was aching now, and she wanted it to end.

Why could she not hold herself together?

She tried, but it felt as though she was unraveling, like a badly sewn hem with a thread left loose so that one had only to grab it and tug for the entire hem to come down.

"What happened that has you so frightened of London?"

CHAPTER SIX

"LOR, PLEASE. I don't want to talk about it."

He cursed inwardly, realizing there was more to Cammy's fear than a general dislike of being gawked at by the peers who would seek her attention. It wasn't about her shyness or her young years, either. She was eighteen and would turn nineteen next month. He'd learned that much from conversations with her aunt and sisters.

Many young women were married and had children by then.

Perhaps gaining confidence through age and experience might have helped her overcome whatever troubled her, but she was still far from that, and her distress was no small thing.

He reached out to take her hand.

She drew it away. "Effie only brought up breakfast for me. I ought to ask her to bring up something for you."

He frowned and stopped her when she tried to rise. "Are you afraid of me?"

"No. Of course not." The notion sincerely startled her, which gave him some relief. He would never gain her confidence if she did not trust him unquestioningly.

"Then talk to me. I will always protect you, Cammy."

"I know. It is in your nature."

"Big ape. Possessive arse." He leaned forward and smiled at her. "It has its advantages. You know I will never let anyone hurt you."

She nodded. "Tonight, Lor. We'll talk about it tonight."

"Promise me, love." He hadn't meant the endearment to slip out, but he wasn't about to take it back or pretend it was something less than it was. He was falling in love with Cammy. Or had already fallen in love with her.

Probably the latter.

He wasn't doubting his feelings, only that they had come upon him so fast, they'd caught him by surprise. He'd known her only a few weeks. Not even a month. Would learning her secret anguish make him love her less?

She was staring at him in wonder, probably doubting she had heard him right.

He arched an eyebrow. "Care to say it back to me?"

He knew she wouldn't. Nor would he be hurt if she did not. It was too soon for both of them.

She reached for her cup of tea and busied herself drinking it.

"It's all right, Cammy. You needn't say anything to me." He kissed her on the forehead. "We're going to finish reading that book together after breakfast. I'll be back in a few minutes."

He went into the inn's dining room and grabbed a handful of freshly baked scones and a cup of coffee for himself.

He returned with them and paused at the door. Cammy was still seated at the table, fork now in hand, merely picking at her food.

He shut the door behind him and settled once more in the chair beside her. "I'll trade you a scone for those eggs," he said, keeping his manner light.

She nodded and nudged her plate over to him.

They ate in silence, something he did not mind at all. He was used to being on his own and was not much for talking even when in company.

Cammy surprised him by breaking the silence. "*The Book of Love* says we must always be honest in our feelings. It teaches us how to look at a thing and see it for what it truly is, not what we hope it to be."

They had discussed this in their first conversations, so he knew there was more to her point and did not interrupt her.

"While you were tossing Maplethorpe across to the other inn, I tried to calm myself by making lists in my head."

"What were those lists about?"

"You, of course. And us." She stared down at the apricot scone she had picked apart. It sat uneaten in a crumbled pile on her saucer. "You are a good fit for me, Lor…at least, you are pleasing to my senses, and heaven knows you are the sort of mate any woman would want. Strong, protective, able to keep the wolves from the door."

"I hear a 'but' coming on."

"Read the chapters on connections and expectations. Those expectations, in particular, are very important to me. Read on about marriage and the bonds we develop over time that make it thrive. As well, the character traits in us that will destroy a marriage. What flaws are we willing to accept? Which flaws will destroy all hope of happiness?"

"You left out compromise." He reached out and took her hand. "Isn't this one of the pillars of a happy marriage? Truth, trust, respect, faithfulness, willingness to compromise."

"Would you be willing to compromise if I refused to live in London?"

This was the heart of it, the one demand she would not give in on. Were he merely an agent for the Crown, it would not be a concern. But he worked closely with the Foreign Office and, at times, the Home Office on matters of security for the Crown and England. He was privy to the most sensitive information. He regularly met with cabinet ministers and military leaders at the highest levels. His opinion was often sought after and highly valued.

He had to remain in London, at least for now.

He had to be within easy reach if summoned by the Duke of Wooton or one of Parliament's cabinet ministers. It was not even unheard of for the king to summon him.

"My work is there, Cammy. I cannot walk away from it." This was his demand, the one requirement he could not give in on.

"But your assignments take you all over the country, sometimes abroad as well. What difference would it make where we lived?"

"I'm more than merely a tracker in service to the Crown. Do you think I received a knighthood merely for my talents as a bloodhound?"

This obviously surprised her. "What more do you do?"

He wasn't ready to tell her all of it yet. "Let's set the discussion aside for now. We can talk about it once we finish reading the book together."

He glanced out the window, eager for the pelting rain to stop. But it seemed the storm had not yet lost its strength, and they might be trapped here tomorrow as well. He stifled his frustration. He wanted to marry Cammy as soon as possible.

He wanted to marry her and sort out their differences while bound to each other as a married couple.

She was already finding reasons why their union would not work.

He was not going to allow this to happen.

This was the ruthless part of him, but he was thinking of her as much as he was thinking of himself. However, he was not dismissing her concerns at all. Obviously, something had happened to her that scared her so much she was willing to give up her happiness to avoid ever having to face this frightening thing again.

So, what was the connection to London when she had spent her life in Barnstaple?

What was he missing?

He finished his breakfast, waited for her to take the last, paltry nibbles of hers, then piled their plates on a tray, and set it outside their door. He latched the door, more to keep Cammy from darting away, but she did not have to know that. She thought he was latching it to keep others out.

They were going to have an uncomfortable conversation. He would not let Cammy run away from their chance at happiness.

He removed his boots, then took out *The Book of Love* and settled on the bed with it.

"You want to read it there?" Cammy eyed him suspiciously.

"My back is stiff from sleeping on the floor. Sitting in that chair is no better. Do you mind? I just need to stretch out on something soft for a while."

She accepted his excuse and settled beside him, sitting up while he lay beside her. "Read the next few chapters to yourself, Lor."

He did not press her about reading with him since she was familiar with its contents and could recite them to him by heart. "All right."

The observations discussed about men and women in these chapters were not hard to comprehend. He quickly pored through the pages on the senses, understanding how one could be so captivated by the look of someone that they overlooked all warning signs of faults. He also read about connections, those threads that bound them to each other and strengthened as they shared memories over time.

He and Cammy already had several important connections. Family members married to each other. Similar upbringing, similar hopes, and dreams. Importance of family life.

Expectations were the stumbling block, but it was not as dire as Cammy had made out to be in her mind. They both wanted a true marriage, the two of them building a life together. The difference of opinion was in where that life together would be built.

As for flaws in either of them that might destroy a marriage, he did not think there were any that would. Neither of them had excessive behaviors that the other could not tolerate. No gambling problems. No hard drinking. Neither of them would break their marriage vows. So this left the smaller problems, the little quirks that got under each other's skin. He had not seen any of those either, not in the time they had spent together.

Surely, he would have noticed something about her that raised his hackles by now. People could not be thrown together for extended periods of time without something coming to the surface.

He knew what was important to him and could make his own list of the little traits that would irritate him.

He was not a talker, so he did not want to be burdened with a woman who chattered incessantly.

He often liked to be on his own to think, so he could not be with a woman who constantly demanded his attention.

He'd spent days with Cammy and enjoyed her company. She did not talk too much. Often, he had to be the one to draw her out. She was not snappish or condescending to him or anyone else, for that matter. She had a sweet heart. Her laughter was soft and enchanting. In short, he found her delightful.

Beautiful, charming, clever, and compassionate.

How was she not perfect for him?

He reached out and took her hand, entwining her fingers in his. Even her hand was soft and small, just perfect. "Cammy, whatever it is that is scaring you about London...we'll work it out. There isn't anything that will interfere with my marrying you."

He felt her tense immediately.

"Lor, once we are married, you will have the power to tell me where we shall live. I cannot live in London. I will run away from you if you make me."

"Do you think I would ever force you? Purposely make you miserable? We'll work out a solution. Isn't this what compromise is all about?"

"A husband holds all the power. Why would you listen to me after we exchange wedding vows?"

"Because I want you to be happy. I want you in my life." He would do whatever it took, even if it meant living apart for much of the year. It was far from a perfect solution, but he would rather be with her for one month out of the year than not at all.

"Compromise," she murmured, moving closer to him. He took that as a good sign. "You are better at it than I am, Lor. But I will try. Just don't be angry with me if I cannot summon the courage to meet you halfway."

"I'll never be angry with you."

She laughed, but it was a gentle laugh, not bitter or harsh at all. "Yes, you will. How can we always be in agreement? I'm sure we will raise our voices on occasion or be irritated by something the other one says or does."

"Those are small things. We can't expect perfection in each other."

"I think you are as close to perfect as anyone I have ever met."

He jokingly winced. "Don't say that. I am bound to disappoint you then."

"No, you would never. I am aware you can be apishly protective and possessive, that you can be ruthless when you think you need to be. You like to be on your own, but you are also very good around people. You've been quite tolerant of me."

"Cammy, you've been an angel."

"Hardly but thank you. You are also competitive by nature. You must have irritated your brothers to no end, always trying to do whatever they were doing, and determined to best them at it. Is this not what younger brothers do?"

He tweaked her chin. "Perhaps. What about you? Were you the same with your sisters?"

They had this in common, each being the youngest of three siblings. He was genuinely curious about how sisters behaved. As boys, he, Shayne, and Donal were always poking and pushing each other, always testing boundaries, and competing with each other.

"My sisters treated me as their little doll. They mothered me to death. But I never minded very much. They played with me, read to me, encouraged my painting. They rarely complained when I followed them about while barely able to toddle. But I wanted so much to be with them, doing whatever it was they did. They always accepted me. I don't know if this is in the nature of all sisters, but it was for us. June and Willow are not only my sisters but my best friends. Always encouraging and nurturing. However, there is one thing they did that drove me mad."

"What was that?"

"They loved my hair and were always playing with it. Brushing it, trying out new hairstyles on me. Some of them were ridiculous."

"Ah, quite the villains." He could not wait to run his fingers through those gloriously silken curls. "You know your hair is beautiful."

"I've been told. I never complained when they played with it because I enjoyed being with them. But sitting still while they twisted and curled my hair into idiotic styles was incredibly boring." She shifted even closer to him so that he could feel the warmth of her skin against his. "I know what you are thinking."

He arched an eyebrow. "What am I thinking?"

In truth, he could hardly keep a thought in his head while her soft body was pressed against him.

"That if I truly hated it, I could cut it off. It is just hair, after all. Then others would see there was more to me than a mass of dark gold curls. But I do like my hair. I suppose I am quite vain about it."

He laughed. "You? Hardly. Vanity requires a manipulative aspect to your temperament, and you are the most guileless woman I have ever met. You are beautiful, but you go out of your way not to use it to your advantage. So, you are permitted to like your hair and not lop it off. Do you mind that I find it quite attractive?"

What man wouldn't?

He glanced at their positions.

This looked promising. She had curled herself against his

shoulder.

She must have seen the direction of his gaze and tried to scramble away. "I'm sorry, Lor. I didn't—"

"I'm glad you feel comfortable around me." He drew her back to him. "There is nothing wrong with enjoying the physical attributes. Our liking the look of each other is an important part of what will keep us bound to each other. But I know it is not the only part."

"This is what I resent most," she admitted, her tension easing as she sat beside him. "Everyone thinks of nothing but the physical attributes once they set their eyes on me. I am never more than that. It isn't only the men who do this, but the women, too. I am so tired of being treated as though I am an empty-headed trinket. Then I worry perhaps I am, that they are seeing me as nothing more because I am nothing more."

"Cammy, don't ever believe that."

"It is hard not to."

He set the book aside, then settled back and propped his hands behind his head. "We don't need more reading. We need to get to know each other better. Tell me about yourself. The little details. What is your favorite food? Your favorite color? Favorite time of day?"

She answered those questions easily. "Apple tarts. Purple, but the softer hues such as lilac. Morning is my favorite time of day."

"Why morning?"

"Because of the promise it holds. It's a new start, a new opportunity, the chance for something special to come into your life."

He then asked how she filled her days.

She answered that easily as well, her eyes brightening as she told him about her work with the gentleman who was a Royal Society naturalist. In describing her drawings, he realized that she loved the outdoors and was keen on sketching it. She was not afraid of climbing cliffs to better capture the birds on paper.

"Cammy, were you never in fear of falling?" he asked, sincerely concerned when she described what she did in order to get a good look at her birds. Those heights were dangerous, especially for a woman attempting to climb them in a gown. How did the fabric not get tangled in her legs?

"No, I am rather a good climber. But I do respect the dangers. I sewed a special gown for myself." She described it as a pair of breeches hidden beneath an overlayer of fabric that could be rolled up and tucked in a belt around her waist when she climbed. "Once I am down, I merely untuck the overlayer of fabric, and it falls into place as any gown would, hiding the breeches underneath."

He thought it was quite inventive.

"My parents don't know. Please don't say anything to them when you meet them. They think I draw birds along the beach. They would stop me if I told them what was involved."

"Because they love you and fear for your safety."

"I am careful, Lor. And I don't attempt the truly dangerous climbs. I would never go up the cliff face. There are easier trails to those nests. Tumbling down any of those would not kill me."

"Cammy, that is—"

"Sensible. Is this what you were going to say? Because I always use my common sense. I am not foolhardy. Those hikes to their nesting spots are difficult...yes, that's the best word to describe them. They are not dangerous, just difficult. I also wear proper climbing boots. And what of you? Don't you risk your life every time you go off on an assignment?"

"That is different."

"How? Would I not cry my eyes out if harm were to befall you?"

He cast her a tender gaze. "Would you, Cammy?"

She sighed. "Yes. This is another important consideration, Lor. The work you do. It is fraught with peril."

"I know. And it is not going to change anytime soon. You might have chosen not to marry me because of my line of work, but this isn't about me. It is about protecting you. Once we are married, you will have the protection of my name no matter what happens to me."

She remained silent a long moment, then rolled to the side of the bed and sat up.

"Cammy?" He reached out to her, taking her hand and making certain to keep his touch gentle, for she was obviously overset.

"I said I would tell you tonight, but I'm ready now."

He sat up, as well, but said not a word. He was afraid she would change her mind if he so much as breathed.

His eyes widened as she began to unfasten her gown.

"Help me, Lor."

He undid the laces, his breath catching as she proceeded to fumble with the ties of her corset next. He helped her with those as well.

She was not done yet, slipping the chemise off her shoulders. "Help me, Lor," she repeated in a whisper.

He had been with women before.

He was quite adept at helping them shed their clothes.

But he was not prepared for Cammy…well, he was able to help her, easily slipping the garments off her—the gown, corset, and chemise—nudging them down to her waist. But he was not quite prepared for how deeply his heart was involved.

It wasn't about lust, although his was full-blown and savage now that he'd caught an eyeful of her beautifully shaped breasts.

What was she doing?

He quickly tamped down his low-brain frenzy and resolved not to touch her unless she asked. She was precious to him, and he did not want to make a mistake.

"Draw my hair aside," she said softly.

He took those beautiful, thick curls of gold and gathered them in his hands, still marveling at how much she trusted him to bare herself to him. That's when he saw it, a long, mottled line of red that stretched across her back. He recognized it as a whip mark, one that must have been viciously applied to cause this extensive damage.

Anger tore through him.

He wanted to shout in rage. "Who did this?"

"Who do you think? Some lord who believed he was above the law."

"What's his name?" he asked, his voice shaking with rage.

"I don't know. He and some friends were passing through Barnstaple. They were arrogant and thoughtless. He, in particular, was as bad as Lord Belfy and his friends. We all did our best to keep out of their way for the duration of their stay. They did not remain in Barnstaple very long. When I saw them leave town, I thought they were gone for good. So I set off to draw my birds. It was morning, and I looked forward to being able to sketch them again."

"Only he hadn't gone?" He tried to keep his voice calm, but he was too furious to manage it.

"His friends had moved on to their next destination, but he'd been delayed for whatever reason. Perhaps he had stayed behind purposely to follow me. I was alone on my way to the cliffs. He must have thought his rank allowed him every privilege. He approached me."

She circled her arms around herself as though wanting to withdraw inside herself.

Her voice was hollow as she spoke. "You can guess what he wanted. I fought back, of course, and defended myself by landing a kick where it hurt him most. But in successfully fighting him off, I had angered him. When he realized he was not going to have his way with me, he stumbled over to his horse and drew out his whip."

Pain tore through Lorcan.

"I hadn't expected him to whip me. I never realized anyone could be so cruel. I screamed, but I was too far out of town to be heard by anyone. However, a farmer's dog heard me and came to my rescue. He bit that lord hard on his buttocks. The poor dog was whipped, too."

She took a deep, trembling breath and continued. "The wretched fiend. I know I ought to feel bad about him being mauled by Mr. Ogilvie's dog, but I don't. He got what he deserved. But he wouldn't stop whipping either of us. I was in too much pain to fight back by then, almost unconscious with it."

"Cammy…dear heaven."

"Fortunately, the farmer's dog still had fight left in him and bit that miscreant lord hard again. Anyway, it was enough to scare him off."

Lorcan wanted to take her in his arms and hold her forever.

She was now shivering as she spoke. "He leapt on his horse and rode off as if the devil were on his tail. I'm sure sitting in his saddle had to be painful for him. I hope he remains in excruciating pain to this day. I know it is not charitable of me, but it gave me great pleasure to see his clothes ripped and his bottom bloodied. I hoped it would hurt him for weeks, years even. I wanted him to live with the reminder of what he had tried to do to me."

She began to raise her chemise to cover herself. "Now you know why I want nothing to do with those London lords. I shudder to think what might have happened to me had the farmer's dog not come to my rescue."

So did he.

To see that raw mark against her soft skin had his blood boiling and his heart in chaotic turmoil. In lowering her garments, she had not only revealed her body to him, her soft shoulders and those magnificent breasts he had longed to see and explore, but her soul.

She was beautiful beyond belief.

But this wasn't about his desires.

This was about the secret ache she had carried all this time and the trust she held for him in order to confide it. He would never do anything to betray her.

"I hid the damage to my gown by tossing my cloak over my shoulders, then made my way home and burned the gown. That was easy enough to do. But trying to cleanse the whip marks on my back proved much harder. Some of them were superficial and hadn't broken through my skin. But this one in particular…this one was bad. I'd fallen to my knees, helpless. He just struck and struck, the same spot, over and over."

"Did you not seek a doctor to—"

"No, I dared not tell anyone. They would have reported the incident to my parents, and then I would have been forbidden to go near the nesting birds again. I treated the wound as best as I could. Juniper walked in and saw what I was doing. I had to tell her what had happened since she saw the lash marks and would not let it go until I confided in her. She tended to me. But she is the only one who ever knew. I swore her to secrecy. The fiend was gone. He had not…violated me. Even if he had, he would have gotten away with it because of his status. I would have been the only one ruined. Juniper understood and kept silent. Not even Willow knows."

She wiped a tear off her cheek and took a shaky breath before continuing. "I wanted to tell Willow when she got hurt a few weeks ago and was so overset about the wounds to her arm. She was afraid they would leave scars and worried that Shayne would be revolted by them, that he would not want her."

"My brother would never abandon her over such a thing as that. He loves her too much."

She nodded. "Still, it is something she feared. But I quickly saw how little it mattered to him. So I kept quiet about my own scar. She did not need to hear about it while she was suffering from her own injuries."

He ached to hold her and kiss her, but now that she'd let her secret anguish spill, she was eager to cover herself again. He helped her don the corset and was as gentle as could be when lacing her gown.

"Now you know why I don't want to be in London," she said, her body still trembling.

He was seething.

Even his hands were shaking with anger as he tied the last of her lacings.

"I thought I could manage it if all three of us were together, but with Willow and Juniper now married…I cannot do it, Lor. I simply cannot."

"Nor will you ever have to. We'll figure it out. I promise you, Cammy. There is no question we must marry, but I will never make you go through that pain again."

"You don't mind that I will not go to London? But what about your work?"

"I cannot leave it behind. There will be a solution." He took her onto his lap and wrapped his arms around her. "There must be."

She flung her arms around his neck. "I'm glad it was you who came after me."

He smiled, although his heart was still in turmoil over her ordeal. "I would have killed anyone else who tried. Being a possessive arse has its advantages."

He held her in silence for several minutes, willing to hold her all night if it would help in any way. She remained clinging to him. He felt the moisture of her tears against his shirt. "Thank you, Lor. I'll be all right now."

"Are you sure?" He doubted she would ever get over the harrowing experience, but perhaps it would not interfere with her happiness quite so much, especially now that he was aware of it and could help her deal with any rough moments.

"Yes, you may not believe this…it felt good to unburden myself to you. But I don't want to think of it or talk about it anymore. I can't, Lor."

"I know, sweetheart."

She was surprised by his use of the endearment, but she should not have been. He had called her "love" earlier. This what she was, *his love*.

She wasn't ready to accept it yet.

"Since the rain has not stopped, and we are trapped here for another day, Lor," she said with forced brightness, "any suggestions on how to occupy our time?"

He understood her need to lighten the conversation. "I do, but you will likely slap my face at the games I would suggest."

She laughed as she dried the last of her tears. "I always knew you were wicked."

He kissed her on the forehead. "I am only teasing. You will always be safe with me. I hope you know that."

She nodded. "I do."

He did not want to be anything but gentle with her after hearing the reason for her running away. The physical pain was bad enough, but she had buried her anguish so deep inside, it had gnawed at her soul until almost devoured her entirely.

He would never allow that to happen.

He intended to discover the identity of the fiend.

What would happen next, he didn't know.

But there was no need to discuss it now and further overset her.

Showing him the scar had taken so much out of her. "I'll see if I can scrounge up a deck of playing cards. Do you play, Cammy?"

He must have said something right because she cast him another sweet smile.

Lord, this girl got to his heart.

"In fact," she said with an impish smirk, "I am a bit of a cardsharp."

"You are? Well, that's interesting. Shall we play for stakes?"

She nodded. "Name it, but be warned, I shall probably win."

"Then I had better set the wagers to my liking." He was glad she was ready to move on and set a lighter tone after what had been an excruciating conversation for her. "Very well, loser must kiss the winner."

"And what does the winner get to do to the loser?"

"Undress the loser."

She gasped, then shook her head and laughed. "You are a

wicked hound, Lorcan Brayden. That is utterly… I get to undress you?"

He grinned. "If you win. And if I win, I get to undress you."

But he turned serious in the next moment and caressed her cheek. "Cammy, I am in jest. I will never do anything to you that makes you uncomfortable. If I win—"

"You won't."

He emitted a bark of laughter, quite liking her saucy confidence. "If I win, just say the word, and I will not collect on my wager. It is only meant to be in fun."

She looked up at him, her eyes gleaming with mirth. "Oh, I think undressing you will be ever so much fun."

CHAPTER SEVEN

B LESSED SAINTS!

Was she really going to undress him?

Lorcan had worried about how Cammy would feel after revealing her secret to him. He was honored and heartened she had trusted him enough to tell him of her hidden pain, but also concerned his prodding had raised those insidious demons she had been trying so hard to suppress.

However, as they played cards, he began to appreciate her resilience. She was trouncing him and thoroughly enjoying herself. He liked this impertinently confident side of her and hoped sharing the incident with him had freed her of the worst of those agonizing memories.

It was a lot to ask.

One conversation was not going to heal her.

"I think I shall have you remove your shirt first, Lor," she teased, watching him lose another hand to her.

"I shall have you remove the pins from your hair," he replied as she dealt him another two cards and took two for herself.

There were aspects to her that he had never realized existed. She was a talented artist and quite nimble with calculations, in addition to being beautiful and sweet. He was at fault for not noticing her abilities sooner, of course. But one look at her and his brain turned to pudding. Whose wouldn't? No wonder she felt frustrated when everyone complimented her on her beauty and ignored everything else about her.

She wanted to be seen for the person she truly was, not treated as an object to be set upon a pedestal and gawked at.

"Hit me," he said, for it was late afternoon, and they had spent the last few hours playing a game of *vingt-un*.

She was surprisingly quick with numbers and on the verge of wiping him out.

Indeed, this innocent lamb was about to strip the wolf of his clothing…assuming she was daring enough. He certainly had no issue with losing to her. After all, he'd set the wagers. However, he had never seriously considered he might lose.

They were playing for spillikins, a game of pick-up sticks. But they were using the thin sticks as currency. He had borrowed them and a deck of cards from the well-stocked gaming room at the inn.

Cammy giggled. "Are you sure you want me to deal you another card?"

He arched an eyebrow. "Are you counting them?"

"Perhaps. Obviously, you are not, or you never would have asked for another. Do you wish to take it back?"

"No. Hit me."

"You do realize I am about to win the last of your spillikins."

"Yes." He leaned closer, his lips quirked upward in amusement. "I am eager to see what you intend to do about it. I think I shall always enjoy losing to you. But you purposely distracted me."

She eyed him innocently. "How did I do that?"

"With your angel eyes and siren's body. You used me as your test frog, and it worked. So mark that down as a successful experiment."

She stifled a laugh and glanced at *The Book of Love* perched atop the bureau. "I don't know what you mean."

"Shall I read back that first chapter on the male low brain and how easily it falls into a lustful frenzy? You held your cards to your chest, which is quite magnificent, as you well know. You took deep breaths, drawing my attention to the swell of your breasts each time I had to decide whether or not to go for a card."

"Are you accusing me of interfering with your mathematical abilities?" She snorted mirthfully. "They are surprisingly dismal, by the way."

Oh, he loved to hear her laugh. "Only when I am in a low-brain frenzy, which I was throughout the game because of your nefarious ploys. So be it. The question is, are you going to claim your prize?"

She blushed furiously as she dealt him his last card. It was a jack of hearts and sent him over the count of twenty-one.

She cleared her throat. "I told you I would win."

"Indeed, you did. As loser, I owe you a kiss. May I claim it now?"

She nodded. "I like your kisses."

"I know." He took her hand and raised her to her feet, then wrapped his arms around her waist to draw her delightful body up against him. "Close your eyes, Cammy."

"Oh," she whispered, her face taking on a dreamy expression.

He watched her eyelids flutter closed, the dark lashes a lovely contrast to her pink cheeks.

"Now, put your arms around my neck."

She reached up and circled them at his nape. "Lor, I—"

He crushed his mouth to hers, the need to taste her thrumming savagely through him. But he held back his ardor, for she was still vulnerable, and he did not ever wish to push her beyond what she was ready to willingly give. They had enjoyed themselves these last few hours, neither of them able to overlook the sexual tension building between them.

By confiding her pain to him, Cammy had woven a powerfully intimate thread between them. Their hearts were now bound to each other, although he was not certain she understood this yet. Hopefully, this kiss would show her. She had said she liked his kisses. He felt much the same about hers. They were refreshingly honest and particularly sweet because they were meant to be shared with him alone.

This intimate knowledge had also stirred a desire for a deeper physical intimacy, not only for him, but he suspected for her as well.

However, she was shy.

When teasing him, she'd blushed furiously and was uncertain how he would take their suggestive banter. Not that it was all that risqué. But she had never been so forward with a man; that much was obvious.

He liked that she was comfortable enough to be playful with him.

He also liked that she was attracted to him physically beyond kisses.

He knew the telltale signs.

The light flush of her cheeks.

The nibble of her lip.

The way she leaned toward him throughout their play and the genuine enjoyment she seemed to take from their time together.

But he would remain careful not to demand too much of this lovely girl.

The pain of her first encounter with that wretched lord had scarred her inside and out, and was still raw. More so now that she had spoken of the incident for the first time since it had happened.

He licked his tongue lightly along the seam of her lips to nudge them open.

She moaned in sweet surrender.

Lord, he had to get her home to Barnstaple and marry her quickly because this restraint was killing him. But he indulged a moment longer, probing her sweet, plump mouth and enjoying the feel of her breasts pillowed against his chest.

He was a big man, and she was only of average size. Yet, they fit perfectly against each other. They would always fit perfectly to each other; this is something he knew simply from the way their bodies had responded from their first meeting.

He tasted tea and apricot scones on her lips.

"Cammy, sweet heaven." He wound his fingers through her silken locks, wanting to draw her atop him and surround them both in those golden strands as he taught her the pleasures of love. But he knew his limitations. Another moment and he would have the clothes off her, soon followed by his, and there would be no holding back.

He groaned as he eased his mouth off hers, but he did not have the strength to let her out of his arms yet. Of course, she had only to say the word. But her eyes, as she opened them, were as bright as candles and her smile was soft and captivating.

He cast her a naughty grin in return. "Care to claim your prize now?"

Her cheeks turned crimson, and she suddenly appeared frozen. "Lor…how far am I supposed to go?"

"In stripping me of my clothes? As far as you wish."

"And if I demanded you take off all your clothes?"

"Then that is what I'll do. I am not the bashful one. Obviously, you are. I don't mind, Cammy. This is meant for your enjoyment, not to scare you."

"Do you mind if we put it off? I don't think I am that adventurous yet." She flicked her tongue lightly across her lips. "But I think I will be ready tonight."

He caressed her cheek. "There is no expiration on your prize. Claim it whenever you wish."

Although Cammy had a siren's face and body, at heart she was a traditional girl with a strong set of moral values which—to his chagrin—included not undressing in the afternoon and certainly no sex.

Probably none before their marriage vows were spoken.

Not that he intended to claim her before then.

She was innocent and deserved to be so until her wedding day.

They were in enough of a mess without compounding it. Yes,

she would be ruined either way, but it was important to him that she could hold her head up with pride and assert her purity. He hoped it would never be necessary.

There were other ways to pleasure her, and he meant to show her those, but not until she was truly ready.

He kissed her lightly on the forehead. "You owe me nothing, Cammy. Whatever we do must always be done willingly."

"Except for the marriage part."

Was she still worried about having trapped him? Which she had not, but he could not seem to convince her otherwise. "I've told you, I knew what I was doing. I went after you fully aware of the potential consequences and ready to accept them."

He strode to the window and peered out. "The sky appears to be brightening, just a light gray now. No longer that thunder-cloud overcast to it. The rain is easing up, too."

She came to his side to peer out. "Oh, thank goodness. Does this mean we will be able to leave tomorrow morning?"

"The roadways will be thick with mud, trees will likely be down, and there will be entire areas of the road flooded. But it is worth a try. We can stop at the next coaching inn if travel proves too difficult. I think we are both eager to get out of here." He shook his head. "Not that I minded a moment with you. I just want us to move on, get you home, and us married."

"Lor, you must be feeling so trapped. I don't mean with me but being stuck inside this little room for so long. Shall we have our supper downstairs? For a man who so enjoys the outdoors, you must be as restless as a caged lion. We should be safe enough from prying eyes if we ask for a private dining room. Besides, that odious Mr. Maplethorpe is no longer here to disturb us."

"Speaking of the man," Lorcan muttered, gazing out the window in time to see Maplethorpe scurry out of the Reaper's Tavern and furtively make his way to the nearby stable.

What was that mean-spirited little ferret up to?

A sudden chill ran up his spine, for there was something in his expression that had Lorcan wondering...was the petty oaf going to tamper with Berengaria?

"Cammy, stay right here. Don't open the door to anyone but me. Not even anyone claiming to be on the inn's staff."

Her eyes rounded in surprise. "Where are you going?"

"To check on my horse. I'll be right back. If I think it is safe enough, I'll secure a private dining room for us before I return."

She took gentle hold of his arm. "Lor, what is going on?"

"Nothing. I need to check on Berengaria. It's the truth." Just not all of the truth and she knew it.

"And nothing to do with Mr. Maplethorpe? I saw him crossing to the stable."

He sighed and ran a hand through his hair. "I am not going to harm him. But I need to be sure he won't do anything to harm my horse. He's just the slimy sort to plan a malicious trick."

"I'll come with you."

He put his hands on her shoulders. "Let me handle it. I promise you, the worst I will do is kick his scrawny arse back to his lodgings. All right?"

She nodded with reluctance.

"Watch from the window, if you like. But don't be obvious about it. Just peek from behind the curtain. I don't want him noticing you and getting ideas." He gave her shoulders a light squeeze. "I'll be back shortly."

He left their chamber and strode downstairs, trying to keep his rage in check. Men like Maplethorpe and that vicious lord who had tried to take advantage of Cammy made his blood boil. They deserved a good pounding. But Cammy was watching and would not forgive him if he beat Maplethorpe to a bloody pulp.

Of course, he would never do any such thing unless that officious ferret meant to harm Berengaria. He strode out of the inn and into the tapering rain. The courtyard was a mess of mud and marshy puddles, but he easily skirted the worst of the muck and made his way to the stable.

It was dark inside, only the faintest glow of light coming from a lamp near the back stalls. He crept along quietly, his eyes soon adjusting to the dimness and his manner gentle with the horses he passed along the way, who were snorting and snuffling in their stalls.

Maplethorpe was too busy pouring something into a bucket of oats to notice his approach. What was he about to give Berengaria? "Here, my pretty. Come have your feed," the vile man was crooning as his filly nervously shied away. "Does your owner think he can toss me out with impunity? I'll show him. He'll—ack!"

"He'll do what, you sniveling coward?" Lorcan grabbed the bucket along with Maplethorpe and called for the ostler.

Several grooms also came running in response.

Lorcan handed one of the young lads the bucket. "He's poisoned it. Dispose of the contents very carefully. Don't let any of the horses near it. And I want a guard posted to watch over Berengaria."

"What of this slimy cove?" the ostler asked, rushing over to him as well. "Rest assured, he will never be allowed to step foot in here again. Shall I summon the magistrate?"

"I haven't done anything!" Maplethorpe shouted. "You cannot prove I ever meant to harm your horse. I'll charge you with assault, Brayden!"

"I am quaking in my boots." He dug into the man's breast pocket and removed a vial that was almost empty. "No harm, you say? Then I suppose you won't mind drinking the remains of this harmless vial. Go ahead, Maplethorpe. Or is it not so harmless? And I am certain the magistrate will easily determine that it matches the poison found in the bucket of oats. I'd like to see you explain that."

Unable to respond, he tried to break loose. Failing that, he took a desperate swing at Lorcan.

Lorcan easily dodged his fist. "You are only making it worse for yourself, you idiot." He dragged the man outside and tossed him into the mud. "That's a second warning, Maplethorpe. Go back to the Reaper's Tavern and pack up. I want you out of town before sundown. If you dare linger…there'll be no third warning. I'll break you in half."

The ostler followed closely behind him. "Mr. Brayden, what about the magistrate?"

"No need to summon him unless Mr. Maplethorpe will not agree to leave." Lorcan shoved the worthless specimen back in the mud when he tried to get up. "You are getting out of town immediately, aren't you?"

"I'll see you in hell, Brayden!"

He wanted to kick the idiot into the mud again but held back since Cammy was surely watching. He turned to the ostler instead. "If he isn't out of here by nightfall, then yes. Summon the magistrate, and I shall press charges."

The ostler grunted in satisfaction. "Very good. Do ye hear that, lads? We go straight to the magistrate if this villain isn't out of town by dark."

Lorcan fixed his angry gaze on Maplethorpe. "Is there something about this warning you do not understand?"

The man spouted more curses. "Rest assured, the duke will hear of this!"

"Indeed, he will. I'll be sending off a report to him on the next mail coach that comes through here." He turned away and grunted in disgust. He was angry, but not only for the harm the little ferret had attempted to perpetrate on his horse.

There was something else going on here.

What was he up to?

Lorcan's instincts were on heightened alert, his senses on fire, for there was something foul afoot.

Did the Duke of Wooton know he was here?

He turned to address the ostler. "Make certain he never gets close to any of the horses again. Watch out for him. He's a vindictive prig."

Maplethorpe sputtered as he staggered to his feet. "My horse is in there."

The grooms and ostler now surrounded him as Lorcan

stepped away. "Ye heard Sir Lorcan," the ostler growled, outraged that anyone would dare harm the precious beasts under his care. "Send over one of the boys from the tavern once ye are ready to leave. He will deliver yer mount to ye. If ye dare enter my stable again, my boys and I will make certain ye do not walk out alive. Poison, indeed! What sort of man carries such a thing around?"

Lorcan felt Cammy's eyes on him and knew she had probably overheard everything, certainly everything after he'd tossed the duke's clerk into the mud. He had shown remarkable restraint. He only hoped Cammy thought the same.

He thanked the ostler, tossed him a few extra coins, and marched back to the inn. He quickly made arrangements to dine in one of the private dining rooms, then climbed upstairs to their guest chamber and knocked at the door. "Cammy, it's me. Let me in."

The door flew open, and she dragged him in. "Did he really try to poison Berengaria?"

Lorcan nodded.

She clutched a hand to her chest. "Why do men do this? Seek to harm the innocent?"

He shrugged as he shut the door, latched it, and then stepped over to the window to watch Maplethorpe hauled back to the tavern. The little man's expression was venomous. Lorcan hoped his sneers and a few shouted curses were all he would do to release his impotent rage. He did not want the ostler or his grooms to be hurt by that malicious ferret. "It gives them a false sense of power. This is what weak men do, seek to hurt the defenseless."

"And you, with your strength and the respect you command, embody everything he detests. I'm glad you caught him before he could harm your horse. Are you all right, Lor?" She came to his side and gently ran her hands over his shoulders and arms.

He arched an eyebrow. "If I tell you I am fine, will you stop touching me? Because I surely like having your hands on me."

She cast him a wry smile. "Oh? You like this, do you? Even while you are fully dressed?"

"That oversight can be corrected."

"Lor! I am in jest! It is still afternoon."

He chuckled. "Is it? What was I thinking?"

She cleared her throat. "I give you fair warning, however. I intend to claim my prize tonight."

This girl had a way of evaporating his anger.

He kissed her lightly on the lips and cast her a wicked grin. "Is it night yet?"

"No, you low-brain fiend. Not even if you draw the curtains and douse the candles. You will have to be patient and wait until evening. Why do I get the feeling you will enjoy this prize even more than I?"

"Nonsense. I hope to give you pleasure beyond your wildest dreams." And he meant it, but his mind was still on Maplethorpe. He needed to be certain the duke's ferret actually left town.

It still troubled him the man was here.

The duke was in London; Lorcan knew this much for certain. So why was this insignificant clerk in Clifton and walking about with a vial of poison? Did he have more? And who was he planning to use it on?

"Lor? Why are you suddenly frowning?"

"Just thinking, Cammy." As he continued to peer out the window, he recognized an older man standing off to the side and furtively studying the Reaper's Tavern.

Was Lord Crimmins on his way to meet Maplethorpe?

Now that was interesting.

What were those two plotting?

CHAPTER EIGHT

"Lor, you were distracted throughout supper, and now you are back at the window. What is going on?" Cammy stared at his broad back, waiting for him to turn around and respond. But he was not paying attention to her.

Despite his distraction, he'd eaten enough to choke a horse.

Well, he was a big man and obviously had a big appetite. He'd done an able job of polishing off his mutton chops, and everything else piled on his plate. Leeks, carrots, roasted potatoes, along with that hefty serving of meat simmering in its own juices.

He had been so preoccupied, she doubted he'd even noticed what he had inhaled. They were back in their chamber now, and he was still lost in his own thoughts. "Lor?"

"Hmm…"

This was the twilight hour, a time when the sky turned beautiful shades of pink, gold, and lilac. But with the rain still falling, albeit a much lighter drizzle now, there was nothing but a blanket of gray to mark the sinking sun upon the horizon.

Cammy wanted to light a candle since night was about to fall, and it would soon be too dark to see her own hands waving in front of her.

"No, Cammy. Don't light it."

He was obviously worried about something in the offing, no doubt concerning that troublesome Maplethorpe fellow. "All right. But will you tell me why?"

He ignored her, once more staring at the activity in the courtyard.

"Lor?"

He grunted.

"Lor, did you hear what I said?"

"Sure. Sure. That's nice."

She sighed. "I am standing naked behind you."

He continued to fix his gaze on the courtyard. "Yes. Fine."

"Completely naked. Utterly starkers. Shall I entertain you by doing Salome's dance of the seven veils?"

"That's...what?" He turned around, his mouth agape as he realized what she was saying. He laughed softly. "You naughty thing."

"I thought that might gain your attention." She grinned impishly, for she was still dressed, of course. Fully clad and had no intention of disrobing while his attention was elsewhere.

"Did you just say what I think you said? Every one of my bodily organs is in spasms now."

"And yet, I still do not think I have your full attention."

"Give me another moment, Cammy. Blessed saints, my blood is on fire. You shouldn't say such things to me. I think my heart just stopped." He groaned and held out his arm to her. "Come here, love."

He tucked her against his side as he continued to peer out, careful to keep them both out of the line of sight should anyone standing outside bother to look up. She doubted anyone could see them even if they did stare straight up at their window. Lor had made certain to keep them well hidden.

And despite his blood being on fire, he was still concentrating on the scene below. So much for her powers of seduction. Assuming she had any over him or would know what to do if he suddenly responded.

Men usually tripped over themselves to be near her. She was not used to having to work for masculine attention. But she would have her work cut out for her with Lorcan. He was passionate about his duty to protect the Crown and could not resist any mystery that cropped up related to that duty.

"I recognize Mr. Maplethorpe," she whispered, not certain why she was keeping her voice low. But it did feel as though they were in the middle of a clandestine operation on behalf of the Crown. Judging by the intensity of Lor's gaze, she was certain of it.

She wasn't going to do anything to put him in jeopardy.

"The other man with him is Lord Crimmins. He was involved in a bit of intrigue last year but somehow managed to talk his way out of it. I never trusted him, though."

"Seems you were right. What are they passing off to each other?"

"Maplethorpe's just given him information in exchange for a bribe. The only question is, was Maplethorpe acting as the lure under the Duke of Wooton's authority, or is he committing treason? Since the arse tried to poison my horse, I am inclined to believe His Grace has not brought him into any clandestine operation, and that little ferret is acting on his own."

Cammy burrowed a little closer, inhaling the delicious scent of him. Male, musk, and a hint of apple and cinnamon, which was the fragrance of the soap she'd taken with her when fleeing for home. "He must know you are on to him. Why would he go through with this rendezvous then? Has he not considered that you will come after him?"

He shrugged. "The man is full of himself. He thinks he will talk his way out of this scrape. He'll lie to me and have me believe he is on assignment for the duke. Then he'll run off like a scared rabbit."

"Lor, don't be so casual about it. He must be worried about you giving him away. What if he intends to kill you before he runs off, or has Crimmins do it? Surely, you must have thought of that."

"I have."

"Then why not summon the magistrate?"

"Because if this is a Crown operation, I do not want outsiders brought into it. And I do not mean that Maplethorpe is working for the Crown. The man is incompetent and completely untrustworthy. Likely, the duke is aware and allowed him to steal a particular secret. He'll have agents following the little traitor to get to whoever bribed him."

"We now know it is Lord Crimmins."

"Indeed, and now the duke will want to know who Crimmins reports to because he does not have the intelligence to be more than a low-level go-between. I want to nose around and find out more. I'll do that as soon as Maplethorpe packs up and leaves."

"And if he does not get out of town within the hour?"

He shrugged again. "We'll see."

She nudged out of his arms and stared up at him. She always knew he was fierce, and his work was dangerous, but she had not fully appreciated all it entailed. "Lor, what does that mean? Are you going to kill Maplethorpe? And Crimmins?"

"Of course not. I bring men to justice. I do not mete it out on my own like some sinister, avenging angel."

"But would you kill if you were under orders?"

"Cammy, I am under no such orders. I visited my brother because I am on holiday. I helped him deliver Lord Belfy and his cohorts to Exeter prison while still on holiday. And I chased after your glorious, feathered backside while hoping for a few days to actually enjoy what was left of my supposed days off. That's it. Nothing more."

Her stomach was now twisted in knots. She wanted to believe him, but how could she know for certain? "Would you tell me if you were assigned to kill someone?"

He sighed. "No. But I give you my word of honor that I am not here on any mission, and I am no one's hired assassin. I do not kill in cold blood, not even for the Crown. Ah, there. Their exchange is done. They've just parted ways."

"What happens next?"

"I don't know." He led her away from the window and spoke

to her in a soft, seductive voice meant to distract her. "Let me help you undress."

She eyed him warily. "Why?"

"Don't you wish to be more comfortable?" His hands slid around her waist.

Goodness, he was devastating when he turned on the charm.

"Are you offering because you are in a low-brain frenzy to undress me? Or are you doing this so I cannot follow you out when you suddenly hop to your feet and leave? Besides, I won the card game. If anyone is to be undressed, it is you."

He kissed her brow and sighed. "I must be losing my touch. Give me twenty minutes. I need to see what these two conspirators do next. When I return, you will have my full attention."

"What are you going to do to them?"

"Nothing sinister, Cammy. I only intend to watch them and make certain Maplethorpe rides out of town. Then I'll see who Crimmins meets next. As I said, those two are low men on the espionage ladder. All I need to do is make note of who appears on the next rung up. I'll send a message to the duke as soon as I gain that information and will pursue it no further until I return to London."

"You won't do anything more here?"

"Not another blessed thing. This isn't my assignment. I know better than to interfere in what may be an active investigation. But in kicking Maplethorpe out of Clifton, I may have damaged a Crown trap. If so, I'll help the duke fix whatever it is I've ruined. But not before I marry you. That is my top priority."

He lowered his mouth to hers and gave her another of those deliciously scorching kisses that left her weak in the knees and feeling warm in her belly. He was purposely distracting her with kisses. To her shame, it was working.

All thought fled the moment his warm lips planted on her mouth.

She was still giddy when he ended the kiss, the effect utterly devastating as he gazed at her with his seductive, silver eyes.

They burned through her like embers, fiery and smoldering.

He grinned, obviously well pleased.

"Yes, Lor. You are irresistible. Now go." She latched the door after him and rushed to the window to peer out, wanting to keep an eye on him because he was far too fearless about walking into danger.

But she never saw him leave the inn or cross to the Reaper's Tavern.

Nor did she see more of the two men who had exchanged packets in the rain.

She sighed as she continued to stand watch. The rain was little more than a cool mist, and its vaporous swirls obscured the courtyard. Even so, she should have been able to make out the shape of a man walking across it.

But Lorcan must have been born with the instincts of a jungle cat, able to wend his way unseen in shadows like a predator on the hunt. His mother must have had her hands full taking care of him. Cammy could not even imagine what he was like as a child.

But he'd grown into a powerfully handsome man.

Smart, seductive, and dangerous.

After staring at nothing for what she estimated was about ten minutes, she gave up and settled on the bed to remove her shoes and stockings. The room was still plunged in darkness, but she dared not light even the smallest candle. Her eyes drifted shut as she stretched atop the mattress and waited for Lorcan's knock to allow him back in.

It could not have been more than another ten minutes before she heard a light rap at the door and Lorcan's comforting voice. "Cammy, it's me."

She rushed out of bed and opened it. "What happened? Did you find out anything? Isn't it safer for both of us to know? This way, I—"

He kissed her, at the same time nudging her inside and kicking the door shut. "Ready to collect your prize?"

She felt the heat and hard length of him as he drew her up

against him and kissed her senseless. Heavens, was he trained in the art of seduction? Because he was very good at it. She almost believed he was insanely wild for her.

"Lor…" She *eeped* as he nibbled the little pulse at the base of her neck. "Oh…my."

His hands seemed to have a will of their own as they roamed along her body. "Cammy, what you said before…"

She was breathless, and her words came out in a heaving sigh. "What did I say?"

"I want you naked with me."

"Oh…my. Yes, Lor. But…do you mean it, or are you just saying this because you don't want to talk about what you found out?"

"I didn't find out anything. They've both disappeared. Their horses are gone, too. Good riddance. If they have any brains, they'll be riding hard to Portsmouth to hop on the next vessel sailing across the world before the duke's agents catch up to them and haul their scrawny arses to the Tower." As he spoke, he made certain the door was securely latched, then lit one of the candles and turned back to face her. "Ready, love?"

"I have more questions. What if–"

He gave her another scorching kiss that melted the clothes off her. Well, his hands were expertly working to unloosen her stays and lacings. Her clothes did not simply disappear of their own accord.

She tingled as he worked the encumbering gown and corset off, one by one, and felt them slide down her body to pool at her feet. "I want you, Cammy."

How was it possible this exquisite man could want her enough to marry her? "The feeling is mutual, Lor."

He eased away, still keeping hold of her hands as he led her closer to the bed. "Claim your prize, love."

She swallowed hard, suddenly finding her chemise quite cumbersome as well. But she was not taking it off yet. First, she was going to undress him.

Heaven help her!

Was this really happening?

She seemed helpless to resist, even though she knew his sudden eagerness had more to do with wanting to distract her from asking more questions than lusting for her. Although clearly, there was quite a bit of lust involved, if the gleam in his eyes and the heat radiating off his taut body was any indication.

Did she really want to put a stop to his seduction simply to pry information about a sensitive Crown matter?

How much did she want to know of this intrigue?

Not that Lorcan would ever tell her.

He could not possibly be at liberty to tell her anything.

More important, he was a loyal agent and would go to his grave before divulging ministry secrets, even to her.

She gave up asking more questions and turned her attention to the matter of removing his clothes.

Mercy.

Her hands shook from inexperience and a hefty dose of delight. She knew whatever she lacked in finesse would be overlooked by Lorcan since he knew this was her first time doing…what exactly were they going to do?

How far did he mean for them to take her prize? Merely stripping him of his clothes? All of them? What would happen from there?

His hands gently fell over hers that were presently fisted in his shirt and crushing the fabric. "We are not going to do anything you are not comfortable doing, Cammy. Never forget that."

She nodded. "That's the problem, Lor. I don't think I will be afraid of anything we do while I am in your arms."

He caressed her cheek. "You are safe with me and always shall be."

"I know. I know this to the depths of my soul." She removed his jacket and then untucked the shirt from his waistband and tried to pull it over his head. But he was too tall, so he had to remove it for her.

She watched him, took in the sleek grace of his movements, and inhaled the musky heat of his body. The man seemed built of granite. Hot granite, if there was such a thing. She trailed her hands lightly over his muscled arms and broad shoulders, along the taut planes of his stomach. Oh, his body was magnificently contoured, divinely rippled. There was a sensual aura of danger as he stood beside her, and she took in his brutally beautiful physique.

His fists were as big as boulders.

But his touch was exquisitely gentle. "What next, Cammy?"

"Um, your boots."

He sat on the bed.

She watched the strain of his back muscles as he drew off his boots, socks, and withdrew an alarming number of weapons hidden within the lip of his boots and in his clothing.

Her head was spinning.

He grunted. "A hazard of my occupation. One has to be prepared for anything and everything." He studied her expression a long moment. "Come here," he said, gently drawing her onto his lap.

What was the expression? Out of the frying pan and into the fire?

Was it sinful of her to want to be scorched?

"Lor…"

"I am not doing this to distract you from snooping, Cammy. They are gone. If our presence has interfered with any investigation, I will discuss it with the duke. There is nothing more to be done but concentrate on claiming your prize. Hopefully, you will find me to your liking."

"Mother in heaven," she murmured. "Is there a doubt?"

He smiled.

"Lor, is this how it is supposed to be? My body is awash in sensations. The book spoke of the five senses, but I had no idea exploring them could be so overwhelming."

He closed his arms around her so that she was nestled against him. His skin was hot and smooth. "What are you feeling, Cammy?"

She curled her fingers in the spray of dark hair across his chest. "Excited. A little scared. I'm taking all of you in, the look of you…" His silver eyes were devastatingly attractive. "The scent of you."

He chuckled. "I've been using your soap."

"But it smells different on you. Nice, more manly."

He nudged the chemise off one shoulder and kissed her there. "Yours is apples and roses. Light. Fragrant. Delicate."

"Your touch shoots tingles through me. Your voice does the same. It's as though I am becoming trained to respond to you, like a dog learning commands. But I am not explaining it right. It is not about master and subservient. It is about my heart recognizing and responding to yours."

"It is no different for me."

"But you've been with other women."

"Been with them but never been in love with them."

She inhaled sharply. "Are you in love with me, Lor?"

He nodded. "From the moment I set eyes on you."

She laughed.

He growled softly. "Why are you so surprised?"

"Because all you did was ignore me. On occasion, you grunted at me when you could not escape directly responding to me. I did not think you even knew my name. Or ever wanted to know it."

He slid the chemise off her other shoulder and kissed her there. "I knew who you were. I wasn't ignoring you. I wasn't ready to trust my heart."

"And you are now?"

"Completely."

Her own heart was pounding wildly. This was so different from anything she had ever experienced before. She had never understood what it meant to be in love until Lorcan.

And she did love him deeply. Only, she was afraid to say it

back to him.

Wasn't it too soon for either of them to know for certain?

How could he be so confident in his feelings? Was he simply saying these things because they were trapped and had to marry?

She did not think so.

Lorcan was genuine. If he felt something, he told you. If he did not feel anything, he would tell you, as well.

"What happens next, Lor?"

"That depends." His voice had turned low and seductive, and his gaze turned from smoldering to fiery.

"Depends on what?" She was still seated on his lap, his powerful arms circled around her.

"On whether you will allow me to remove your chemise."

"My chemise?"

He was the one supposed to be undressing.

Well, he was undressed save for his trousers.

And she did not think they would stay on very long after her chemise came off.

Not that it mattered, for she was ruined already.

A mere article of clothing would not save her honor.

But most of all, she loved him. Even if she was not ready to say it to him, she could not deny it to herself. "Yes, Lor. You may."

A slow smile crept across his lips as he slipped it off her and set it aside.

She was embarrassed and clung to his shoulders. "What happens next?"

"This." He closed his mouth over her breast and suckled lightly.

The candle's fiery gold flame flickered beside them, enveloping them both in its soft light as Lorcan introduced her to sensations she had never experienced or ever knew existed before this moment.

He cupped her breast and took obvious pleasure in the way it filled his large hand. As he flicked his tongue across its rosy peak, she felt herself heat up like that candle's golden flame.

She breathlessly moaned his name and clutched her hands to his head.

He kept up the onslaught, his lips and tongue working magic. But his hand did not linger very long on her breast before he began to slowly slide it down her body, setting little fires everywhere he touched.

He paused when his hand came to rest on her inner thigh.

"Cammy, I love you," he whispered, moving it upward to touch her intimately.

She almost leapt off his lap in surprise. "Lor…"

"Trust me, love." He lifted her in his arms with little effort, his muscles hard and beautifully sculpted as he set her on the bed so that she was lying flat on her back. He stretched his long, lean body beside her, his desire barely tethered as he propped on one elbow and gazed at her so tenderly, it stole her breath away.

"I do trust you."

His lips returned to her breast to tease and suckle it, and at the same time, his hand eased between her legs to stroke her until she thought she might scream from the pleasure of it. "Lor, please…"

She did not understand what it was she was begging for, only that she needed him with a shuddering hunger and wanted…needed…was about to explode with a desire more powerful than any she thought could possibly exist.

"You're almost there, love." He kissed her on the mouth.

Almost where?

She placed her hands on his massive shoulders and held on tight as an enormous pressure began to build inside of her. She'd seen storm waves upon a turbulent sea, their silent crests surging ever higher and higher. She now felt something like those waves surging inside her body, strong and intense but also as fragile as froth and foam.

Lorcan's touch.

He carried her to unexplored heights.

She moved urgently against his hand, pressing herself to it, and completely out of rhythm to the stroke of his fingers upon her intimate core. She could not help it, for she was drowning in a flood of sensations and ready for something...something... She dug into his shoulders, responding wildly as he once more closed his mouth over her breast, and his fingers stroked the slickness between her legs.

She cried out.

She heard herself, raspy and breathless as a splendid force rocked through her body. "Lor...*Lor.*"

"I'm right here, sweetheart." He wrapped her tightly in his arms and covered her mouth with his, their kiss long and deep and boundless.

She felt his love pour into their kiss.

She poured hers in as well, hoping to convey what she did not have the courage to say in words. It was all happening so fast. It was all so magical. She placed her hand against his cheek and felt the rough bristles of a day's growth of beard.

This was Lor, rugged and manly.

She studied his face, loving its fierceness and feral beauty.

After a moment, he sank back against the mattress and drew her atop him. His arms closed around her like gentle, iron bands holding her to him. Her hair was a wild tumble, and several long strands fell over his arms to cover them in a blanket of gold.

Silently, he drew her hair to one side and began to stroke along the scar on her back with exquisite care.

A tear rolled down her cheek.

"Are you all right, sweetheart? Am I hurting you?"

She shook her head. "It's the scar, the way you touch it."

"I'm sorry. I did not realize it was still tender." He started to move his hand away, but she stopped him.

"The *loving* way you touch it. The scar does not hurt me any longer, not now that you've...we've...done this. I feel free again, as though the chains surrounding my heart have suddenly been lifted off. I had forgotten how wonderful it feels not to fear. But I think this is the insidious nature of these scars. One never realizes how deeply they can penetrate and damage you."

He groaned. "I wish I could have protected you."

She laughed softly, ignoring her tears as they continued to spill down her cheeks. "Then I would not have run away, and you would not have come after me. You might never have revealed how you felt about me."

"I would have, Cammy. It is you who would not have given me a second look while you had dukes, earls, and viscounts paying court to you."

"No, Lor. I would have chosen you. My heart would not have allowed me to accept anyone else."

He kissed her on the forehead. "Good, because we've really dug that hole deep now. I need to get you to Barnstaple as fast as possible for your father's consent."

She rested her hands on his chest and gazed at him. "We raise farm animals back home."

He arched an eyebrow. "Your point?"

"I do know what needs to happen in order to carry a babe. You did not…you know. Is this why you did not allow me to completely undress you?"

He nodded. "Tonight was about teaching you how things could be between us."

"*Mother in heaven.* What a lesson I had. Do men respond as wantonly when taking their pleasure?"

"Yes, perhaps even more so because of our low-brain mating urges. Are you sure you are all right, Cammy?"

She snuggled against him. "Very."

He reached over and blew out the candle. "Good. We had better get a good night's sleep. I'd like to get an early start in the morning. We have a solid day's journey ahead of us." He started to rise from the bed, but she stopped him.

"Lor…"

"Yes, love?"

"Will you sleep with me tonight?"

"Do you want me to?"

"Yes."

He kissed her again and eased back to hold her in his arms. "Then I'll stay."

"Lor…"

"What, love?"

"Do you mind if I stay cuddled against you?"

He laughed softly. "No, I don't mind. You feel like heaven."

"So do you." She squirmed against him. "Lor…"

"Yes, love?"

"Do you think Maplethorpe is really gone and won't cause you any trouble?"

He hesitated a moment. "Yes. I assure you, he won't be causing either of us any more problems."

"How can you be sure?"

"Go to sleep, Cammy. We need to get out of here soon after daybreak."

She did not press him further.

After all, he was a trained agent of the Crown and understood these things better than she ever would.

Still, it troubled her.

How could he be so sure Maplethorpe would not come after him?

CHAPTER NINE

A SHARP RAP at their door shortly before dawn had Lorcan immediately rolling off the bed and reaching for the pistol he kept hidden in the lip of his boot. "Who is it?"

"The magistrate," came the reply.

"Damn it." He quickly tossed on his clothes and donned his boots, then took another moment to make certain the spare pistol he kept hidden in a special pocket of his jacket was properly loaded. In the meanwhile, Cammy had also risen and quickly put on her chemise before scampering back in bed and covering herself with the sheet.

She was now staring at him in panic.

He stifled a pang of disappointment, very much wishing he could have slowly wakened her with kisses instead of having them leap out of bed to deal with whatever new mischief was at their door. "It's all right, love."

"Geordie," he said, opening the door a crack and not bothering to hide his surprise at the sight of his longtime friend. "Don't tell me you're the magistrate."

"I'm afraid I am."

"The townspeople must have been desperate," he teased his friend. "Give us a moment to dress."

"Us? I should have known you would have a woman with you."

He frowned, for Cammy must have heard the offhanded

remark. But she also had to know these casual pleasures were a thing of the past for him. "I'm here with my wife."

Cammy *eeped*.

Lord, he hoped she was not going to blab the truth.

Geordie laughingly shook his head. "I'll be damned. Then it's true. I did not believe the innkeeper when he mentioned it to me."

"Give us a minute, and I'll introduce you." He shut the door and quickly assisted Cammy in lacing the ties of her corset and gown as she hastened to make herself presentable. Once she had donned her shoes, he helped her pin up her riotous mane of hair.

Her cheeks were pink, and her eyes still had the sensual droop of sleep.

"Ready, love?" At her nod, he stepped to the door and pulled it open to allow his old friend in. "May I present my wife, Lady Camellia Brayden?"

Cammy's cheeks immediately flamed crimson.

Bollocks.

He quickly introduced his friend to Cammy. "Magistrate Geordie Newton and I go back many years when he was also serving as an agent of the Crown."

"A pleasure to meet you, Lady Camellia."

She cast him a tight smile. "Thank you, Mr. Newton."

He turned back to Lorcan, his grin broad across his lightly scarred face. "I had no idea you had planned on marrying. When did this happen? Ah, it must be recent. Your wife is blushing very sweetly."

He was being polite.

Cammy's face was lit up like a torch.

She was obviously mortified, especially after having lain with him last night and experienced her first sensations of pleasure.

Much as he liked Geordie, he wanted to get him out of their guest chamber before Cammy gave everything away. "We married only a few days ago. What brings you to our door?"

The smile left his friend's face. "I'm here because of the

duke's clerk, Maplethorpe."

Lorcan stiffened. "He came to you? You know the man's a deceitful little…did he complain that I tossed him out of this inn?"

"He isn't about to complain of anything. He was found dead an hour ago."

Cammy gasped.

Lorcan invited his friend to step fully inside, for they needed to have a serious conversation, and he did not want them to be overheard. Whoever had killed Maplethorpe might now be considering killing him and Cammy. "How did it happen?"

His friend glanced nervously at Cammy. "Perhaps we ought to have this conversation in private."

"No," Cammy said. "Please, you needn't worry about my delicate sensibilities. Oh, or were you worried about discussing confidential Crown matters within my hearing?"

Lorcan settled beside her and took her hand in his. "Go head, Geordie. You can say anything to me in front of Cammy."

His gaze flitted from one to the other, then he shrugged and proceeded to relate all he'd learned. "One of the stable boys noticed a riderless horse feeding on some gorse in a meadow not far out of town just before dawn this morning. When he approached, he saw Maplethorpe on the grass amid a pool of blood. His throat had been slit. By the condition of his body, I'd say it had happened no more than an hour before the poor lad found him. Lor…" He arched an eyebrow. "I need to know…"

"It wasn't me."

Geordie eyed him dubiously. "You and I really ought to talk privately downstairs."

Cammy gasped. "You think he did this?"

"Lady Camellia, I do not mean to overset you. But it is my duty to ask questions. Is it not true this man made unwelcome advances toward you?"

"Yes, but…"

"It's all right, love." Lorcan squeezed her hand in comfort, although he was not certain she took it as that. "I kicked his scrawny arse out of the inn for this reason. He grudgingly settled at the Reaper's Tavern. All I did was toss him out."

"Not quite all," Geordie reminded him. "There was an incident with your horse."

"The bastard tried to poison Berengaria in retaliation. Yes, I wanted to beat the bloody stuffing out of him, but I wasn't going to do it with my wife watching. She has a gentle heart and would not approve. So I merely warned him to leave town before nightfall or…" He paused and groaned. "I threatened to come after him if he was still around. But I had no intention of wasting any more time on him. I told the ostler that if he was still around after dark to call you in, and I would press charges."

"Lor, he insulted your wife and tried to poison your horse. How do you think that looks to me?"

"I don't care how it looks. The man was a nothing, an imperious little speck who got involved in a dangerous game and did not understand the lethal rules of play. Someone killed him, but it wasn't me." He glanced at Cammy. "I'm sure you've noticed how beautiful my wife is."

Geordie's neck and ears turned red, a sign of his embarrassment. "I did. Who wouldn't?"

"That's right. She is extraordinarily beautiful."

Cammy frowned at him.

"My point is," he said, once more squeezing her hand, "given the chance to be with her or chase that little ferret out of his hiding hole, I am going to choose being with her every time. If I took offense at every man who ogled my wife, there would not be a man alive in England today."

"But he made untoward advances."

"Which she ably fended off."

Cammy tipped her head up with pride. "I am not helpless, Mr. Newton. I will admit that I was grateful for Lorcan's timely arrival, but I was already fighting him off successfully. I do not appreciate your thinking of me as some delicate, wilting flower who hasn't the brains to defend herself from—"

Geordie emitted a laughing groan. "Point taken."

Lorcan grinned. "As for Maplethorpe, I was just making certain he would not bother her again. Not by killing him but by kicking him out of the inn. Nor was I going to harm him, even after his attempt to poison Berengaria. I was afraid my unexpected presence here had compromised one of the duke's operations, and I was going to do nothing more to interfere."

"Then you believe the Duke of Wooton is involved?"

"I think so. Obviously, the duke would never personally involve himself in these low-level assignments. But it is also possible he was completely in the dark. I'm not sure."

"Truly? You think he was unaware? He's a pretty sharp man."

Lorcan nodded. "Yes, I know. It may be that he knew Maplethorpe was stealing secrets and purposely put out a lure, some planted information, hoping the little ferret would take it and sell it. Nor do I know whether any of the duke's agents are in town and tracking Maplethorpe's movements. I only hope my unexpected presence did not botch an operation, assuming there was one going on and they were here to watch it unfold. But I am not leaving my wife's side to investigate further. We are heading out of town today."

Geordie held up his hands. "You know I take you at your word. But even if it had nothing to do with your wife or your horse...dash it, Lor. Give me your oath. Were you...was it..."

"My assignment? No. Upon my word. We had not even intended to be here. Cammy was meant to be on the coach to Barnstaple, and I was to follow her. But in her distraction, she got on the coach to Gloucester instead. Fortunately, I caught up to them. You can confirm this with Matthais. He was driving the Gloucester coach. That's how we ended up here. No other reason."

Cammy cleared her throat. "I can vouch for Lorcan's whereabouts. He did not leave our room at all last night."

"Lady Camellia, he might have slipped out while you were asleep."

Her face burst into flames again. "No…you see, we…we did not sleep…much."

Geordie tossed him a rakish grin. "Ah."

Lorcan arched an eyebrow. "Are we done?"

His friend nodded. "Yes, of course. But will you help me, Lor? Please. If you did not do it, do you have any idea who did?"

He nodded. "Now, I will need your oath. This is likely a Crown matter, and you cannot talk about it to your deputies."

"You have my word. Even though I am retired from service, once an agent, always an agent. It does not ever leave one's blood. Lor, please. Give me a clue. I will not reveal whatever you tell me in confidence. But I have to know. The man is dead. He stole a ministry secret…or thought he had. What happened next?"

"He turned a packet over to Lord Crimmins."

Geordie inhaled sharply. "Crimmins? I knew that bounder was guilty of treason. So he was involved?"

Lorcan nodded. "Up to his eyeballs."

"Then we have another problem."

He frowned as he fixed his attention on his friend. "And what is that?"

"Crimmins was also found dead not far from Maplethorpe's body. He was also still warm."

"What? Damn it, Geordie." Lorcan surged to his feet to confront the man he considered a friend. "Why did you not tell me sooner?"

"I had to be sure it wasn't you, Lor." He held his hands out in supplication. "You are the duke's most trusted agent. How was I to know for sure you weren't somehow involved?"

"With Cammy beside me? Do you think I would ever place her life in danger?"

Geordie continued to hold out his hands. "Don't hit me, Lor. But I have to ask this next question. You know I do. Are you truly married? Or is she also an agent for—"

Cammy burst into tears. "Lor!"

He groaned and quickly took her in his arms. "She is not an agent," he said, glowering at his friend. "For pity's sake, is it not obvious? Do you have any more insults to throw at the woman I love?"

"No." He raked a hand through his hair. "Lady Camellia, my sincerest apologies. But I had to ask. I have a double killing on my hands. Lor, I could really use your help in this."

"I don't know any more than I have told you. If you want my opinion, either the duke had them silenced, in which case, you will never be permitted to discover the identity of the agent who committed the deed. Or they were silenced by the treasonous parties the duke is hunting. In which case, the duke will still never permit you to discover—"

"I know. I'll hit a wall either way."

"All I can say is that you have my word of honor, I was not involved." Lorcan was angry, but he could not allow it to show, or Cammy would burst into tears again. "Some holiday," he muttered. "I'll be glad to return to the peace and quiet of work. I assume we are free to go?"

Geordie nodded. "Do me a favor and send word to me once you have spoken to the duke on this matter. I'll continue to poke around and see if I can find any other traitors skulking about my town. But I expect they will all be gone by now."

"As will any agents of the Crown, assuming any were involved."

"Lor, I'll send word if anything odd pops up that might be helpful to the duke's operation. But I would appreciate a return favor. I'd like to be able to close this investigation and calm the townspeople."

"If the duke allows it, I certainly will write to you and tell you all I find out."

Geordie shook his hand. "Sorry about the circumstances, but it was good to see you again." He then turned to Cammy. "Delighted to meet you, Lady Camellia. I am certain you do not feel the same, but I hope we shall meet under more pleasant circumstances next time."

Cammy merely nodded.

Lorcan remained in the doorway, watching Geordie stride downstairs before he shut the door and turned to Cammy.

She was seated on the bed, her head now buried in her hands. "That was frightening. What if the magistrate hadn't been one of your friends? You might have been locked up for a double murder."

"Which I did not commit." He knelt beside her. "Even if I had committed it, the Duke of Wooton would have had me released. I was never in any danger of being hanged for those killings."

She looked up at him. "How can you be sure? It would only have taken a few angry townspeople and a noose."

"No one was going to come after me for the death of two unpleasant strangers. Even if they had, I carry a Crown badge. No magistrate would have held me. No outraged citizens would have strung me up."

"My hands are shaking."

He enveloped them in his. "I am truly sorry, Cammy. This is not how I would ever plan on spending time with you. But it only makes our trip to Barnstaple that much more urgent."

"Yes, we've been lying to everyone about my being your wife."

He kissed her brow. "That is what truly scared me, the worry you might give away our situation."

"Lor, you lie about it so easily."

"So, you think I can easily lie about everything else? I was with you all of last night, Cammy. Blessed saints, you know it is true. I couldn't keep my hands off you."

The mere thought of the pleasure he had aroused in her fired his blood. He had brought her to passion not once but twice last night. Cammy was beautiful beyond belief, not just her body but her gentle and open heart.

Watching her respond to him had been incredibly satisfying and also agonizingly frustrating. He ached to be inside her, to fill her and claim her for his own. To love her with his body as well as his heart.

"Except you did go out. Shortly after nightfall."

"Yes, to spy on Maplethorpe and Crimmins. But that was almost eight hours ago. These killings are fresh."

"Do you know who did it, Lor?"

"No, and I do not want to know. I want to get you home and get us married." He left her side and began to gather their meager belongings. He picked up the red leather book they had left atop the bureau and tucked it safely back in her pouch.

Trust was the foundation of any marriage, so the author had said, and Lorcan agreed with that assessment. But how was he to get Cammy to trust him now? She believed he was the consummate liar. Hell, perhaps he was. But only in his line of work.

He was never going to lie to Cammy in their marriage.

They lingered at the inn for another hour before heading out. They'd dressed in a rush and hadn't taken the time to properly wash or eat or otherwise prepare themselves for their journey. While Cammy did so now, Lorcan took a moment to seek out the innkeeper and ask for provisions to be packed for them. They would need to eat, especially if the weather held them up again before they reached the shelter of a comfortable inn.

He also took a moment to step outside. The storm had passed, and the sun was breaking through the thinning layer of clouds.

He would have liked to wait a little longer for the roads to dry, but they had lost too much time already.

He crossed to the stable and had one of the lads saddle Berengaria, then left instructions for the lad to lead her out of the stall and tie her reins to the post just outside the inn's front door.

Berengaria appeared healthy and unharmed. She was straining at the bit, eager to be out of her confining walls and on their way.

As for Cammy, he was not certain what was going through her mind.

When he returned inside, she was seated beside the innkeeper's desk, quietly awaiting him. He groaned inwardly, knowing she was troubled since she did not look up as he approached. Even afterward, she remained quiet as a mouse as he secured her travel pouch and then lifted her onto the saddle.

Nor did she acknowledge him when he mounted.

To his relief, she did not resist when he drew her up against his chest and circled his arms around her waist. The delicate scent of her filled his nostrils, for she had used the apple and cinnamon scented soap he loved on her. It mingled with the warmth of her skin, sweet and fresh and pure. "Will you hate me the entire way to Barnstaple?"

She sighed and relaxed against him. "No, Lor. You know I don't hate you."

"But I've lost your trust, and I think that is far worse."

"You haven't lost my trust."

He said no more, and she made no further attempt to protest as they rode out of town. Their progress was slower than he would have liked because they had to make their way around fallen tree limbs, mud as deep as one's ankles, and puddles as large as lakes. Despite the obstacles that would plague them for hours yet, Lorcan was determined to press on.

He did not want Cammy talking herself out of marrying him.

"Lor, can we stop soon?" she asked after they had been riding for much of the day.

"Of course." His mind had been elsewhere all the while. He'd hardly noticed the sun burning through the remaining layers of clouds as the hours progressed. It was now beating down on them in all its radiant fury.

Cammy was flushed and perspiring.

Berengaria, usually strong and frisky, was flagging as they rode on.

"There's a stream not far from here." They could refresh themselves. "Can you hold on for another five minutes?"

She nodded.

In truth, they all could do with a rest.

If Cammy was done hating him, they might take a dip together. They had time since they were not going to make it to Barnstaple today. The storm had left the roads in poor condition and almost impassable.

He had planned for this and intended for them to stop in the town of Highbridge. They would reach it well before nightfall.

He'd stayed a time or two at a pleasant inn called the Hare and Hound.

He recalled the food was excellent and the guest chambers quite comfortable.

Yes, they would sleep there tonight.

Then on to Barnstaple tomorrow, but not before they stopped at his brother's estate, and he sent word to his brother in Taunton. Cammy's aunt and sister were waiting at the Ashcott Inn with Shayne, anxious for Cammy's safe return.

Perhaps it would have been kinder to ride to Taunton before heading westward, for it was only an hour or two out of their way. But a note from him assuring them all was well would serve the same purpose. And who was to say the diversion to Taunton would be quick? Once there, Cammy might refuse to ride on to Barnstaple.

He couldn't risk that, especially now that she was coming to understand the nature of his work and not liking the dangers involved.

Perhaps it was not fair of him to take the decision out of her hands, but they had to marry. There was no question about it. Too many people had seen them, too many knew they had shared quarters as husband and wife.

Blessed saints, he'd touched her as only a husband should touch a wife.

Was she going to ignore this?

Would she ever accept his duties for the Crown?

Or would it forever interfere with their wedded bliss?

CHAPTER TEN

L ORCAN RODE UP to the Hare and Hound with Cammy in the late afternoon. They could have pushed themselves to travel a few hours longer, but it made little sense to do so. The heat was sweltering, and the air was humid enough to suck the soul out of anyone. Even Lorcan's sturdy filly was too tired to trot.

This inn was a safe stopping point.

He dismounted and helped Cammy down as the inn's ostler rushed out to greet them. "Sir Lorcan, good to see ye again. Will ye be staying with us tonight, sir?"

Lorcan nodded. "Yes, Fergus. I hope so, if there is room for us."

The ostler glanced at Cammy.

"This is my wife, Lady Camellia." It amazed him that even in her state of exhaustion, she managed to look beautiful.

"Well, I'll be. Someone finally tamed ye, did they? A pleasure to meet ye, m'lady. The inn's crowded, but I'm sure they'll find room for ye."

"Good. My wife is feeling a little queasy." He'd noticed her hand resting on her stomach. An upset stomach was a natural response to heat exhaustion, and Cammy was surely feeling it. She looked flushed and did not appear too steady on her feet, waddling a little as she walked.

The ostler must have taken it as indication she was carrying his child. "Ye don't waste time, do ye, Sir Lor?"

Lorcan choked back a laugh at the look of horror on Cammy's face, for she'd quickly caught on to what Fergus meant.

Fergus remained happily unaware, continuing to chatter as he handed Berengaria over to one of the stable grooms. "Ye take good care of that beautiful beast, lad. I'll be seeing to the lovely lady. Ye can see she is in a delicate condition. Never ye worry, m'lady. We'll get ye comfortably settled in the common room while yer husband sees to yer accommodations. Ye must be thirsty. Hungry, too, now that ye are eating for two."

Cammy's eyes betrayed her panic. "No, I…oh, no it's…thank you."

She cast Lorcan a look of surrender.

He shrugged as he tucked her arm in his to escort her inside. "There's no help for it. On the bright side, we're bound to get one of their nicer rooms out of it."

Which is indeed what happened.

The innkeeper and his wife, their maids, and even the kitchen staff spent the next hour making certain the guest chamber was to their liking, bringing up a tub and water for Cammy to have a good soak, bringing up refreshments, extra pillows, offering to clean their boots, refresh their clothes, and anything else they could think of to spoil him and Cammy.

Being married and having a child on the way had its advantages, he decided. But he knew these compounding lies were upsetting Cammy. "You've been most generous to us, Mr. Gormer," he said, shooing the innkeeper and his curious staff out of their guest chamber so they could finally be alone. "I shall summon you if we require anything more. As you can see, my wife is exhausted. She would like nothing better than a quick bath and a long rest."

The man had a rotund belly and an equally rotund face. His cheeks were perpetually pink, perhaps from tippling a bit too much, but his nature was pleasant whether in his cups or fully sober. "Anything for you, Sir Lorcan. We'll never forget how you saved our children from the burning schoolhouse."

Cammy stared at him in surprise. "You did?"

He shrugged. "Anyone would have done the same."

"No, Lor. They wouldn't," she said in a whisper that sounded reverential to his ears. Well, he wanted her to like him, to respect him. She had seen the uglier side of his occupation—the greed, corruption, and that double murder which had shaken her quite badly. Why should she not also see the good he did, the lives he saved, and families he preserved?

"Shall I help you out of your gown?" They were now alone, and that tub looked awfully inviting. He would take a soak once she was done.

"Yes, please." She turned to give him access to her lacings. "Lor, why did you not mention this to me?"

His hands paused on her ties. "What, that I actually save lives? I don't like to talk about what I do, the good or the bad."

"It would have helped for me to understand you better." She slipped off her gown and allowed him to assist her with her corset, as though it was the most natural thing in the world, and they were an old, married couple.

He liked that she no longer resisted this intimacy that would normally be shared by a husband and wife. "What is so hard to figure out about me? The work I do is meant to save lives. Sometimes that means stopping those who would harm others."

He knew by her expression she was thinking of the murders of Maplethorpe and Crimmins. "Cammy, I had nothing to do with the killing of those men. It was not my assignment. Nor do I think other agents did this. We like to capture our traitors and spies alive. One cannot get information out of a corpse or trade hostages if one side has nothing to trade."

She did not appear to be convinced.

He sighed and continued. "All signs point to the conspirators. Crimmins's contact is the likely killer. He probably saw me arrive at the inn and immediately feared I was on to Maplethorpe's treachery. Maplethorpe then compounded his error by approaching you, inadvertently causing his conspirators to leap to another conclusion, that he was not betraying Wooton at all, but working for him."

"But he wasn't."

Lorcan shrugged. "It matters little now whether he was or not. Had he avoided us, he would be alive today."

"Do you really think so? Everyone seems to know you in these parts. The mere sight of you would have scared them all."

He sighed. "Perhaps. I hope I did throw their plans into turmoil. Is it so terrible that traitors should turn on each other? I would rather have them kill each other than harm the innocent."

"You make it all sound so reasonable."

"Because it is. Life is not always pretty, Cammy. That scar was not put on you by any law-abiding citizen. The lord who hurt you, these are the sort of people I go after. My heart aches that I could not have been there to stop him."

"I know, Lor." She threw her arms around him. "Everything is happening so fast, and none of it is what I expected. I do not mean to give you a hard time. In truth, I am thinking of myself and how little I've done to contribute to anything beyond my immediate family. The more aware I become of what real life is about, the more I realize how much you do and how sheltered and ignorant I have been."

"Sweetheart, that isn't so." He cupped her face in his hands when she eased away to look up at him. "It is beauty like yours, and I am not speaking of your outward beauty, Cammy. It is good hearts who save the world, who inspire hope when all is lost. Your drawings, I am sure they are wondrous. They will stir others to explore and seek knowledge."

She smiled up at him. "You should be a politician, Lor."

He growled. "Don't say that. I've already been asked, but I'd rather muck stables than stand in the House of Commons and deal with the muck that abounds there."

"All the more reason why you are needed there."

He kissed her on the nose. "No, but I know someone who would be perfect."

"Who?"

"Why not you?"

She laughed and drew away. "Don't be ridiculous."

"Why should you not be?"

She glanced down at herself. "Have you suddenly gone blind? I am not a man."

"Praise heaven for that. Who says you must be one? Laws can be changed. I expect there are more women in England than men, certainly after all these years of war on the Continent and elsewhere around the world. Why should you not have a say in the future of our country?"

She regarded him with astonishment. "You surprise me."

"Why, because you think of me as a grunting ape?"

She blushed. "I know now that you are much more than that. And you did grunt at me, don't you dare deny it. How was I to know it was done on purpose to keep me away?"

"That plan failed spectacularly, didn't it?" he said with a laugh. "Not only are we married, but we are awaiting our first child."

She winced. "Don't remind me. This deception is awful."

He turned away to give her privacy while she removed her chemise and stepped into the tub. "I know. We'll remedy it soon."

He heard a light splash as she sank into the water. He tried *not* to imagine her lathering her body but failed utterly, of course. The innkeeper had sent up a pitcher of lemonade. He grabbed a glass and poured some for himself, gulping it down in the hope it might quench this insatiable thirst he had for Cammy.

"The water is delicious. I'll be finished soon, and you may have a turn."

"I'm in no rush. Take your time."

"Lor…"

"Yes, Cammy."

"You don't have to stay turned away. I mean, you've already seen all of me."

He let out a long breath, understanding what her statement meant. It wasn't about sex. It was about acceptance. When making the list in her head of reasons not to marry him, she had decided there were several compromises she could not make. The first was living in London. The second, after those double murders, was his line of work.

She had hardly spoken to him today, and he knew it was because she was fretting about having to marry him. Her silence on their journey meant she was trying to figure out a way out of this coil.

By allowing him to turn around, she was now accepting him for who he was, finally seeing the good in the man he was and what his line of work allowed him to accomplish for the betterment of society, not merely the bad aspects of it. "I'll help you wash your hair."

She laughed. "You are as bad as my sisters."

He chuckled. "Oh, no. I am much worse. They merely wanted to play with your hair. I have no intention of stopping there."

"Lor!"

"I don't mean now. Only once we are truly married. I am not taking you outside of marriage."

"What would you call…you know…the way you touched me last night?"

"A hint of the pleasures to come. I can wait, Cammy. For you, I will always wait." He glanced at her and saw that she had her arms crossed over her bosom to cover it. He respected her modesty, but she had only covered her breasts. He had a clear view of her back, and the red scar slashed across her pale skin.

He bent and kissed her softly along that thin line of red.

"You are the oddest man I have ever met, Lor. How can you be an ape one moment and so tender and enlightened in the next?"

He shifted to face her and kissed her on the nose. "It's a gift."

She shook her head, laughing again. "That's true, although I think you only meant it in jest. Your line of work frightens me, and yet I don't know anyone more suited to it than you. You've probably killed men—"

"Only if they come after me first. I've told you, I am no one's hired killer."

"My point is, you can be lethal when you have to be. You like to be in charge. You are protective by instinct. You are naturally comfortable being surly and abrupt. But you are also surprisingly tender, eloquent when you want to be, and a champion of women. I think this is the most important thing to be learned from *The Book of Love*. The right spouse will never stifle you but encourage and inspire you to be the best that you can be."

"Lean your head back. I'm about to dump water on your hair."

She sputtered as some of it dripped into her mouth since she was still trying to talk to him. "Lor!"

"What? I told you to put your head back."

"I know, but I wasn't through complimenting you."

He handed her the soap. "I'll rinse you off once you've lathered your hair. You were not complimenting me so much as coming to terms with what you perceive are my faults. But I do appreciate your moving me off the 'can never marry that apish fiend' list and finding me acceptable."

She looked up at him, ridiculously cute with her hair piled up atop her head and soap all over it, dripping into her ears. "Are you angry with me again?"

"No, I have never been angry with you. Why should I be? I understand it is important we accept each other for who we are, the good qualities and the bad."

"You seem to have an easier time of it than I do."

"Because I know what I want, and I especially know what I don't want. Experience has given me that knowledge." He nudged her head back and rinsed the lather off her hair. Cammy had the ability to look silly and sweet, and at the same time, irresistibly sultry.

Once she was rinsed off, he turned to grab a drying cloth for her. "Here, wrap this around you." He helped her out of the tub as soon as she did so. "Shall I brush your hair?"

She grinned. "No, I can manage by myself. Your turn in the tub. And I wasn't finished with my remarks."

He arched an eyebrow. "Go ahead. I'm listening. But are you going to turn away?"

"Oh, no. Not on your life. You've seen all of me, so it is only fair that I do the same. And I did win that round of cards. You said my prize did not expire."

"It doesn't." He began to remove his clothes, stifling a laugh when her face turned crimson the moment he removed his shirt. "Tell me the rest of what you wanted to say." He began to unbutton the fall of his trousers. "Cammy, why the silence?"

Suddenly, she was looking everywhere but at him. "What?"

He still liked that innocence about her.

Now that she was looking away, he dropped his trousers and stepped into the tub. "You had more to say to me."

She sighed. "Oh, Lor. I think women must also have low brains. One look at you, and all thought has flown from my head."

She hadn't seen all of him, just his upper torso when he had removed his shirt. He liked that he could fluster her. They would need to maintain this strong attraction to each other if she could not bring herself to live with him in London. He would never cheat on her, nor would she cheat on him, but those long months of separation would surely weigh on them.

Perhaps things would change as she gained confidence in herself.

After bathing and eating their meal, they meant to remain in the beautifully appointed quarters for the rest of the day and leave early the following morning. All was proceeding smoothly until Cammy suddenly gasped and began to shove one of the drying cloths between her legs. When she drew it away to inspect it, the cloth was stained in blood. "Oh, my courses,"

What the hell?

He'd grown up in a household of men.

He did not know how to respond to such things.

Worst of all, Cammy had nothing with her to do whatever it was women did when they bled. She hastily rang for one of the maids. Since everyone at the inn believed she was with child, the maid scurried out and told one of the other maids, who in turn told the innkeeper's wife.

Chaos now erupted.

They all thought she was losing the babe.

Within moments, women began to pile into their quarters. A few tried to kick him out, but he had no intention of leaving, and they soon realized moving him was harder than moving a mountain, so they gave up.

Instead, he shooed most of them out since there was nothing they could do, and were merely gawking.

He raked a hand through his hair in consternation.

Deception was sometimes necessary in his assignments, and he carried it off without a twinge of remorse. But this was different. Lying to these women who were there to support and comfort his 'wife' was simply cruel.

Yet, he could not allow them to know the truth.

Nor could he allow Cammy to confess the truth.

He needn't have worried. She was shocked and silent. Her expression was taken for sorrow in losing a child she never had in the first place. His gut twisted, for even he felt awful about the unintended consequences of their deception.

A quiet tear streamed down Cammy's cheek.

Soon, she was not the only one crying. The innkeeper's wife and the two maids he had allowed to remain in the room were also overset and tearing up.

When they finally left to allow Cammy to rest, he released the breath he had been holding. "I'm so sorry," he said, drawing a chair to her side as she lay in bed looking utterly miserable.

"Lor, these lies keep getting worse and worse."

"I know."

"Everyone must know by now there is no child. They must think I am the most horrible person in the world. What can I say to make things right?"

It turned out she had no need to say anything. No one blamed her for any deception. Instead, they were kinder than ever. "Sir Lorcan," the innkeeper's wife said gently, taking him aside a few hours later when she came to their door to peek in on Cammy and see whether they wished supper to be brought up to their room, "it is obvious your dear wife is hoping for a child and allowed her wishes to get the better of her. Do not be angry with her for leaping to a false conclusion because her courses were late. It happens. Please do not blame her."

Did he have to hear this?

He cleared his throat, knowing the kindly woman was awaiting a response. "I love her, Mrs. Gormer. She knows I do." Well, at least that was the truth. "I do not blame her."

"I am relieved to hear it. Sometimes a lass hopes for something so much she almost wills it to be true. But take heart, it will happen."

He ran a hand across the nape of his neck, for he was now breaking into a sweat. "I just want her to be all right."

"She will be. The poor lass. Is she still distraught?"

"She is recovering. I'm sure she'll be hungry by the time our supper is brought in. Thank you for all you've done." He nudged her out before Cammy broke down and confessed all. She was not asleep and must have heard everything, even though he and Mrs. Gormer had kept their voices to a whisper.

"Dear Lord," he muttered. "Glad we got through that."

It was his habit to look around wherever he stayed because he liked to know who was there and if they posed a threat. He took a moment to walk downstairs, but all was quiet. Nothing odd leaped out at him when he sent Mr. Gormer on a made-up errand so he could peruse the inn's register.

The good-natured man returned moments later with an ale in hand. "There ye are, Sir Lorcan."

"Thank you." He spent another moment chatting with the amiable man, his purpose to make certain there were no ill consequences to their deception. Not for his sake but for Cammy's.

He needn't have worried.

Everyone was genuinely sympathetic. Despite the maids and innkeeper's wife knowing Cammy was not carrying his child, somehow that rumor still persisted, and guests were now coming up to him and extending their good wishes to him and Cammy.

He did not bother to correct them.

Explanations would compound their lies and make things worse.

He told Cammy about the gossip when he returned, and she pressed him with questions.

"Lor! I cannot take it," she said with a moan, sitting up in bed.

"You must, just a little longer. We'll be on the road by break of day and won't have to see anyone before we leave."

But Cammy's face was once more buried in her hands. "What are we going to do?"

He knelt at her side. "Nothing changes. We continue on our journey. You marry me."

The silence between them was charged.

Her despair was a palpable, living thing, a great beast that now stood between them and happiness.

He understood her concern.

So many lies.

He hadn't lied this much, even during his dirtiest assignments for the Crown.

She looked up and cast him a look of utter despair.

Bollocks.

He understood that look. She had placed him back on the 'can never marry the apish fiend' list.

"Nothing changes," he insisted. "I want you for my wife, Cammy."

"How could you? Have I not been a burden to you the entire

way? And look at us now? Deceiving all these kind and generous people."

"We'll be married within a matter of days. Blessed saints, why do you care what anyone else thinks?"

She glanced up. "It isn't about them. It is about me. I was not a liar until you—"

He realized what she abruptly stopped herself from saying. "What? You were not a liar until I turned you into one?"

"I know you were only doing what you thought was best for my protection."

"And what is wrong with that?" He had a greater tolerance for this sort of thing. One could not succeed in his line of work if one insisted on being honest with everyone they met. Intrigue and espionage did not work that way.

She sank back atop the bed. "I don't blame you for any of it."

"Good to know." But she did blame him for the callousness the work he performed for the Crown had bred in him.

That night, she suggested he sleep on the floor beside the hearth.

He did so without protest but moved to the bed beside her when she grew restless in the middle of the night, and he could see she was in a lot of discomfort. "Just for a little while, Cammy. Let me hold you in my arms."

"All right."

She finally fell asleep in his embrace.

He slept fitfully and awoke to find his hand splayed across her belly. He recalled it had seemed to help the cramping that was intense enough to have her body curling into a little ball to defend against the pain.

She had not slept well, except perhaps those last few hours when he lay by her side. He noticed dark circles under her eyes come morning.

He cast her a worried frown. "Can you travel today?"

The weather was clear, no sign of rain, and the oppressive dampness had disappeared during the night and been replaced by a cooling breeze from the north. She nodded. "Yes, I am eager to be on our way."

He gathered their belongings and then carried her travel pouch downstairs, while she saw to whatever it was she needed to do for herself. He knew nothing about these things. The innkeeper's wife noticed him pacing. "Ah, you are distressed by your wife's situation. It is natural. She will feel a little out of sorts. Sometimes travel makes the cramping worse. But it will clear in a few days."

He nodded and was forced to listen while Mrs. Gormer went on about these womanly concerns. Cammy must have seen his pained expression when she finally joined them. She cast him a wry smile.

He breathed a sigh of relief as he set her on the saddle and climbed up behind her.

After a quick farewell, they rode away.

Only after they were out of sight did he bother to pull up on the reins. "Cammy, are you truly all right?"

"Yes, Lor."

"Just tell me if you feel the need to stop at any time."

"I will."

"Because all you have to do is ask."

She shook her head and laughed. "I think you are more comfortable dealing with murder plots than dealing with the nature of a woman's body."

"Lord, yes," he admitted with a groan. "I don't know what to do for you. I'm afraid to touch you for fear I'll hurt you."

"Lor, it is not a wound."

"Fine. But you'll tell me if anything hurts?"

She nodded.

They rode on in silence.

As afternoon turned into approaching night, Lorcan was never happier to reach his brother's estate. At first, only the rooftop and chimney stacks were visible. But not long after, Shayne's manor house came into view, standing grand and proud against the pink and gold hues of sunset.

Berengaria was perhaps happiest of them all to reach Shayne's home. She suddenly perked and increased her pace as they rode up the elegant drive.

"We're here, Cammy," he whispered, for her eyes had drifted shut a little while ago, and he hadn't the heart to disturb her rest since she'd gotten so little of it last night.

She blinked them open, and a genuine smile broke out for the first time all day.

It was nice to see the unmasked joy in her eyes, even though he knew it wasn't for him.

To his surprise, Shayne, Willow, and her Aunt Charlotte came running out of the house to greet them. He thought they had remained in Taunton at the Ashcott Inn awaiting word. But the town and inn were only a few hours from here, and Shayne must have realized they were likely to pass by here first.

Cammy's aunt and sister wrapped her in hugs the moment he set her down. "Cammy! Thank goodness you're safe! We were so worried about you!" her sister cried, tears gleaming in her eyes.

Her aunt was also crying.

In the next moment, so was Cammy.

Lorcan left them to their reunion and walked Berengaria to the stable. Shayne strode beside him. "Glad you found her."

"So am I," Lorcan said. "She climbed onto the wrong coach and was headed to Gloucester instead of Barnstaple."

His brother nodded. "So, I learned shortly after you'd taken off. But I was also told you knew and had gone north to stop that coach. Willow was a wreck, crying for days. I suppose the storm delayed your return."

"It did." Lorcan handed Berengaria to one of the stable hands and made certain they were out of everyone's earshot before filling Shayne in on all that had happened. The scent of hay and horseflesh carried on the cooling breeze as they sauntered back to the house.

He confided almost everything to his brother, only leaving

out the more intimate details of his time with Cammy.

But his brother was no fool. "Bollocks, Lor. You shared a room with her?"

"I wasn't going to leave her alone and risk having her run away again, or risk some oaf noticing her and attempting to break into her room because he knew she was in there alone."

Shayne said nothing, obviously awaiting the inevitable pronouncement.

He sighed. "Yes, I am taking her to Barnstaple next. I hope we can leave tomorrow. We need to marry as soon as possible."

His brother frowned. "Lor, you didn't…"

"Take advantage? No, I didn't." He understood his brother's concern. "But there is no question we must marry to save her reputation. I'm known in those parts. People recognized me. We had to pass ourselves off as husband and wife."

"Are you all right with it?"

He snorted. "More than all right. I'm in love with her. Is it not obvious? But she hasn't decided about me."

Shayne clapped him on the back. "I'm sorry. I guess we all got it wrong. Willow was sure she was in love with you."

"She is," he said, glancing in the direction of the women who had been standing by the entry and were now about to enter the house. He held Shayne back a moment to finish their conversation. "But as you know, after reading that book they toted around, sometimes love isn't enough. She hasn't quite come to terms with my duties as an agent of the Crown. And she is serious about not wanting to step foot in London. I'm not sure how we'll work it out, but I want to have that discussion with her once we are husband and wife."

His brother stared at him, a frown marring his brow. "Are you sure? What if you cannot work it out?"

"We have to," he said, his own expression grim. "I love her, and I know she loves me."

"Blessed saints, Lor. You cannot dismiss these issues. I don't care how much you care for each other. It does not mean you are right together. How will either of you ever be happy if you cannot find a compromise?"

"Stop spouting that damn book at me. I've read it. I know all about compromise and expectations. I know what's at stake."

"Do you? Because it seems to me you are ignoring all the warning signs and plowing ahead without caution."

"No, I'm not. I love her. There is nothing I would not sacrifice for her." In his heart, he knew this was true. He was not blind to the impediments, but Cammy was the beauty in his life, and he did not intend to lose her.

He glanced at the sky, studying its stunning hues, the golds and pinks against the pale blue expanse. The fading sunlight was brilliant at this hour, magnificent as it glistened off the manor's rooftop.

Cammy was like this glowing light, an incandescent burst of sunshine in his day.

How could he explain it to Shayne? Did he not feel the same about Willow? The eagerness to be around her. The peace that filled him whenever he was.

He must have had these feelings, for he had been an immovable mountain, not budging from Willow's side when she was hurt. How can a love like that be ignored?

"And what of her?" Shayne asked, regaining his attention.

Lorcan cast his brother one of his lethal stares, eager to end the conversation. "What do you mean?"

"Does she feel the same way? Will all your sacrifice be enough?"

Lorcan did not know.

"Because that's the real question, isn't it?"

CHAPTER ELEVEN

"CAMMY, WHY DID you run off?" Willow asked as she and their aunt led her upstairs to one of the bedchambers that had been readied for her. The room, a mix of peach and pale blue silks, and dark, polished furniture, was surprisingly elegant but in a cozy and charming way.

Her tension eased despite the questions Willow and Charlotte were tossing at her. She and her sisters had been raised to marry for love. Of course, a man's wealth did play a part, but only a small part. Intelligence, kindness, faithfulness, willingness to protect those he loved, were just as important, if not more so.

But she was pleased that Willow had found herself a man with all these qualities and a surprising bit of wealth.

Lorcan had mentioned he and his brothers shared in their investments. Did it mean he was just as wealthy as Shayne? She set aside the thought, for all the wealth in the world would not sway her to marry a man she did not love.

Of course, she loved Lorcan.

But she was not ready to say it to him yet.

"Give me a moment to wash up, and I will tell you every-thing."

Charlotte groaned, no doubt worried all these nights alone with Lorcan had led to something irreversible. But in this, Lorcan had been surprisingly gallant and refused to claim her outside of marriage.

Had he made advances, she would not have resisted, for the man was devastatingly appealing. But it spoke well of his character that he had not attempted any such thing. He was a protector, even if it meant protecting her against himself.

It felt odd not to share a bedchamber with him.

She tried not to think of it and ignored the pang of regret now squeezing her heart. Perhaps…no, he would not sneak a visit in the middle of the night, certainly not under his brother's watchful eye. But she wondered where they had settled him. There were at least five or six bedchambers that she had counted along the hallway and probably more in the opposite wing.

If it were up to Charlotte, she would have had him placed in the barn, as far away from her as possible.

Not that it would stop him if he wanted to see her.

Willow must have been reading her thoughts. "Shayne has plenty of rooms in this big house. His first task after acquiring the place was to set aside two of the larger bedchambers for his brothers. They are a close family, just as we are. He wanted them to treat his home as though it were their own, to have a place to leave their belongings, and come and go as they pleased.

"That is generous of him."

"After their parents died, he wanted to make sure he and his brothers would never drift apart. As eldest, he felt it was his duty to hold the family together."

Cammy nodded. "He seems to have done that rather well."

"I think so, too. I admire him for it, especially since they are all strong and independent. Donal and Lorcan still work for the Crown and are sent wherever there is trouble. It would be so easy for the years to pass by without them getting together. Donal has been at the Earl of Monkton's estate tying up loose ends over the death of the earl's wicked brother."

She knew Willow referred to Lord Belfy.

"Donal will return tomorrow, sometime in the early afternoon, I think. Shayne might ask Lorcan to hold off your journey to Barnstaple for another day, so the brothers can spend an evening together. Do you mind, Cammy?"

"No, not at all." She had a lot to say to Lorcan as well but would not seek him out tonight. She would wait until morning. She did not like the way they had left matters between them. Not that it was his fault. She was the one who had been wavering, unable to shake off her uncertainty, still mired in doubt and fear.

It was important for her to explain to him what had been going through her mind. So many experiences were new to her, and she dared not get anything wrong. Her future happiness was at stake. So was his.

For a fleeting moment, she considered speaking to him tonight, but she dismissed the idea.

In truth, she was tired.

She also needed time to think.

Besides, she had an important matter to discuss with Willow and Charlotte. No more secrets between her and her family. She needed to tell them about her scar and why she was so afraid of London and the marriage mart. She would attend to it as soon as she had washed up and changed out of her dusty travel gown.

Part of growing up was learning to stop hiding from her fears and start conquering them.

"Willow," she said, noting her sister's happiness now that she was married to Lorcan's brother. It shone in her eyes. June had been the same when marrying Augustus. This is what she wanted for herself. "Would you happen to have a spare gown for me? Some undergarments, too. I ran off with nothing for myself. And I'll need rags. I…poor Lorcan. I thought he would faint when I started my monthly bleeding."

Willow was clearly struggling to smother a chuckle. "Yes, I have all the clothes you'll need. Just because you were gone did not mean Mrs. Albright and her seamstresses stopped making new gowns for us. But why did you run away, Cammy? We were all frantic with worry."

"I know. It is time I showed you the reason." She turned her back and sought Willow's help in unlacing her gown and corset.

"This is something I should have confided in you long ago. Only June ever knew of this because she saw me sneak into the house right after it happened. I could not reach…well, I had to tell her since she immediately sensed something was wrong and would not leave me alone until I confessed."

"Confessed?" Willow cast her a worried glance.

"I do not know the name of the lord who did this to me, nor do I ever want to face him again. I told June that I did not get a good look at my assailant other than to know he was no one local."

Willow and Charlotte gasped when she revealed the mark across her back.

She told them how and when it happened. "I was afraid Mama and Papa would forbid me from drawing my birds if they ever found out. I wasn't going to let that beastly lord take this away from me, too."

"Oh, my dear!" Charlotte took her into her embrace. "You should have told us at once. That wicked man would have been brought to task. When I return home, I shall go directly to the inn where those fiends were staying and get his name. I'm sure he made enough of a bad impression that no one will have forgotten him."

Willow nodded. "I'm glad Mr. Ogilvie's dog managed to take a chunk out of his backside. I hope that bite festered and gives him constant pain. It is no less than he deserves. I wish you had told us sooner. Why didn't you? I thought we shared everything."

"We did. But I couldn't talk about this. I wanted to bury it deep and forget it ever happened. It was so shocking and frightening to me, the mere mention of it makes me physically ill even long after the pain of those lashes has gone away. Look, my hands still shake."

Charlotte sniffled. "Oh, you poor dear."

"I told Lorcan about it. He is so easy to talk to. And yet, I haven't been kind to him." Cammy's hands were still shaking as she poured water into the basin on her bureau, dipped a cloth in it, and began to soap it up with another of the scented Farthingale soaps made by her cousins in Oxford. It was Willow's favorite scent, orange blossoms.

"Why do you think you have not been kind to him?" Willow asked.

"I know I haven't been." She swallowed to relieve the ache in her throat. It had turned tight and painful as she spoke of the incident. "I've pushed him away because he is so casual about facing danger. Nothing frightens him. And everything frightens me. I feel so cowardly."

Charlotte frowned. "Has he accused you of this?"

"No, he's been wonderful to me. He makes me feel cherished. But his kindness only makes me hurt worse. He is so strong and confident, and I…I don't even know what I am. He is steel and fire. I am pudding and mush."

"Nonsense." Willow put an arm around her. "You are my very brave sister."

Cammy shook her head. "Oh, no. Do not cast me in a good light. I wish I could be as brave as you are, but I'm simply not. I wanted to tell you about my scar when you were injured by that shattered glass. Then I thought, how could I add this burden on you when you were in so much pain of your own?"

"I wish you had."

"I should have, especially when you were overset about requiring stitches. I could have shown you my scar and assured you that you would heal. But I still hadn't healed, had I? So how could I assure you? Besides, Shayne hardly left your side, so I could not talk to you in private."

Charlotte tsked. "I was here, too. I wish you had mentioned it to me. All the while, I thought you were behaving childishly when you were doing nothing of the sort. What you suffered was a severe shock to your body. This happens to soldiers in battle sometimes."

"But I was at home, not on a battlefield."

"The attack you suffered was as severe. It affected everything you did from that day on. That you are able to speak of it now is a sign of your strength. It is a healing step, Cammy. Hiding it was not cowardly. It was you struggling to maintain the essence of who you are, your compassion and gentleness, even after being victim to that brutality."

She set aside her washcloth and tearfully ran into her aunt's arms. "June was worried about leaving me. She was ready to give up Augustus for my sake. But I pretended I was fine, and she needn't worry about me. I would never have forgiven myself if she had stayed behind for me and missed out on her happiness."

"And was this not a brave thing, too?" Willow said, caressing her cheek when she once more picked up her washcloth to continue rinsing the dust of her body after the day's ride.

"I never thought of it as brave. You know I would never do anything to interfere with your or June's happiness."

"What will you do next, Cammy?"

"There is no question about her next step," Charlotte said. "She's spent the night with Lorcan Brayden. More than one night. Surely, he understands what he must do. Marriage is the only alternative. If he has not offered, then Shayne must speak to him at once."

Cammy's fingers tightened on the damp cloth. "He has offered. We only stopped here because he wanted to leave word with you that he had found me, and I was all right. Then he intended to take me straight to Barnstaple and speak to Papa."

Charlotte eyed her shrewdly. "Then where is the problem? Why are you not pleased? When we were staying at the Ashcott Inn, I sensed you liked him very much. Has something changed?"

"No. I still like him…very much indeed."

"Child, what are you afraid of?"

"I don't know. Perhaps of failing him, of disappointing him because I cannot be as brave as he is. Perhaps I am making something out of nothing. I'm not sure there even is a problem." She shook her head. "I need to talk it through with Lorcan. But not this evening. We've had an eventful journey, and I need some time on my own to think."

Willow glanced at her travel pouch that was perched on one of the chairs by her bed. "Are you going to read that book?" she asked, digging through the pouch to draw it out. She now held it up as though it were a treasured artifact.

Cammy studied its binding, the faded red so familiar and somehow comforting. "No. I've read it so many times with you and June. I've also read much of it with Lorcan. It is now time for me to think for myself."

Charlotte patted her hand. "Dearest, just remember that none of us is perfect. Nor will the one who steals your heart always be perfect. Love is about sharing the path your life takes you on. After all is said and done, it is your heart that must guide you. But just remember this, do not push Lorcan away because you are afraid to disappoint him. This is not the right way to think about how love works."

Willow frowned. "Or are you worried that he does not care for you as much as you do for him?"

"It is not that." Cammy blushed. "He has said he loves me."

Willow gasped. "He said it to you? Lorcan? Stoic Lorcan? The man whose fierce gaze can drop a man cowering to his knees?"

Charlotte broke into a beaming smile. "Precisely my point. It is no small thing for a man of his nature to admit his feelings for you. He is no glib rascal. To say this to you…well, he must have felt it to the depths of his soul. So, think of how miserable he would be if you were not beside him to share his life's journey."

Cammy nodded. "I think I have been a great fool."

"No, my dear. It is not too late to set aside your doubts and let him know how you feel. But not tonight. As you say, it is late, and we are all weary. Get a good night's rest and talk to him first thing in the morning."

She nodded. "If Shayne has not convinced him to stay here another day, then he will want us to leave early for Barnstaple. We'll have plenty of time to talk along the way."

Once her sister and aunt had left her chamber, she ate some

of the fruit and cheese the housekeeper had brought up, drank some of the cider to ease her parched throat, then fell into bed with a sigh of exhaustion.

They had arrived at sundown, which at this time of the year did not occur until ten o'clock in the evening. It was almost midnight by the time she went to bed and nearly one of the o'clock before she finally stopped tossing and fretting and fell asleep.

The sun also rose early in the summer season, and Cammy made certain to keep her drapes open so that it would shine into her bedchamber soon after sunrise. As hoped, she was awakened by the soft light falling across her face.

The hour was early, but she scrambled out of bed, eager to see Lorcan.

She had missed having his arms around her and his big body to warm her as she slept.

Shayne's housekeeper had set out several gowns and their undergarments for her last night. She quickly washed up and was debating whether to ring for one of the maids to help lace the gown she'd selected, a lovely travel gown of dark green muslin with white lace trim at the collar and sleeves, when one of them silently stepped in. "Oh, Miss Cammy, I did not mean to disturb you."

"Not at all," she said, "I was about to ring for you, Aggie. Will you help me with these lacings?"

"Of course." Aggie was a kindly, middle-aged woman who had been in service with the prior owner of the manor and had remained on after Shayne had acquired the place several years ago. Apparently, most of the servants had stayed on and were well pleased with their new master, judging by the cheerful disposition of the few on the staff Cammy had met.

Aggie also helped her to pin up her hair, leaving it in a loose, twisting bun that she found quite flattering to her features. Her eyes seemed bigger, her mouth softer, and the angles of her face appeared more graceful. "Don't you look lovely, Miss Cammy?"

She hoped Lorcan would feel this way.

"Is anyone else awake yet?" She tried to sound casual, making no specific reference to Lorcan, but Aggie was not fooled.

The woman could not contain her affectionate smirk. "The master and your sister are still abed. So is your aunt." She paused, purposely making no mention of Lorcan.

"Aggie…"

"Sir Lorcan has already had his breakfast and gone off."

"Gone? Do you know where?" Weren't they supposed to leave for Barnstaple this morning? Shayne must have convinced him to stay on here another day. Or had she done such a thorough job of pushing him away that he wanted nothing more to do with her and rode away?

No, it was not possible.

He would never leave her to face ruin.

"He's only gone fishing, Miss Cammy. I'm sure he'll return in the early afternoon."

Was this the excuse he'd given everyone? "But we were…never mind." She felt ready to cry. "Will you please let my sister know I need to speak to her as soon as she wakens?"

"Of course." Aggie put away her nightclothes. "But I'm afraid it won't be for at least another hour yet. She and the master usually rise at seven, and it is barely six now."

"I see." She took a deep breath. "Let them know I've gone for a walk and will be back shortly. Which way to the fishing spot?"

As soon as Aggie had given her directions, she left her bedchamber and hurried out of the house. The morning dew was still on the grass, and the air still held traces of the cool of night breeze. But the day would assuredly turn hot, for the sun was already beating down on her with unusual intensity for this early hour.

She glanced up and saw not a cloud in the sky.

This was rare for summer, she thought, cutting across the manicured lawn dotted with grazing sheep. A short while later, she came upon a wooded glade and heard the sound of a rushing stream.

She was headed in the right direction.

Following the sound, she soon reached a clearing. It was a small patch of open field alongside the stream, but still surrounded by the woods. Several trees had sprouted beyond the glade and came up to the edge of the water, their silvery-leafed branches bowed gracefully over the swiftly moving current.

She stood at the edge, taking in the cool spray as she searched for Lorcan.

Her breath caught when she noticed him seated on a fallen log, fishing pole in hand. He was casually dressed, wearing a coarse linen shirt and dark breeches almost as dark as his fishing boots. The white shirt accentuated the broadness of his back and his trim, tapering torso.

He appeared quite relaxed as he flicked the line in and out of the shimmering water to lure a fish.

She approached him quietly, taking a moment to study the waves of his dark hair and the way the ends seemed to curl caressingly around the nape of his neck. She itched to run her fingers through his hair, ached to touch him.

"Are you going to stand there gawking at me, Cammy? Or will you come sit beside me?"

Honestly, the man had eyes in the back of his head.

She hadn't made a sound.

How had he known she was there?

He also seemed able to read her mind, she realized as he spoke his next words. "I caught the scent of your soap. Orange blossoms."

"But that's Willow's scent. I only used it because this is the soap she gave me. How did you know it wasn't her?"

"At this hour? My brother is besotted with your sister. He isn't going to let her out of bed for at least another hour yet. Not before they—"

"Lor!"

"I wasn't going to say anything lewd."

She settled beside him, ignoring the poke of decaying bark against her backside. If he could tolerate it, then so could she. "What were you going to say?"

"I merely intended to observe that Shayne likes to review estate documents in the undisturbed privacy of his bedchamber. He has those delivered along with his coffee each morning. Now that he and Willow are married, I expect he shares his business concerns with her over a pot of coffee before they set about their day."

She laughed. "I don't believe you. I've seen the way they look at each other. Estate documents are the last thing on either of their minds. If they are drinking in anything, it is the sight of each other."

"You're right." He winked at her and grinned. "You look beautiful this morning, Cammy. Did you get a good night's rest?"

"Yes." She glanced down at herself and blushed. "Lor, may I talk to you?"

"Of course." He lodged the fishing pole between two sturdy branches of the fallen tree where they were seated and turned to her. "Take all the time you need. You have my complete attention."

"Since I found you here fishing, I assume it means you do not want to leave for Barnstaple today."

"Do you mind? Donal is due back this afternoon, and it is important to Shayne that we spend time together. These past few weeks were supposed to be a restful break for the three of us."

"I know. Instead, you've spent it helping Shayne subdue Lord Belfy and his cohorts, deal with a carriage house fire, a deranged guard, and a runaway idiot."

He growled low in his throat. "You are not an idiot, Cammy."

"I was. Thoughtless. Panicked. Scared rabbit. But I do not want to be that scared rabbit anymore. This is what I wanted to say to you. I let my fears control me, and it almost ruined my chance at happiness."

He drew her close and tucked his arm around her. "You weren't ever going to lose me. I hope you know that."

She shook her head. "Perhaps not immediately, but in time my fears would have made us both miserable. The demands I intended to place on you would have had you twisting and contorting, sacrificing too much just to appease me. But I want you to know, Lor. You are the only one for me. So if it means living in London, I will do it because it is important to you."

He stared at her in amazement. "Do you mean it, love?"

"Yes," she said, eagerly nodding. "Be patient with me, though. I will have to work up the courage to go out and about, especially to attend society affairs. But I have plenty of cousins to look after me whenever you are not around, and at some point, I will gain the strength to stand on my own."

He lifted her hand to his lips and kissed her palm tenderly. "What changed your mind?"

"The realization of just how timid I had become. This is not who I am, Lor. Not that I am anywhere near as courageous as you. But I was ready to give you up in order to avoid having to face my fears." She shook her head and cast him a pained glance. "I cannot lose you. You are too precious to me. So, I chose to give up my fears instead. I refuse to allow that wicked lord to control my life and destroy my happiness."

"Bravo, love." He drew her onto his lap and put his arms around her. "You also have this grunting ape to protect you for always. I won't let anyone hurt you ever again. But I have an important question to ask."

"Go ahead, Lor."

"Will you allow me to do a little investigating when we reach Barnstaple? I want to find out that lord's name."

She tensed. "Charlotte said the same thing."

"You told her? And Willow?"

She nodded. "Last night. My first step in taking back the reins of my life."

He kissed her gently on the lips. "I'm proud of you, sweetheart."

"I still broke into a sweat, and my hands shook the entire time. My throat tightened painfully, but I managed to tell them everything. Willow has probably confided it to Shayne by now. I told her she could."

She snuggled against him, loving the warmth and strength of his body. "All this time, I was afraid to find out that beast's name. I wanted him to remain a shadow, not make him real. But Charlotte is right and so are you. We need to find out who he is. I want us to do it together."

"Are you sure, love? It's a big step for anyone, even the most hardened of us."

She nodded. "I won't be afraid while I am with you."

He gave her another light kiss. "Cammy, once we have his name, you need to trust me to bring him to justice. This is not something you can do on your own. The sad state of our society is such that you, more than he, will be tarnished if the incident becomes public knowledge."

"I understand. He was so arrogant and full of himself. He is likely a peer. That could make him untouchable. You won't…"

"I will not kill him, much as I would love to. But he cannot be allowed to get away with what he did. There are ways to deal with him other than physical force. Do you trust me to handle the matter?"

She nodded and saw the relief in his eyes. "Lor, do what you think best. But I am not afraid of coming forward if this is what it will take for him to be properly punished. I don't want him harming others."

"I'm sure you weren't the first, nor the last. But we'll see what's to be done once I learn his identity. I won't risk bringing you forward if he is a peer of the realm. He'll escape punishment, and you'll be left the subject of nasty gossip. It will accomplish nothing."

She pursed her lips. "This is something that must change, this 'privilege' of peerage. Why should they operate under a separate set of laws? Especially when it comes to criminal matters?"

He grinned. "You ought to tell that to the House of Commons. And while you are at it, how about working on allowing women as Fellows in the Royal Society? If your drawings are as good as I expect they are, why should your naturalist get all the accolades when you have worked just as hard on bringing these findings to light? What do you think, Cammy?"

"We'll see." She laughed genuinely, for Lor was more than she had ever hoped for. Indeed, she would not have to worry about his holding her back. If anything, she would have to rein him in.

Did he seriously believe the Royal Society, that bastion of male arrogance, would ever allow a woman into their midst?

But she liked that he was a man of action and looked forward to the vitality their lives together would hold. "There is something I must do before I go ahead and champion a thousand causes."

His eyes were alight with amusement. "What is that?"

"This." She kissed him fervently, pressing her mouth to his warm lips and hoping to convey how deeply she cared for him. "I love you, Lorcan Brayden. I love you with all my heart and soul. I will love you forever."

He leaped to his feet, still holding her in his arms, and emitted a noisy whoop that frightened several birds out of the low-hanging branches. She heard their startled cheeps and mad flutter of wings as they flew away.

He twirled her around, laughing and joyful, before finally setting her back on her feet.

But he gave her only a moment to find her balance before he drew her against him and crushed his mouth to hers. He kissed her until her toes curled. He kissed her until they were both laughing and breathless. He kissed her until his fishing pole suddenly sailed off the branches where he'd lodged it. "Lor! You've got a fish on the line!"

He grabbed the pole before the current, and the frantic fish carried it downstream. "Come on, love. We'll haul him in together," he said, wading out of the water with it in hand and climbing back onto the grassy bank of the stream. He took hold of her hand and drew her in front of him. "Here, put your hands on the pole. Both hands. Hold it tight. Now slowly pull it back. Good. And again."

"Lor, he's strong! My hands keep slipping down the pole. As fast as I push them up, they slide back down. I can't hold it. I think your pole is too big for me."

"No, it's the perfect size," he said with a soft chuckle, unable to contain his merriment.

She sensed there was a double meaning to his words because he had the wickedest grin on his face when she turned back to stare at him.

"Keep your eyes on the fish," he said, still chuckling. He turned her to face the stream and drew her close so that her back was up against his chest, and he had his arms wrapped around her.

"He's fighting back. I'm not sure I can hold onto him."

"You can do anything you put your mind to doing, love." He kissed her on the neck and began to nibble the sensitive spot where it met her shoulder.

"I'm going to lose the fish if you don't stop doing that!" But she was laughing just as hard as he was. His arms felt so good around her. He was teasing and playful, and this moment together in the sunshine and cooling breezes off the stream felt like heaven.

She was out of breath and disheveled by the time she hauled the large trout onto shore. "Oh, Lor. We cannot kill it."

He rolled his eyes when she maintained her pleading look. "Fine. You are soft as pudding, you know."

"I know. But the day is too perfect to be marred by death."

"We are speaking of a fish. We eat them. For supper." But he quickly unhooked it and tossed it back in the stream. "There, happy now?"

"Yes. Thank you. Now the day is perfect."

"Not quite," he said, drawing her back to the fallen tree trunk and nudging her down on it. He knelt beside her. "Camellia Farthingale, will you do me the honor of becoming my wife?"

She threw herself into his arms, knocking them both down. He fell back gently upon the grass and hauled her atop him, his arms closing around her and swallowing her up in his embrace. "Yes, you wonderful man. Yes, and yes. But you did not have to ask me. Isn't this the reason we were on our way to Barnstaple?"

"I did have to ask you. I want you to know that no one is forcing me to offer for you. I am not marrying you to save your reputation. There is no need for a rifle pointed at my neck to lead me to the altar. I am asking because I love you. I am asking because I can never be happy without you in my life."

"Nor could I ever be happy without you." She began to rain kisses on his face. His cheeks. His chin. His jaw. The lids of his eyes.

He cupped her face in his hands and drew her head down to kiss her on the mouth. When he was through ravaging her lips with his sweet kisses, he sat up and set her on his lap. His eyes were silver ash and smoldering. "Best day's fishing I've ever had."

"Do you mind terribly that I made you toss the trout back?"

"No, love. I've got you, and that is a far better catch." He was about to kiss her again when someone cleared his throat behind them.

Cammy scrambled off Lorcan's lap, her face burning.

Lorcan felt no embarrassment whatsoever. "Donal, you're back early." He rose and strode to his brother, clapping him on the shoulder in greeting.

Donal also had a fishing pole in hand. "I thought I'd join you, but I see your idea of fishing is not quite the same as mine. Good morning, Cammy. Glad my oaf of a brother brought you home safely."

She was still mortified Donal had caught them in the midst of a passionate embrace. "We are going to be married," she said, as though this would somehow make her appear less of a wanton.

He arched an eyebrow. "I expected as much. You spent several days together. More important, several nights."

Lorcan took her hand in his. "I am marrying her because I love her. Just want to be clear on that point. No one is forcing me to the altar."

Donal laughed and shook his head. "Gad, you and Shayne have turned into besotted fools. It's that book, isn't it? The one Cammy and her sisters were toting around? I'm beginning to believe it is magical."

"It is magical," Cammy insisted, gazing lovingly upon Lorcan. "No one escapes finding true love when that book is put in front of them."

He did not appear impressed and merely shrugged. "Who is getting it next?"

A slow smile crossed Cammy's face. "You, of course, Donal. Isn't it obvious?"

CHAPTER TWELVE

"**I** AM NOT taking that book," Donal said between gritted teeth when Cammy repeated her decision the following day, insisting he would be next to receive *The Book of Love*. She and Lorcan were about to leave for Barnstaple, this time in luxury, for they were borrowing Shayne's elegant carriage and leaving Berengaria with him for now.

The carriage had been brought around, and the three of them were now standing in front of the sleek, black conveyance. "Yes, you are," Cammy said with a stubborn set to her mouth that had Lorcan laughing as he watched his brother squirm.

Donal cast him a pleading look, but Lorcan merely shook his head. "Don't look at me. I fell under its spell, didn't I?"

Cammy bestowed a breathtaking smile on him before returning her attention to his brother. "I will turn the book over to you once Lor and I reach London."

"No sense fighting it, Donal. You are doomed." He returned his brother's glare with a grin.

Cammy was not in the least put off by the scathing looks Donal was casting them. "It won't be released to you until your brother and I are married. But rest assured, it will happen. Do you not wish to be as happy as he and Shayne are?"

"I am already happy. Not looking to change anything in my life." He was on his way back to London to report for his next assignment and obviously eager to be on the road. His horse had been brought to the courtyard along with Shayne's carriage.

"You might change your mind once you have it in your hands. You don't have to read it," Cammy said, still ignoring Donal's scowl. "If you don't want it, just return it to my Aunt Sophie. She is going to hold onto it for the next generation of Farthingale daughters. She resides on Chipping Way, next door to your cousin, Romulus. He married my cousin, Violet."

Lorcan stood beside her, still laughing hard. It was not often he had the pleasure of seeing his brother aghast. Cammy thought he and Donal were fearless, for they were cut from the same cloth. His assignments for the Crown were just as dangerous as Lorcan's often were. But his brother looked ashen at the moment. Who knew a book of love could be so terrifying? "You cannot escape it, Donal."

He glared at Lorcan before turning to Cammy. "Haven't you Farthingales all been taken by now?"

She nodded. "Yes, those of us presently of marriageable age. But more will be along in another few years. My cousin, Rose, has two daughters. Alas, it will be at least another decade before they are ready for the marriage mart."

Donal rolled his eyes. "Thank goodness."

Cammy was not through teasing him. "Of course, you are free to marry whomever you please. In my opinion, there have already been too many Brayden-Farthingale matches. I think you ought to seek new blood. Has any young woman caught your eye?"

Lorcan glanced up in surprise as his brother hesitated an imperceptible moment before grinding out a vociferous "No!"

Well, that was interesting.

Shayne joined them on the front steps, Willow and Charlotte following soon after. "Donal, don't forget," he said, handing over a parchment that was rolled and tied with a red bow. "I need you to drop this missive off with the Earl of Monkton before you ride on to London. It shouldn't take long. Let him add his thoughts to the missive and then deliver it to the Duke of Wooton."

"What am I? Suddenly everyone's errand boy?" He grumbled but nodded as he climbed onto his saddle and rode off before anyone added more chores for him.

Lorcan watched his brother until he disappeared around a bend of sheltering trees. "He's ready for love. I saw it in his eyes."

Cammy regarded him hopefully. "Really? How could you tell? He was scowling at us the entire time. Does he have a young lady in mind?"

He nodded. "I think so."

"Who?"

"That I do not know. But I expect we will soon find out, won't we?" He kissed her brow. "Ready for our journey?"

She put her arm in his and smiled. "Eager for it."

This is what he loved about Cammy, the sparkle that shone in her eyes whenever she looked at him. How could he ever know happiness without her? He gave silent thanks she had found the strength to move on after her ordeal.

Of course, he would take note of how she fared once they settled in London. If she could not manage, there was no question he would agree to another solution. Perhaps settling her in Taunton near her sister. He was willing to compromise on many things but losing her was not one of them.

He shook off his concerns.

Cammy had already taken this first important step toward her recovery. He had noticed a lightness in her that had not been there before and was heartened by it. They would deal with each day as it came.

First and foremost, it was time to head off to Barnstaple and obtain her father's consent to marry.

"Lor," Shayne said, wrapping him in a brotherly bear hug. "I wish you and Cammy all the good fortune in the world."

Lorcan gave him a playful punch on the shoulder when he finally drew away. "I appreciate the loan of your carriage. Not that I minded having Cammy ride on my lap." He tossed her a wink. "But I don't think her parents will appreciate our appearing at their front door looking quite so cozy."

Cammy blushed.

Since she had already said her farewells to her sister and aunt, he lifted her into the carriage and took the seat beside her in order to stretch his legs on the opposite bench. The hour was early yet, but it would take them two long days of travel to get to Barnstaple. Two excruciatingly long days. He would go mad keeping his hands off Cammy, but he was determined to do it.

Two more days.

Had they arranged for coaching horses, they could have traveled straight through. But these belonged to Shayne, and he was not going to leave them behind at any coaching inn while they rode on with a fresh team. They would lose time having to stop every few hours to water, feed, and rest them, but it could not be helped.

They were not long on the road to Barnstaple before he realized he was not built for enclosed spaces. Even though the benches were well padded and the carriage well sprung, the roads were not in the best of shape, and the jouncing and jostling were most uncomfortable.

As the hours rolled on and the day grew warmer, he began to fidget. Cammy had been gazing out the window to admire the scenery, the green hills and flower-dotted meadows, but now turned to him. "I'm sorry, Lor. You must feel trapped. And it is hot in here, even with the windows down. I think there is more dust blowing in than air. Perhaps we ought to have brought Berengaria along for you. You could have been riding her instead of closed up in here with me."

"There isn't anywhere else I'd rather be." He took her hand. "I'm all right, love."

As night fell, the carriage pulled into the courtyard of an elegant coaching inn. Since it was fairly late, most of the other travelers had eaten and were already settled in their quarters. This suited Lorcan, for the fewer people who saw him and Cammy, the better.

She tucked her arm in his, and he could feel her tension mounting as they approached the innkeeper to register for the evening. He was almost sorry Charlotte had refused to accompany them. He could feel Cammy's discomfort as their lies continued. Perhaps he should have insisted her aunt serve as chaperone.

Charlotte had been quite vocal about her feelings on the matter. "I have no intention of returning to Barnstaple only to turn around and head back to Taunton, then on to London where we should have been weeks ago. You do not need me. The damage has already been done."

Yes, Cammy's aunt was a practical woman.

She was also a terrible traveler, and this was no time for unexpected delays.

Besides, he liked being alone with Cammy. It did not matter that he had no intention of acting on his low-brain lust until they had exchanged marriage vows. Just having her with him was all he needed.

But now, he was faced with another problem.

Stupidly, he'd neglected to discuss the matter of sharing accommodations with Cammy. He had assumed she knew they would. Still, he could see she was quietly fretting, and he felt awful about it.

But taking two rooms was out of the question.

Not that he feared she might run away, for they'd gotten past that days ago. But a young woman traveling alone with a man, namely him, even if taking separate quarters, was still more scandalous than pretending to be husband and wife.

Cammy cast him a slight nod to convey she understood.

He covered her hand with his as she held onto his arm and gave it an encouraging squeeze. "My wife and I were hoping you had a room available."

"Yes, of course." The innkeeper eyed Cammy curiously. "Miss Farthingale, isn't it? That is, you are one of the Farthingale sisters. I recognized you from your earlier travels. Your parents were guests here not a week ago. They mentioned their two eldest daughters had married but said nothing about their youngest. Felicitations, I had no idea all three of you were wed."

Cammy turned scarlet.

"Yes," Lorcan quickly said, leaning forward to sign the register and block the innkeeper's view of Cammy's lit-up face. "We had planned on waiting, but what can I say? One gets caught up in all the wedding madness, doesn't one? We saw no point in delaying for ourselves. This is why we are on our way to Barnstaple. Her parents are not aware. Since they missed our ceremony, we thought it would be nice to have a quiet blessing done at their parish church that they could attend."

"Sir Lorcan," the innkeeper said in awe, reading his signature.

"Yes. Mr. Wren, is it?" He glanced at the sign upon the wall which had the name of the inn—The Bird in Hand—and his name, Mr. Wren, etched on it. Was it a pun on birds?

The man chortled jovially. "Robin Wren, that's me. My son is Hawk, and my daughter is Sparrow. My wife," he said, glancing around and lowering his voice, "is Margaret, but I call her Magpie because she is always squawking at me." He then made the most unflatteringly cacophonous cawing sounds and flapped his arms.

Cammy covered her mouth to keep from laughing.

"Oh, Lor," she said the moment they were safely alone in their quarters, a modest but comfortable room with a bed hardly big enough to accommodate the two of them unless they pressed close. "My sisters and I stopped here with Aunt Charlotte a day or two before we reached Taunton. No wonder the innkeeper knows my family so well. This was a stopping point for all of us. But I was in such a fearful panic back then, I paid no mind to where we were. And is his name not too funny? We are named after flowers, but I think it is not so bad as being named after birds."

She continued to chatter as he took off his boots and shirt and while he washed up. "Lor, that was a clever thing you said about our having a private ceremony at the church for the sake of my parents. I would not have thought of it. I'm glad you did. Still, I cannot wait to be through with these lies."

"I know, love."

She sank onto the bed with a sigh of resignation. "I will be happy when we are truly married."

"Me, too." He sat on the bed beside her and patted the mattress. "It's small, isn't it?"

She nodded. "But we can fit if we squeeze together."

He cast her a wry smile. "Oh, no. You are far too tempting, and I will never be able to keep my hands off you. I'll set up a pallet on the floor for myself."

"You don't have to," she said shyly.

He ran his finger along the line of her jaw. "Yes, I do. Hopefully not for long, only another night or two at most."

She put up little protest and rose to wash and ready herself for bed. He helped her undress, his body racked with unfulfilled desire as he struggled to touch no more than the lacings as he undid them. But it was a losing cause, his hands strayed where they should not.

Cammy did not seem to mind, smiling at him when she ought to have been admonishing him. "See, you cannot trust me," he said with a groan, forcing his hands off her.

Her eyes sparkled with merriment.

She grew prettier with every passing hour, not only in her physical appearance, which was spectacular, but in heart and spirit, as well. He could not recall ever craving a woman's company as he craved hers.

It was odd how everything felt right when he was with her.

He was a solitary man, liking to be left to his own thoughts. But he had never minded listening to Cammy chatter.

She had the loveliest voice.

He found it soothing.

He found her enchanting.

He also liked that her eyes were no longer clouded with fear, and hoped this newly acquired fortitude would not slip away once they reached London. Life without her would be dismal, but he would never insist on her staying if she were miserable.

He kissed her as she climbed into bed and kissed her again because he loved the touch and taste of her. "Sweet dreams, love."

She cast him a well pleased, starry-eyed look. "You too, Lor."

He stretched out on his pallet, his body in pain and unable to relieve it while she was a mere arm's length away.

When he awoke in the morning, he felt a soft lump beside him. He grinned, for Cammy was curled beside him, spooned with her front to his back and her arm wrapped around his chest.

He was a light sleeper and should have been reaching for his knife the moment he sensed a presence creeping closer. But even in sleep, he must have recognized her and allowed her to draw near. This deep recognition amazed him. He thought it would be something that developed over years, not within a matter of days.

She began to stir as he lifted her in his arms to carry her back to bed. "Lor?" she said with a sleepy purr that shot fire through him.

"It's early yet, love. Sun's not even up yet. I didn't want to leave you on the floor."

"It's all right. I'm awake." But she lazed in bed while he left her side to wash and dress. However, she did not linger long, and within the hour, they were both ready to face the new day.

He led her downstairs to the inn's common room for a bite to eat before they set off for Barnstaple.

They thanked the jovial innkeeper and bid him farewell, then hurried out laughing as his wife swept past them, cawing like a magpie over something poor Mr. Wren had forgotten to do. "Oh, my heavens. Will I ever sound like that to you, Lor?"

"No, love. Not a chance."

By early evening, their carriage drew up in front of Cammy's home. Shayne and Donal had stopped here not long ago when Shayne had asked for Willow's hand in marriage. Now, it was his turn. He studied the big, rambling house that appeared just as his brothers had described.

Situated on a pleasant overlook on the outskirts of town, the big house looked well-lived in, but had an aura of genteel refinement. He expected it held a host of happy memories for Cammy…save for that brutal incident, of course.

He glanced at her, concerned this is what she might have been thinking as well. But she was all smiles and seemed eager to greet her parents.

Her father opened the front door, frowning as he watched them climb down from the carriage. "Cammy? What are you doing back home? I thought we discussed this, child. You—"

"I will be going to London, Papa. But not for the marriage mart." She looked up at Lorcan and smiled as she took his hand.

Her father eyed him warily. "Am I to understand that you and this Mr. Brayden…?"

"He is Sir Lorcan. He was knighted by the king." Cammy tipped her head up proudly. "Once we marry, I shall be Lady Camellia."

"A lady, is it?" Her father crossed his arms over his chest. "I did not raise my daughters to be full of themselves. Is his status the only reason you wish to marry this man?"

Her mother now joined them, popping her head out of the door. "Don't be ridiculous, my dear. Did you not see the way they looked at each other when we were in Taunton for Willow's wedding? Honestly, men notice nothing."

She nudged her husband out of the way. "Do not stand there scowling at your daughter. Can you not see they are in love? Titles," she muttered with a dismissive shake of her head. "She does not care about his title."

But her father was not quite ready to be pushed out of the way. He looked toward the carriage, staring at it in expectation. "Where is Charlotte? Is she not with you?"

Lorcan felt Cammy's hand tense in his own. "No, she chose to remain with Willow and Shayne."

Her mother's eyes widened. "You traveled alone? The two of

you without a chaperone?"

"Yes, Mama. Please let us in, and we shall tell you everything. There was no need for a chaperone. You see, it is much like shutting the stable door after all the horses have fled."

Lorcan groaned.

Her father turned apoplectic. "What have you done?"

His imagination was now running wild, and he looked ready to throw a punch. "Mr. Farthingale, it is not what you think. She isn't ruined, not in how you imagine."

"I did not mean to alarm you, Papa. Lorcan has not touched me in *that* way. Dear heaven, he is far too honorable. But things happened, and it was all my fault."

"What things?"

Her face turned scarlet. She really was terrible at hiding her thoughts and feelings. "Papa, let us discuss this inside. But rest assured, it was merely the appearance of ruination. Again, all my fault. That is all I meant by it."

Her father mopped his brow. "The *appearance*? So he never touched you?"

"Papa! Braydens are honorable. Surely you know this, having met his brothers. Please, barring our way will not help anything."

He stepped aside and ushered them into his study, while Cammy's mother hastened to the kitchen to order refreshments brought in for all of them. Her father's face was a frightening shade of purple, and he was still casting Lorcan looks of bloody murder.

Lorcan had not coupled with Cammy, but he'd had his lips and hands all over her, and her father suspected it. No doubt because her father had done the same with Cammy's mother, because this is what men did or hoped to do with the woman they loved. But this was his daughter they were talking about, and therein lay the sin.

He supposed he would behave worse if one of his daughters came to him claiming she was ruined.

For this reason, he remained calm and settled on the sofa

beside Cammy. He kept her hand firmly in his, for he was reluctant to let go of her until matters were resolved. He did not want her fleeing to her old bedchamber in tears.

Not that he thought she would, but one never knew what could happen if things got heated.

Once tea and cakes had been rolled in and the door shut to lend them privacy, Lorcan began to relate what had happened. He told them about their daughter's running off and inadvertently taking the mail coach to Gloucester instead of Barnstaple. However, he left out the reason why she had run off. The telling of the attack that had left a deep scar across her back and in her soul was something Cammy herself needed to tell her parents.

He would step in if she faltered.

But she managed to get through all of it as she related her harrowing experience and told them about the scar.

He was proud of the way she held her resolve.

Her parents were stunned and in tears by the time she finished her story. "Why did you not tell us?" her father asked, his hands shaking as he reached for his cup of tea, although Lorcan suspected the man needed something far stronger to calm his nerves.

"You would not have allowed me back to the cliff nests to draw my birds."

"For your own protection! That man might have killed you! I'll see that wretched lord hanged, even if I must exact the punishment myself."

"There is no need," Lorcan said. "I will take care of it. It is my right as Cammy's husband."

Her father had worked himself into a state. "Which you are not as yet!"

"This is why you must give your consent, Papa," Cammy said, maintaining remarkable poise. "We have been passing ourselves off as husband and wife all across Devonshire. There is no help for it. You must consent. Lorcan and I shall deal with the matter of that foul lord. He will eat you alive if you go after him.

He almost destroyed me, and I will not allow him to do the same to you. Leave it to Lorcan to deal with that wretched man. Give him the right to do it as my husband."

"And what of Viscount Montague?"

Lorcan looked up in surprise. "Who the hell is he?"

Cammy pursed her lips. "He is the Royal Society Fellow I told you about who was researching our local birds."

"Research, my arse," her father grumbled. "Why do you think he was so eager to have you assist him with his birds? He did not give a damn about your drawings. He was working up the courage to court you."

Cammy's eyes widened. "No, it isn't so. He respected my work. It wasn't about me, Lor. He never regarded me in anything other than a fatherly way. He is twenty-five years my senior. As old as my father."

"Gad, how did I raise such a clueless child?" Her father shook his head. "Do you think an old man does not recognize beauty when he sees it? How can you think he was besotted by your drawings? Perhaps it is my fault. After all, I should not have been so dismissive of a title. You could have been a viscountess."

"That is ridiculous." She turned to Lorcan in confusion. "Lor?"

"You are exceptionally beautiful." He believed her father was telling the truth. He also believed Cammy had no inkling the man admired her. But to dismiss her drawings as irrelevant was a slap in the face to her.

She stood up, her hands now curled into fists by her sides and her eyes revealing her heartbreak. "If I already had a suitor, then why would you send me off to London when you knew I had no desire to leave home? Good heavens, I was in tears about it for weeks. Or did you not like Lord Montague?"

"I liked him very much. I thought he was an excellent prospect for you."

"Then why did you send me off? Wasn't Lord Montague's desire to court me reason enough to keep me home? And how can you—my own father—dismiss my drawings as meaningless?"

Her father harrumphed. "I like them, Cammy, dear. But surely you understand…Lord Montague was never going to include them in his books."

She gasped. "Are you serious? Did he tell you this?"

He cast her a pained look. "This was to be a Royal Society publication. They would never allow a woman to receive credit for the illustrations. So he had an artist in London copy the drawings you sent to him."

"What?" She clutched her heart, at the same time emitting a soft cry. "That man's name will appear as illustrator on his books? That man will take credit for all my hard work? He thinks he can copy the passion and love I put into my sketches?"

"I'm so sorry, child. I thought Lord Montague had told you. He'd led me to believe…I thought you knew this is how it would work."

Lorcan put his arms around her as she stood gaping at her father, but he still felt helpless. And angry as hell. That bit of treachery was worse than any ruination she might have endured. It was a stab that pierced her soul.

She had almost lost her life, been left permanently scarred because of Lord Montague's casual neglect to tell her what would really happen with his publication. Her parents had accepted it as well, saying nothing about it to Cammy, never considering any of them ought to have taken a stand in support of her work.

Her father reached out for her, but she burrowed closer to Lorcan.

So, he turned in despair to his wife, who appeared equally ashamed. "We are so sorry, Cammy. We went along with it, never bothering to consider how important it was to you, thinking all along you were aware. We did not see the harm since he was paying us for those drawings. We've set the payments aside in an account for you. It is yours when you come of age. We were never going to touch your earnings. My dear, tell her the rest of it."

Her father nodded. "We insisted on your going to London because the viscount asked it of us. He admitted his admiration for you and asked for permission to court you. But he assured us that if you did not care for him, he would be a gentleman about it and introduce you to other bachelors of suitable wealth and distinction."

Cammy sank back in her seat. "I am going to be ill."

"He is in London now, eagerly awaiting your arrival," her father added lamely.

She shook her head and laughed. "Why did he not say a word to me when he was here in springtime? Or write to me first and ask *me* if I wished to marry him?"

She turned to Lorcan, pain brimming in her eyes. "I would have refused him, of course. It was never a possibility. And not to care about my drawings? To pass them off to a stranger to copy them? I almost died because I wanted to get those sketches done and sent off to him. He never even cared about them."

Lorcan took her back in his arms. "Cammy, I'm so sorry. The man is obviously an unmitigated fool."

"No, I am the fool." No one said anything as she burst into tears.

This was not the way Lorcan had envisioned the direction of this discussion. He now worried that the progress Cammy had made in getting over the vicious attack was about to come undone with this second blow.

He ran his thumb across her cheeks to wipe away her tears. "Show me your drawings, love."

"You don't have to coddle me, Lor. I know they are good. And even if everyone hated them, I would still draw for myself because it is something I must do. This need is as much a part of me as my blood and my bones. It feeds my soul, and I do not care what anyone else thinks. I can no more stop drawing than I can stop breathing or eating."

She groaned and continued. "I am so angry with myself for being so gullible. Why did I not think of this? The Royal Society has never accepted women in their hallowed halls, so why should they accept them in their books? And Lord Montague is one of them, isn't he?"

"Cammy, dear. He did wish to marry you," her father said.

She shook her head emphatically. "No, Papa. The only reason he wanted me in London was to show me off to his friends because I am a pretty trinket to him. I expect he would have proposed once he was certain I fit in with his elite crowd. But if I did not, he would have dropped me like a stone."

"You are being harsh, Cammy," her mother said gently. "Lord Montague does care for you."

"No, Mama. He cares for the idea of a beautiful woman on his arm, one his friends can look upon with envy. Nothing more. If he truly cared for me, he would have fought with the Royal Society to have my drawings included in his work even if they were awful, which they are not." Her eyes shimmered as she looked up at Lorcan. "You would have fought for me."

He caressed her cheek. "Always, love."

She turned to her parents. "Do not waste another moment, Papa. Go with Lor to the parish church. You need to give your consent to our marriage. It is not negotiable. We will head to Scotland to marry if you refuse. But I would rather our journey end here and not require a mad dash to Gretna Green."

Her mother exchanged a glance with her father. "Yes. There is no recourse, my dear. They must marry as soon as possible."

He nodded. "I know. At least Sir Lorcan is willing to do the honorable thing."

Lorcan's gut churned. "No, this is not good enough. Mr. Farthingale, let me be clear on my feelings for your daughter. I am not marrying her for the sake of protecting her good name. I am not marrying her because it is the honorable thing to do. I am marrying her because I love her more than anything on this earth. She is not merely *in* my heart. She *is* my heart."

Cammy cast him a sparkled smile. "Thank you, Lor. I feel the same way about you. We are two halves of the same heart. No one shall ever separate us."

Her father groaned. "Charlotte and her Samuel all over again. What is it about young love? Very well, we shall see to it first thing in the morning."

"And be married immediately afterward," Cammy insisted.

Her mother smiled. "Three daughters married in under a month. That is quite something."

"Mama, what is more important is that we have all made love matches."

"I know, my dear. Come here, Lady Camellia. Give your foolish parents a hug and forgive us for being so stupid. You girls have done far better for yourselves than anything your incompetently meddling parents could have accomplished."

Cammy threw herself into her parents' arms.

Her father melted. "Oh, my sweet child."

Lord, were they all going to cry again?

Lorcan expected he would turn into a blubbering fool where his daughters were concerned. Only, he would be fiercer than a Hun with their prospective suitors. He had never been a softhearted man and would likely be a fire-breathing dragon by the time his daughters came of age.

He hoped they would not turn out as breathtakingly beautiful as Cammy, or he would be beating suitors off from a very early age. Better that their girls look like him and have thick, black bristles on their chin that needed shaving every day. Perhaps broad shoulders, too. And fists the size of boulders.

Bollocks.

It would just be easier if they had boys.

Cammy poked him in the ribs to regain his attention. "Lor, you have the fiercest expression on your face. What are you thinking?"

He caressed her cheek. "Just about raising a family with you."

She cast him a heavenly smile. "Won't it be lovely?"

"Yes, love." He chuckled lightly. "Exactly what I was thinking, how lovely it would be."

She shook her head and gave a mirthful laugh. "I am getting to know you, Lorcan Brayden. You were worrying about our daughters and contemplating ways to dispose of their suitors. Am I right?"

He arched an eyebrow. "Possibly."

CHAPTER THIRTEEN

BY AFTERNOON THE following day, Cammy stood beside Lorcan in the small parish church to which her family had belonged ever since she was born. Measured in distance, her journey had taken her to Taunton and back.

Measured in happiness, her journey had been boundless.

She had left home a frightened little girl, scarred in heart and soul, and entirely lacking in confidence. She had returned a woman, her fears conquered and treasuring this man beside her, for he understood her heart as no one else ever could.

She struggled not to turn into a watering pot, but she was overwhelmed by the intensity of her feelings for Lorcan. How could she not cry for joy? Life with him would be blissful and filled with promise. "I take thee, Lorcan Brayden, as my husband to love and honor…"

"And obey," the minister whispered.

"No," Lorcan muttered, "she thinks for herself."

She choked on her laughter as the minister's face paled.

Lorcan took her hand. "I take thee, Camellia Farthingale, treasure of my heart, as my wife, to love and honor from this day on…"

Then they were married.

They should not have kissed each other as deeply as they did, especially in front of the poor minister and—good heavens—her parents. But relief flooded through them with the force of a tidal wave, and they were each desperate to cling to the other.

As they stepped outside, the sun chose that moment to break through the clouds and shine down on them. "Oh, my dear." Her mother gave her a hug. "I hope you shall be very happy."

"I know I will be." Cammy looked up at Lorcan.

Even when finely dressed, he had a brutish look about him. Broad mouth, piercing silver eyes, nose broken a time or two. Dark hair worn a little too long. Big and muscled. He was a man, not a gentleman.

She cupped a hand to his cheek. "I love you, Lor."

His gaze softened, and he smiled at her.

She realized he was not going to say anything more to her while her parents, the minister, and several parishioners were looking on. He had called her the treasure of his heart when exchanging vows, slipped that in so naturally, one would think it was part of the traditional exchange of vows. This was all he would say to her for now. He was a private person and not one to share his thoughts with strangers.

But later that night, when the two of them were alone in the room he had reserved at one of the finer Barnstaple inns for their wedding night, he took her in his arms and kissed her tenderly. "I am going to show you how much I love you in every possible way."

"I look forward to it, but there is something I must do first." She smiled at his look of confusion. "I have yet to claim my prize for beating you at cards."

He laughed. "You could have claimed it long ago. But I'm glad you saved it for tonight. There is no way either of us will keep our clothes on tonight."

She blushed. "Lor!"

"Can't help it, love. I've held off for so long, and now my body is on fire for you. It's been that way ever since I first saw you."

"I thought I was always the high-brain girl for you."

"You were. You are and will always be. I never want you to

doubt it." He turned her around and began to unlace her gown. "But blessed saints, you set my body off like fireworks whenever I look at you."

Then he was kissing her neck.

Suckling the sensitive pulse at the base of it.

Running his hands lovingly along her body.

Skimming his lips across her back at the spot of the scar, his touch exquisite and tender.

They were going to investigate that lord's identity in the morning. But tonight was just for them, and she did not want to think of anything or anyone but Lorcan.

He unpinned her hair and ran his fingers through her curls before starting to remove her garments. She closed her eyes and felt the gentle slide of his fingers along her skin, the caress of his knuckles as he stripped her down to her chemise.

He stepped back a moment and began to remove his clothes, his silver eyes never leaving her face as he undressed with a casual grace, peeling off each layer and leaving her heart in palpitations.

He cast her a wicked grin after removing all but his breeches. "Well, Cammy? Ready to claim your winnings?"

She swallowed hard and blushed furiously. "Yes, Lor. Take it off."

He did, and then removed the chemise off her body so that they stood unclothed before each other in the softest candlelight.

Had she ever doubted he would look like a bronzed god?

She ran her hands up and down his body, unable to resist.

She put her lips to his chest to taste him.

"Bollocks," he said softly. "I'm not going to last if you touch me." He wrapped her in his arms and carried her to bed, his gaze fiery and his touch shooting tingles through her as he prepared her for what was to come.

But she was unprepared for the powerful rush of sensations that swept over her as he explored her body with a prowess borne of experience. "Lor, dear heaven," she whispered as his hands and lips worked her body with relentless precision.

His mouth closed over her breast, and he suckled her, did things with his lips and tongue that shot fire through her body. She was in raptures. She could not think. She could not breathe. She could only crave. Only yearn and hunger for him. "You taste so sweet, love," he said in a husky murmur.

He moved lower, performed his hot magic at the intimate spot between her thighs. He roused the most sinful sensations, left her singed and scorched. Left her burning for him.

She cried out softly as the pressure inside her body built to a molten intensity. She was on the precipice of something wonderful. "Lor!"

"I know, love. You're ready for me." He shifted over her, and she felt him slowly push inside her slickness, gently at first, for he was never going to hurt her. She took him in eagerly, for their bodies, as well as their hearts, simply knew they were meant to be together.

He thrust deep inside her, making them one.

He thrust again, penetrating deep into her soul.

She wrapped her arms around him and took him, all of him, desperately held onto him as she shattered and dissolved into starlight.

"Dear heaven," she whispered and moaned his name. "Lor."

This is how she felt, sparkling and soaring.

The moon's silver rays filtered into their room and fell across his handsome face. He was smiling at her. "I love you, Cammy."

He called her a diamond, his jewel.

The treasure of his heart.

She watched in wonderment as his gaze turned smoldering, and he soon followed with his own powerful cries of ecstasy as he reached his release.

When he was done, he collapsed atop her, as satiated as a satyr. After a moment, he propped on his elbows to absorb the bulk of his weight and not crush her. "That was nice," he said, his voice hoarse and gritty.

She ran her hands along his body. His skin was hot and damp

to the touch. "How do you feel, love?" he asked, although he had to know the answer, for her face always gave her away.

"Amazing. Wonderful. Was it truly nice for you, Lor?"

"Yes, the best."

"I'm glad. I wasn't sure what to do, so I just closed my eyes and felt you."

"Blessed saints," he said with a rumbling chuckle. "I surely felt you, too."

He rolled onto his back and brought her atop him, his smile arrogant and his touch so wonderfully tender. "I love you, Cammy."

"It feels good, doesn't it?"

He arched an eyebrow. "The sex?"

She laughed. "That was good, too. But I was talking about not having to lie about our situation now that we are truly husband and wife."

"Husband and wife," he said in a whisper, running his hand through her hair. He buried his fingers in her tumble of dark gold curls. "I never gave serious thought to marriage. Wasn't sure I ever would marry. Then you came along, and I knew you had to be mine. And I wanted to be yours." He groaned softly. "I have never wooed a woman, never had the need before I met you."

"I'm sure you had only to crook your finger, and dozens would come running."

"It was easy when I did not care. But with you, my heart was involved from that first moment. I am not glib. I do not spout poetry. I grunt, just as you accused." He stroked her hair. "I saw you for the beauty you were but did not know how to show you the man inside me and how much I cared about you."

"You did. Words aren't necessary for that. Your actions were enough. You would have died to protect me. I knew it in my heart. Not to mention, I thought you were utterly gorgeous." She caressed his cheek. "You still are. More so as I get to know you. And I know you would never have cheated me out of my art."

He winced. "I'm sorry for what Lord Montague did to you.

He probably thinks he was being generous by paying you. But he missed the point entirely."

She shook her head. "I will get over the disappointment. I have plenty of drawings and will make something better out of them. Perhaps I needed to learn this lesson."

"Don't say that, Cammy. There is no excuse for what he did. He bought your silence. He did not fight on your behalf. He hoped to marry you, and yet he did not know you at all."

"But you do, don't you, Lor? Even though we've only known each other a few weeks. Lord Montague knew me for years and never saw beyond my face."

"It is a beautiful face. Your body's not bad either."

"So is yours, and I'm sorry I mentioned my drawings. Tonight is for us. About us."

"My thoughts exactly." He rolled her back under him. "I think I've neglected you shamefully."

She laughed. "Lor! It's only been minutes. Are you...can you...is this supposed to..."

"Yes, yes, and yes." But he turned serious. "Unless you don't wish to—"

She stopped him with a kiss. "Merciful heaven, I do wish. Every part of me cries out for you."

She saw the silvery firelight in his eyes.

Then she closed her eyes and allowed sensation to claim her, the hot touch of his body, the salty taste of his skin, the warmth of his breath, and the deep timbre of his voice as he said he loved her.

She opened her eyes and admired the sight of his coiled, straining muscles as he entered her again. But she allowed her eyes to flutter closed a moment later as molten heat built up inside her, and she was once more lost in bursts of starlight.

He followed soon after with his own release.

She awoke the following morning to find herself curled around his arm like a vine clinging to a sturdy oak. This was Lorcan. Big. Hard. Powerful.

She huddled closer.

He turned toward her and kissed her on the brow. "Good morning, love."

She purred sleepily. "Good morning, husband. Have we slept away the entire morning?"

"No. It is only a little past eight."

"Early still."

He got up and crossed to the window, drawing the drapes aside as he peered out.

Cammy watched him move with the silent grace of a predator, his body big and sleek. But he was also a protector, and it felt so good to know he would always be there for her. Not to fight her battles for her, but to support her as she learned to stand up for herself and fight them on her own.

Sunlight spilled into their bedchamber as he held the drapes aside. She sat up and drew the sheet up to cover her bosom. "Looks like it will be a beautiful day."

"No, love." He grinned and dropped the drapes back into place, darkening the room again, although some of the fabric had remained drawn aside and allowed a little of the sun to filter in. "I'm sure we'll have a blinding rainstorm and won't be able to leave our bed for days yet."

She laughed and held out her arms to him. "Come back to bed then. Let us not waste another moment in sheltering together."

He claimed her again as the morning's soft light shone outside their window.

When they were done, she drifted off to sleep for a little while longer. But she was too excited to sleep, and they had things to do while in Barnstaple. They were to have supper with her parents, and she wanted to get the dirty work out of the way long before then. They needed to discover the identity of the beastly lord who had attacked her. It was an important step for her to take, one that she was ready to face, albeit with trepidation.

She was not warrior strong yet. But Lorcan was steadfast at her side and ready to support her as she conquered her fears.

"Love, you're trembling." He came up behind her and circled his arms around her body.

She nodded.

"I can investigate on my own," he said, his voice deep and gentle. "You could have tea with your mother instead. I won't be disappointed in you, Cammy. It is only a day after our wedding. These should be happy memories. I don't want them to be marred for you."

"I will let you know if it becomes too much for me. I don't want to hide behind my fear anymore. I want to know who did this to me. I am ready to find out."

He looked pained but agreed.

She finished putting herself together, then grabbed her gloves and reticule as Lorcan escorted her out of their room. He looked simply magnificent, his eyes a deep silver against the dark superfine of his jacket.

She had on a simple gown of dark blue muslin taken from the armoire in her old bedchamber. It was one among a dozen "Barnstaple gowns' she had to leave behind when first embarking on her journey to London. They were not deemed fine enough for town wear.

But this gown was among her favorites and suited the seriousness of the occasion. One did not investigate criminals while dressed in cream silks or tea rose satins. But she did not wish to look morose either, so she brightened it by adding a white lace fichu at the collar.

Odd how things worked out.

She and her sisters had packed several trunks full of elegant clothes designed for their London debuts. Those had all burned in Taunton, at the Ashcott Inn's carriage house fire. Now she was back home and had all her comfortable clothes. These were more to her liking. No doubt more to Lor's taste as well, for he did not care for preening society misses and was not at all impressed by their finery.

He kissed her on the cheek. "You look beautiful. Ready?"

There were several inns in town that catered to the upper classes, including the one in which they had spent their wedding night. They checked with their innkeeper first and quickly determined the lord in question had not stayed here.

Cammy was relieved. She did not like the idea of being under the same roof as that evil man.

They moved on to the next inn but had no luck. The third yielded what they sought. "I remember those lords," the innkeeper at the Rose and Lion Inn said with a moue of distaste. "Arrogant lot, but mostly well behaved. Except for one of them. He was a dangerous knave. Gave my maids a hard time."

"He may be the one we are looking for," Cammy said, describing him as best as she could remember. Speaking of him was not easy for her because she had worked so hard to forget him and that awful day.

"I know who you mean. Lord Milkwood. Sour Milk is what I called him. Nasty piece of work. In line to inherit a dukedom, or so he claimed. Duke, my arse. Forgive my vulgar mouth, m'lady. He skipped out without paying his bill. The others paid up, though. Gave my maids no trouble. A bit demanding, but they behaved themselves like gentlemen. Ain't got nothing against them."

He gave their names to Lorcan when he asked.

"But Sour Milk? He was bad." The innkeeper suddenly caught himself. "You friends of his?"

"Not at all," Lorcan said, withdrawing his badge. "Tell me all you know about him."

The man's eyes widened. "Are you chasing him down, Sir Lorcan?"

"Yes."

"I am not surprised. The man may have a fancy title, but he's a common criminal. Skipped out, as I told you. And hit one of my maids, he did. Would have beat her bad if his friends had not heard her screams and pulled him away. And for what? She refused to give him a kiss. We have good girls working here. He could have gone down to the docks if he wanted that sort of thing. Begging your pardon again, Lady Camellia. Good thing he did not catch sight of you and your sisters. Nasty piece of work he was."

"Yes, good thing." Cammy tried not to sound ill.

Lorcan took hold of her hand.

"That's about all I can tell you," the innkeeper said with a shake of his head. "I hope he gets his comeuppance."

Lorcan nodded. "He will."

There was ice in his voice and a steel glint in his eyes. Cammy suppressed a shudder because she was not quite sure what Lorcan intended to do once he'd caught up to Lord Milkwood. He was a trained agent for the Crown. He had denied he was an assassin for the king, and she believed him. But this was a personal matter. Was he capable of slitting a man's throat to avenge her?

Especially a rotter such as Lord Milkwood?

Even she wanted to kill that man.

"Lor…"

He groaned as he led her out of the inn. "Cammy, do not look at me like that. I do not kill for the Crown. All right?"

"Yes, we are all right. I believe you. I know that fierce look is part of your effectiveness when working an assignment. I'm sure people start spilling their guts when they think you will kill them unless they do. That lethal glare works quite well. But my concern is that this Milkwood affair is very personal to you. You are not a cold-blooded killer, and I do not want you to become one because of me. What will you do when you find him?"

"I don't know. Depends on how much dirt I can dig up before I confront him. Being heir to a duke puts him in a powerful position."

She held him back as they walked along the street toward their inn. "Then don't confront him. Not for my sake. I don't want him giving you trouble."

"I am not afraid of him."

"I know." She frowned and shook her head. "You are fearless. But I am not. Let me be afraid for you. He seems the sort who would not hesitate to shoot you. So, turn over whatever you learn to the Duke of Wooton. Let him take care of that wicked man. I don't want him hurting you. Knowing I was the cause… I would never forgive myself if you were harmed."

He arched an eyebrow to make light of it. "Then I will make it a point not to be harmed. I'll be careful, I promise. I am always careful." He pointed to a tea shop. "Our work is done for the day. Care to stop in? Investigations can be hungry work."

"All right." She looked up at him and smiled.

"What?"

"I'm happy, Lor. That's all. I'm so glad I am married to you."

His expression turned tender. "Same here, love."

They entered the charming establishment and were immediately congratulated by the elderly proprietress, who knew Cammy's family quite well. They spent another few moments accepting well-wishes from several patrons who also knew Cammy and had heard of her marriage.

He was not surprised by the warmth of their greeting.

Her family was well known and obviously well-liked. Cammy had grown up with many of these people. "Thank you," he heard Cammy repeat over and over again.

Finally, they were led to a quiet corner where they shared tea and an appealing array of lemon tarts, ginger cakes, and apple crumbles. Lorcan was silent as they sipped their tea and enjoyed this selection fresh from the oven and deliciously warm.

"Lor, is something the matter? Why are you frowning? I thought our day was most productive."

"I was thinking of our return to London," he said, toying with his cup. "I am so rarely there, usually off on lengthy assignments. I have a small apartment for myself in Bloomsbury. It isn't suitable for us as a married couple. But it served my purposes until now since all I needed was a place to lay my head whenever

I was in town."

"I've heard Bloomsbury is where students, scholars, and artists reside. Sounds perfect for us."

He pursed his lips. "It was good enough for me as a bachelor, but I don't think it will be right for us. I am often away on Crown investigations, although I will now ask for those which will keep me in London as much as possible. But I do not get to pick and choose my assignments. His Grace," he said, referring to the Duke of Wooton, "will place me wherever he needs me most."

"I understand. I can always stay with my Aunt Sophie and Uncle John, or any of my cousins, when you are away."

He cast her a wry smile and covered her hand with his. "Cammy, love. That is not my point. What I am trying to say is that I will buy us a townhouse close to your family, much as my cousin, Romulus, did for your cousin, Violet."

She laughed. "Romulus bought that house before he'd ever met Violet. Indeed, I believe he'd owned it less than an hour before they inadvertently found themselves compromised, and he had to marry her. But it all turned out well."

"I was thinking of doing something similar for you. Their house is on Chipping Way, next door to your Aunt Sophie and Uncle John. I don't know that there are any homes available on that small street, but perhaps close by. Or we can find something close to any of our family members."

She cleared her throat. "Lor, they live in the finest neighborhoods."

He nodded. "Yes, and I want the same for you. I want you to be protected and surrounded by those who love you. A home with a nice garden where you might set up your easel. Some place big enough for a studio inside the home so you can paint undisturbed during the winter months. Big enough for your parents and sisters to stay when they come to visit."

"But I shall settle just as comfortably in Bloomsbury. I don't need to live in the most exclusive London neighborhoods. Would Mayfair not be..." She cleared her throat, uncertain how to broach the subject of their finances.

His frown turned into a smirk. "You think I am poor?"

Her eyes rounded in surprise. "No…it's just that…I never gave it a thought. But now that you brought it up…no, it is not important to me. We needn't discuss it."

He gave her hand a light squeeze. "Yes, we do need to discuss it. You are my wife and have every right to know what we can and cannot afford. I am not poor. Blessed saints, I think I have married the only woman in England who does not care about my wealth. This is why I found it so easy to fall in love with you. There is not a mercenary bone in your body. It is nice to know you wanted me and not my bank account."

She gasped, suddenly realizing something. "Lor, speaking of which, Papa said he had put aside the funds Lord Montague sent in payment for my sketches. I never thought to ask him how much there is."

He laughed. "As I said, not a mercenary bone. But your father felt compelled to tell me since I was to be your husband. Care to know?"

"No." She put her hands over her ears. "I want you to send it back to him, every shilling. I don't want to know how much is there, or I might be tempted to keep it."

He drew her hands away from her ears. "Cammy, do you not think there is a better use to be put to his funds? He does not deserve to have those payments returned."

"What are you proposing? That I keep it for our children?" She nodded. "That is important. But it churns my stomach to know he provided any of it while depriving me of the recognition my drawings deserved."

She stared at him a long moment, then cast him a wicked smile. "Lor, you wily devil. You want me to use it to promote women artists, don't you? Perhaps set up a show in a gallery. Or…" She inhaled sharply as another idea came to mind. "Something more permanent. Applying those funds to publication of works by women of science or naturalists such as myself. I am only an amateur, of course. But there are others who have made it their life's work to understand plants and animals, who are deprived of a voice to express their knowledge."

He grinned broadly. "Go on."

"What better comeuppance for him than to know his funds provided an outlet for the very women banned from the Royal Society? But Lor, would this be all right with you? Now that we are married, you are the one with the say as to where it is applied. If you need it to—"

"I don't, love. We," he said with emphasis, "do not need it at all. And I do not care what the law says about a husband's ownership of his wife's funds. I will not touch any of it. You earned it and can do with it whatever you like. Our children will have all they need from me. So will you."

She raised her cup in toast and sipped her mint tea with triumphant satisfaction. But after a moment, she began to nibble her lip. "Lor, am I a terrible person?"

He laughed. "Why would you ever think such a thing? You are the kindest person I know."

Heat rose in her cheeks. "No, I don't think I am."

"Tell me, love. What's on your mind?"

"Lord Montague was set in his ways and quite stodgy, but he was not an evil man such as Lord Milkwood was."

"Perhaps not, but allowing someone else to claim your work is not right either."

She nodded. "That's what I thought. It was indeed wrong of him. But...I should not be so happy exacting revenge on poor Lord Montague, should I?"

❤

CHAPTER FOURTEEN

Lorcan was overdue to report to the Duke of Wooton; however, he doubted the duke would do little more than frown at him before congratulating him on his unexpected nuptials and tossing him onto the next sensitive assignment. He and Cammy had remained in Barnstaple for several days after their wedding in order to give her time to pack her belongings and say her farewells to her parents and friends.

They were now clattering up the drive to Shayne's manor house just outside of Taunton, and it gave him pleasure to see how excited Cammy was at the prospect of seeing her sister and aunt again. Once they had settled in, he would leave her to reminisce with them while he returned the carriage to Shayne, picked up Berengaria, and made arrangements for a private coach to take him and Cammy to London.

He expected Charlotte would join them on this last leg of their journey, which suited him just fine. Cammy would have company in the coach while he rode Berengaria alongside them. He had denied it when questioned by Cammy, but she had to know riding in the confinement of a carriage was torture for him.

"Look, Lor!" she said eagerly, her nose pasted to the window as they pulled up to the courtyard of his brother's elegant home. "They're already standing in wait for us."

He followed her gaze. "My brother's grin is too smug. I think I am going to have to punch him to take him down a peg."

Cammy knew he was teasing and gave him a light kick in the shin. "He is happy for us, you wicked man. And I'm sure Willow is responsible for that grin on his face, not us. I doubt he gave us any thought at all."

"Perhaps you are right. You Farthingales are quite distracting." He drew her onto his lap and gave her a lingering kiss before the carriage door was pulled open, and Shayne helped Cammy out.

"I see you survived the journey with my oaf of a brother," he said cheerfully. "Since he had his hands all over you before I opened the door, I can only assume you are now officially wed. Tired of him yet?"

Cammy could not contain her laughter when Lorcan shot back a remark, calling Shayne the emanation from a donkey's arse and wondering how Willow had not bludgeoned him to death yet. Then they embraced each other like two long-lost souls, the insults out of the way and now forgotten as they greeted each other happily. "Is this how all brothers behave?"

"Apparently so," Willow said, eager to hug her.

Charlotte did the same. "How did my brother take to your arrival on his doorstep with this handsome man by your side?"

Cammy shook her head and sighed. "Not well at all, at first. Right, Lor? But all worked out in the end. Mama and Papa now adore him."

Lorcan waited until the women had walked inside and the bags taken upstairs by Shayne's footmen before he told Shayne what else had happened besides their wedding. "Cammy was heartbroken when she learned Lord Montague never intended to publish her sketches along with his monographs. He'd hired someone else to copy her artwork."

"That is unpardonable," Shayne said, incensed as they walked toward the stable since Lorcan wanted to see Berengaria.

"I'll never forget the look of hurt on her face." He shook his head as they approached his filly's stall. "Sliced straight through my heart. She is so sweet and genuine, completely trusted this man. He thought tossing a few coins her way would make everything all right. If he understood Cammy at all, he would have known it was never about the money. We take so much for granted, the privileges we are offered because we are men. When do we ever consider that what is offered to us as a matter of course is so easily denied to others?"

"Why did her parents not warn her this was going to happen?"

Lorcan snatched up a handful of hay and held it out to Berengaria. She'd recognized him and was now bobbing her head and snorting a greeting. He patted her neck as he spoke. "They assumed she knew. Or wanted to believe she knew. Perhaps they did not think of it at all because they did not see Cammy's work as anything important. They do feel terrible about it now but never thought twice about it at the time."

"And what of that other matter?" Shayne ran a hand through his hair. "Did you learn the identity of the man who beat her?"

Lorcan nodded. "Lord Milkwood. Recognize the name?"

"Should I?" He leaned casually against the wooden slats of the wall as Lorcan treated his horse to more hay.

"No, I suppose not. You've been out of the game for a while now. Before I left London to join you, the Duke of Wooton had received reports of a well-heeled gentleman involved in some nasty doings in the less-elegant parts of London."

"And you think it was Milkwood? What of Lord Belfy? Could have been him as well, in which case, we can all breathe easier since he is now dead."

Lorcan nodded. "I thought of Belfy, but he always traveled with his pack of toadies. There would have been mention of others if Belfy were the culprit. Milkwood is cut from the same demented cloth. He had gone to Barnstaple with friends, but they appear to be decent men. Perhaps arrogant, as most lords are. But they held him in check rather than allowed him to indulge his sordid whims. They rode out of Barnstaple on the morning he attacked Cammy. I think they had become disgusted with him and tossed him out of their group."

"With no thought to what he might do next?"

"Right." He gave Berengaria a final pat and strode out of her stall. "But I doubt they imagined he would ever behave in so depraved a fashion, not with a respectable girl. Cammy is afraid I'm going to slit his throat. I've assured her I have no intention of doing that, much as I would like to carve that man to little pieces. I'll give his name to Wooton."

"And let him dispose of Milkwood?"

"Cammy thinks I have ice in my veins, but I am nothing to that man. He is entirely carved of ice. But I suppose it is necessary when the safety of the kingdom rests upon his shoulders."

They said nothing more as they rejoined the ladies.

Two days later, he, Cammy, and Charlotte were on their way to London. He rode Berengaria alongside their coach until they reached the town of Basingstoke. It was not too far from there to London, and he wanted to be seated beside Cammy as their hired conveyance wound its way through crowded Edgware Road and onto Oxford Street before turning onto the quieter Mayfair squares.

He had suggested Cammy spend this first night on Chipping Way with her aunt and uncle since she and Charlotte were expected, anyway, and rooms would have been prepared for them. "And what of you, Lor? Will you stay with me?"

"Yes, if they will allow it."

"Why should they not? We are married now."

He cast her a wry smile. "Indeed, we are. But I also have to report immediately to the Duke of Wooton and will likely be dragged into other matters as soon as I step into his office. He may keep me at the ministry well beyond midnight." He clasped her hand in his. "Especially when I tell him about Milkwood."

"You would tell him without me?" She did not seem pleased by the notion, but he was not eager to put her through the duke's inquiries. Wooton would not be gentle with her; it simply wasn't his way.

"I will bring you to the duke if it proves necessary. But I would much rather have you spend time with your family and let them show you around London these next few days. I'll be with you as much as I can. He won't refuse me when I ask for another month off to settle us in."

"I know we discussed our residing in London." She sighed, and her hand began to tremble as he enveloped it in his. "I thought I was better prepared for this."

"We knew it would take time for you to adjust to life in town. You needn't go anywhere without me. But I'll set up an allowance for you at the fashionable shops. You'll be safe going out surrounded by your cousins. Your Aunt Sophie can make up a list of the best ladies' shops for me to establish credit. Also, I'm sure she knows everyone in town by now and can tell us who wishes to sell their home, where we should be buying our new home, how best to staff it, and all the right merchants to furnish it."

Again, she did not look pleased.

But this was Cammy struggling to compromise and accept her new surroundings. Also, she did not care for material things. She cared for people, namely him. Although he intended to demand time off to be with her, Wooton would certainly exact something from him in return. He only hoped the "something" would not keep him too occupied these next few days. "Or we can do nothing for now and see how well you dip your toe into London life. Take all the time you need. I've told you before, I am willing to give up anything but you."

"I feel the same way, Lor. I'll try my best to make London work for us."

"I know you will, love. And I will be with you as much as I can be. But I am already overdue, and Wooton will not be happy about it. He'll make me squirm a little but ultimately give in to my request for time with you."

They spoke no more of it, Cammy turning her face to the window to peer out. Lorcan hoped it was because she was fascinated with the bustle of the sprawling town as evening approached, but he suspected it was because she was frightened and did not wish him to notice how scared she was.

She now had her hands clasped, a ploy to hide how badly they were shaking. But she also had a look of determination that he found heartening.

He cast Charlotte a glance.

She looked equally concerned.

Within the hour, they arrived on Chipping Way. The street was quiet and charming, cast in the soft hues of fading sunlight, a perfect place for Cammy to relax and ease her way into new surroundings. An attractive, older woman came running out of Number 3, followed soon after by a distinguished-looking gentleman. "Aunt Sophie! Uncle John!" Cammy's spirits picked up immediately.

They had just climbed down from the carriage when a young woman with dark hair and striking violet eyes came running out of Number 1 and hugged Cammy fiercely. "We were so worried something had happened to you. Thankfully, Willow wrote to us and told us all about the excitement in Taunton. Is this your husband? So nice to meet you. I'm Violet, married to your cousin, Romulus."

She gave Lorcan no time to respond before continuing. "Yes, you must be Cammy's husband, for you are big and handsome just like all the Brayden men are. Romulus will be delighted to hear the news. He returns next week while *the Plover* is in repairs. Won't it be wonderful, Cammy? You'll be right next door, and we shall see each other every day. I'll send word to all the cousins. Lily and Laurel are up in Scotland, unfortunately. Heather is, too, but she and Robbie will be back soon. Rose and Julian are at their factory but also to return soon."

Lorcan looked on in amazement, for Violet had yet to take a breath.

"But Daisy, Dillie, Dahlia, Honey, Holly, and Belle are here. Oh, dear. Have I left anyone out? Well, Poppy is with Nathaniel at Sherbourne Manor, but I'll send word to her right away. The Cotswolds is not far from here. How soon do you think before Juniper returns with her husband? Won't it be wonderful to have so many of us together again?"

Cammy was laughing with genuine delight.

The smile she cast him was beaming, and her eyes had regained their beautiful sparkle. "Lor," she said quietly as everyone turned to Charlotte and began to fuss over her, "I think it will be all right. I will be all right."

He placed his arm around her and kissed her brow. "I think so, too. But you have only to say the word."

"You had a fine idea about finding a home for us close by. I don't think Violet will let me be unhappy. Nor will any of my cousins." She studied the impressive townhome that belonged to her aunt and uncle. "I cannot believe my Aunt Sophie does not look ninety and haggard. She and Uncle John agreed to sponsor all of us in our debut seasons. Well, they won't have to do it for Juniper, Willow, or me now. But can you imagine having all five of their daughters and six of their cousins' daughters tossed on the marriage mart one after the other? We would have made it nine. Remind me to leave *The Book of Love* with Aunt Sophie. She will guard it until we are settled into a new home."

He groaned. "That book. Are you really planning on giving it to Donal?"

"Yes, but only if he promises to return it to Aunt Sophie afterward. It needs to stay in the family."

They spoke no more about it when Violet scampered back to their side and dragged them both inside. "You must be thirsty. Parched, no doubt from the dusty ride. Mrs. Mayhew has set out refreshments in the back garden. She is Aunt Sophie's cook. None better. Her niece is my housekeeper. We must ask her if she has any other relatives to recommend for your household. And you must meet my little Hyacinth. She's being tended to by her nanny right now and about to fall asleep, but I will bring her over tomorrow morning when she wakes."

She sighed. "I am talking too much. I do this when I am excited. Romulus just stops my mouth with a kiss when I go on too long. It is very effective. And works quite well to preserve our happy marriage."

They settled in pillowed chairs in the garden under the shade of a sturdy oak. The older members of the family were not out yet, so Violet took a moment to explain the history of the tree. "I'm surprised Uncle John never had it chopped down. His twins, Lily and Dillie, used to sneak out of their bedchamber by climbing down its branches. Climbing back up was no better. They brought all manner of artifacts and creatures into their rooms. Aunt Sophie tolerated most of their antics but drew the line at spiders bigger than the size of one's hand. One of those escaped Lily's container and had the household in an uproar until it was found and safely confined."

She poured lemonade for all of them. "Lorcan…may I call you that? We are family, after all. But I never met you in all the time I've been in London. Whenever Romulus and his brother, James, mentioned you, it was always in hushed tones, as though you were this mysterious phantom spirit to be feared."

"It is my line of work. I've been caught up in some dangerous assignments and had little time to enjoy the family. Most of these investigations took me out of London for long periods of time." He noted Cammy's rising concern. "But no longer. I'll be taking on tamer duties now, staying closer to home."

"Oh, Lor. Are you sure? Will His Grace allow it?"

He nodded. "He will, love."

Violet eeped. "Oh, I'm sorry. You called her 'love,' and I found it quite charming. But do continue. Why do you think the Duke of Wooton will accede to your request when you are probably his most valuable asset?"

"Because I am now married. Commitment changes a man, as he's found out when dealing with his agents over the years. We are no longer single-mindedly determined and daring. We now think of our wives and children and thereby become liabilities to him."

Cammy reached out to take his hand. "But, Lor. You love what you do."

He nodded. "I'll still have plenty of assignments to keep me busy. Just not the ones where my chances of dying are greater than my chances of survival. That's why Shayne retired from service. He grew tired of the dangers involved. Donal is still active, but we'll see what happens now that you are determined to foist that book on him. But it's all right. I think we are all ready for our lives to become calmer. Shayne led the way, but Donal and I were not far behind."

They spoke no more of his work as the elder generation joined them. He was introduced to their Aunt Hortensia, who was one of the most curmudgeonly women he had ever met. She was a little older than Charlotte and far more cantankerous. "Another pair of compromised lovebirds," she muttered with a snort and then cast a frown at Violet, who did not appear at all contrite. "Seems this is a pattern among Brayden men. Romulus had known Violet barely minutes before ruining her. How long did it take you to ruin Cammy?"

John groaned.

Sophie gasped. "Hortensia! Leave them alone."

But Cammy and Violet were laughing. "Aunt Hortensia," Cammy said, holding her side, "it took him ever so long. I began to despair it would ever happen."

"Naughty girl," Hortensia shot back, then surprised Lorcan by smiling with a genuine, doting fondness. "I can see you love him deeply."

Cammy nodded. "I do."

"And you, young man?"

Lorcan winked at Cammy. "I love her to pieces. Ready to make a complete jackass of myself over her."

"Try not to. There are enough jackasses in the family already."

The rest of their conversation passed easily.

Once Lorcan saw that Cammy was settled in and would be well taken care of in his absence, he made his apologies and rose to leave. It had been decided he would return here no matter the hour, so he felt quite at ease when Cammy walked him to the door. "I'll see you later, love. Don't wait up for me. I'll try to get back as soon as I can."

She nodded. "Lor, you were right. I can do this. Are my aunt and uncle not the nicest people? And Violet is a bubble of delight. I cannot wait for you to meet my other cousins."

"Nor can I." He kissed her deeply, then rode off to the ministry. It was early evening, but he knew the Duke of Wooton would still be hard at work. The sun was a fading red ball in the sky as he rode along the Thames toward the ministry building.

He was shown immediately to the duke's private office, a magnificently appointed chamber with windows overlooking the river. "Your Grace," he said with a nod, awaiting permission to sit.

The duke rose instead and came to him. "Good to have you back, Brayden. I heard you came back married. Are you daft, man? You know I cannot spare you. What in heaven's name were you thinking? Never mind, don't answer that. Men in love never think." He motioned for him to take a chair beside his unlit hearth and strode to the ornate cabinet where he kept his impressive array of wines, ports, and brandies.

"What have I missed while I was away?" Lorcan asked, settling into the soft leather chair and accepting the glass of port the duke handed to him.

"Not much. London has been quiet at the moment, save for that madman running around town killing women but not before he brutally beats them. Nasty piece of work. The Lord Mayor is concerned and asked for my help in the matter. We don't usually handle crimes of this sort, but as things are relatively quiet on the blow-up-the-kingdom front, I agreed." He settled into the chair opposite Lorcan's and took a sip of his own glass of port. "I hear your holiday was remarkably busy. I don't mean the marriage part, although how did you ever find time to fall in love while dealing with that scum Belfy and his rabble?"

"Shayne had his hands full with them. Donal and I had to help him out." He grinned at Wooton. "Doesn't count as a holiday since we were working the entire time."

"You could not have been working all the time, or you would not have found yourself acquiring a wife. Obviously, you had time enough to woo her."

"No wooing. She inadvertently compromised us. But make no mistake, it is a love match." Lorcan allowed a few more jests about his falling in love with Cammy, then he turned serious. "I may have information about that madman running loose in London."

The duke, a rather imposing figure of a man with dark hair lightly sprinkled with gray and piercing dark eyes that missed not a thing, not even a speck of dust on a man's cravat, immediately perked his ears. "Tell me, Lor. The man does not contain his misdeeds to women of the lower classes. He has the Upper Crust in his grip of terror as well. What do you know?"

Lorcan related Cammy's incident and the whip mark etched in her back.

He was surprised by the genuine burst of feeling from the duke. "I am truly sorry for what your wife endured. This is what keeps me up at night, keeps me at this unsavory task even though I am sick of it. The cruelty that exists has sucked my soul dry, but I must keep at my job, and will keep at it until I drop dead at my desk. I'll place Milkwood under watch immediately and deal with him swiftly if he proves to be the one we seek."

"Thank you, Your Grace. Put an agent on Cammy, too. If he is the killer, then she is the only one who survived his attack and the only one who can identify him. He needs to be stopped before he ever realizes she is in town."

"I'll put two on to watch over her starting this very night. I am most curious to meet this brave woman who has captured your heart. Bring her around to the King's Arms tomorrow afternoon at four o'clock. They serve an excellent tea. You shall be my guests."

Lorcan understood this wasn't so much an invitation as a demand. One did not refuse a duke, and certainly not this duke who held more sway with the king and Parliament ministers than any other man alive. "It will be our pleasure."

"Good. Now, let's get back to business, the plots against the Crown and the usual assortment of idiots hoping to bring down Parliament. Then there are the foreign spies lurking about to steal military secrets for their country or merely to enrich themselves. French, Russians, Prussians, Austrians, Dutch, Spanish, Portuguese, and so on. I do enjoy those who are out for themselves since there is rarely any violence required to bring them to heel."

"I thought you said London was quiet at the moment." He set down his glass of port. "I need to spend time with Cammy."

"Ah, love rearing its ugly head again," he said in jest, although there was a bit of irritation mixed in. Wooton liked having control over his agents and did not care to share it with anyone, especially not a wife. "You shall have it. But give me your attention this evening. It is relatively quiet, but there is still plenty going on. I want your opinion on several matters I deem of urgency."

"What of Donal? Can he not help?"

The duke nodded. "He has been helpful. The two of you are my best men. But I've already placed him on another assignment that requires all of his concentration. I cannot keep summoning him back to my office. But I will have no such qualms about imposing on you. It is the *quid pro quo*. I give you another month off, but you remain at my beck and call when I need a second opinion."

Lorcan knew he was not going to get a better deal. "Agreed."

The duke seemed genuinely relieved.

He suddenly felt sorry for this man of ice, for that frigid shell of his was obviously beginning to crack under the strain. How much had he given up for king and country? A true love?

Children? Did this man have any enjoyment in life?

As much as Lorcan admired him, he was also determined not to follow in his path. He could not imagine himself without Cammy, holding her in his arms as they drifted off to sleep or waking to her smile and the soft warmth of her body. "Let's sort through these urgent matters, Your Grace. I expect you've heard about my encounter with your clerk, Maplethorpe."

"Yes, the greedy fool."

"So, you set him up to steal a government secret?"

"Of course. He could never have gotten his hands on it unless I allowed it. He led us straight to Crimmins. I knew that arrogant lord was a traitor."

"We all did. It was only a matter of time before he was caught. But what happened? How did they both end up dead?"

"Not by my hand. Crimmins was meeting a foreign agent who panicked when he saw Maplethorpe with you. He thought both of them were working for me and were going to turn him over to me. He killed them before our own agents could stop him. But we have that foreign agent in custody now, and he's spilling his guts, telling us everything he knows. We cannot shut him up," he said with a wry grimace. "I've sent word to Geordie Newton. A good man. He can now close his investigation. I'm sure he wasn't happy to have a double murder in his quiet town."

Lorcan nodded. "Then the matter is now closed?"

The duke nodded.

"Good. Shall we move on to the other problems, Your Grace? Which ones do you feel are most pressing?"

CHAPTER FIFTEEN

LORCAN HAD THOUGHT Cammy would be wary of meeting the Duke of Wooton, so he was surprised when she readily agreed. "I am eager to know him, Lor. He is a man you admire, and I do appreciate how much of a sacrifice he has made in giving you over to me for the entire month. I did not think he would allow me to keep you to myself for more than a day or two."

They were in the bedchamber they shared while at John and Sophie Farthingale's home. The hour was late, well past midnight. Cammy had already donned her nightgown and let down her hair, although it was brushed back in a neat braid he meant to undo as soon as he took off his clothes and got into bed beside her. "Having the month off came with conditions. I am to respond to his summons, no matter the day or the hour. But my role is only to give advice. I will not be required to take on any assignments."

She nodded. "It sounds fair."

"If he keeps to his bargain," he muttered, setting aside his clothes and falling naked into bed. He gathered her into his arms, loving her sweet scent and adored the softness of her body.

She laughed as he undid her prim braid and ran his hands through her hair. "I knew you would do that."

"Then why braid it?"

"Because I was not sure you would return tonight, and it is more comfortable for me to sleep without rolling on my hair and tugging on it each time I turn." She leaned over and kissed him lightly on the lips. "But I am more than happy to endure such hardship since you take such pleasure in having it down. Besides, I think I must sleep like a contented lump whenever I am beside you. I doubt I move at all unless it is to huddle closer to you."

He kissed her back. "If I had an ounce of poetry in me, I would tell you just how good you make me feel whenever you are beside me."

"Just good?"

He grinned. "Very, very good."

She smiled back at him. "Lor, that is all the poetry I need. Sleeping in your arms says it all, I think."

"Just sleeping?"

"No, not just that," she said with a blush. "But that is all we are going to do tonight. I would be mortified if Uncle John and Aunt Sophie heard us."

He expected they had seen and heard far more than the squeaking bed of a newly married couple, but he said no more about it. He was tired, and the Duke of Wooton had given him a lot of information to ponder. They were to meet again in the morning to discuss these affairs concerning the security of England. At four o'clock, he was to bring Cammy to tea at the King's Arms, easily the most elegant hotel in London.

"I'll borrow a gown from Violet," she said in a yawning whisper and soon drifted off to sleep. "I want to look my best when meeting the duke."

Lorcan lay awake an hour longer to consider the problems Wooton had posed him. Cammy's soft body was pressed against him. Although he was not going to touch her tonight, he thought of how perfectly they fit together and how much he loved the way she nestled against him, as though he was her anchor. Her home.

He was so deeply in love with her after knowing her for only a month and being married to her for only a week. No wonder Wooton hated working with married agents. Love, marriage, responsibility to others, those changed a man.

He absently ran his fingers through her hair while she slept. "Sweet dreams, sweetheart."

He kissed her brow and fell asleep himself.

Cammy saw him off the next morning, waking when he did but remaining in bed while she watched him wash and dress. "Shall I meet you at the hotel at four?" she asked, tossing aside the covers and rising as he prepared to leave.

She had a sleepy, rumpled look about her that made him want to fall back into bed with her and sink himself inside her. But he knew it was not possible while duty called. "No, love. I'll come back here to pick you up. Wouldn't want you having to make your way alone."

"In my uncle's carriage? With his driver, Abner, watching out for me every moment?"

He laughed. "Do not be reasonable about this. I need an excuse to leave Wooton's office, or he'll have his claws into me the entire time. Besides, I promised I would spend as much of the day with you as possible. I intend to keep my word."

"I'll busy myself at Violet's for most of the morning. She will love fussing over me. And I will adore fussing over little Hyacinth. I'm sure several of my cousins will just happen to stop by as well. They'll enjoy making me up. I want to look suitably elegant when introduced to your duke."

"Don't let them overdo it." He kissed her. "I like the way you look. I'm sure you will melt his frigid heart with your enchanting smile…and all the other enchanting parts of you."

"Lor!"

"What?" He drew her hair aside and lightly nibbled her neck. "Am I to be blamed for finding you irresistible? Every man in London will feel the same and weep because you are already married to me."

"What nonsense! Go away. Stop making me weak in the knees." She sighed and shook her head. "But hurry back. I'll try to fend off the throng of gentlemen callers lined up at my door." She spoke with obvious sarcasm, for she truly did not appreciate how beautiful she was, nor did she like the idea of gentlemen fawning over her.

He kissed her on the forehead. "Do not be surprised if they do start lining up on Chipping Way. They won't be deterred by something as inconsequential as our marriage."

She rolled her eyes. "I think I am safe enough from those frenzied swains."

Lorcan rode off and spent a busy morning with the duke.

When he returned, Cammy was ready and waiting for him. She told him about her day as they rode in her uncle's carriage to meet the duke at the appointed hour. "I spent most of my time with Violet and little Hyacinth. Dahlia came over as well. She has a talent for decorating and offered to help us set up our household once we find a place for ourselves. Do you mind?"

"Not at all, love." Lorcan escorted her into the hotel on his arm.

He immediately noticed how she captured the attention of all the patrons, men and women alike, as they made their way into the elegant tearoom. "This gown is borrowed from Violet," she whispered. "Of course, it had to be a shade of violet. Do I look all right in it?"

She looked spectacular, and he admired the way the lavender silk hugged her curves. "You look perfect."

Her hair was also styled in a loosely upswept twist that brought attention to the graceful curve of her neck. She had little adornment, just some earbobs and a small necklace with an amethyst stone in the middle of it at her throat.

The duke had reserved a quiet corner table for them, but between Wooton's commanding presence and Cammy's exceptionally good looks, all eyes remained on them as he led her to their table.

As always, Lorcan scanned the crowd to make note of the patrons in attendance and the staff serving them. The duke had likely done the same, for neither of them could ever enter a room without immediately searching for suspicious characters. Who belonged? Who looked out of place? Who was fidgeting?

Nothing appeared out of the ordinary at the moment.

However, he remained vigilant, even though he doubted there would be any trouble here. The King's Arms tearoom was exclusive, and one did not simply show up and expect to be seated unless one was titled or extremely well connected.

He was a nobody as far as society was concerned, but Cammy's looks were extraordinary, and he suspected that had she shown up on her own, some earl or marquess would have scrambled to his feet and invited her to join him.

As it was, they were both now being entertained by one of society's most powerful men.

The duke came around to greet them. "Lady Camellia, it is a pleasure. Your husband has told me much about you."

She cast him a genuine smile that caught the old hound off guard, for he was not used to people actually looking forward to seeing him or being so openly pleased to make his acquaintance. But Cammy did not know any other way to be, and Lorcan had no intention of changing that about her. She was the breath of fresh air that swept into dark corners and cleared away the usually foul stench of London society. "He has told me about you, too, Your Grace."

He arched an eyebrow. "Nothing complimentary, I suppose."

"Quite the opposite. He was all compliments, and I can see why. You are both cut from the same cloth. Men of rare, good character who would sacrifice all to keep us safe. I understand you are known as the Icy Duke, but it takes a warm, caring heart to perform the job you do."

"Thank you, Lady Camellia. Truly. Few appreciate me for who I am. Of course, I do not make it easy for them. I am known as the Ice Duke, to be precise. Some say I have earned that reputation. Perhaps, I have. I say very little, entertain almost not at all. Condescend to most people. And I never smile."

"But you are smiling now."

"Because I approve of Lorcan's choice in you."

"Thank you." She cast him another enchanting smile.

"I never thought Lorcan would be one to woo a young woman. Was he charming?"

"Oh, dear me. No. He did nothing but grunt at me the first few weeks of our acquaintance. However, his every *action* was heroic. How could I not fall in love with him at once? Anyone can spout poetry. Few can save lives."

The duke glanced over her head toward Lorcan. "You chose well. Glad to know not all my agents are idiots."

"Thank you, Your Grace. I am overwhelmed by your praise."

The duke chuckled as he held out a chair for Cammy. "Do sit beside me, Lady Camellia. I think we shall have an enjoyable conversation."

She glanced at Lorcan.

He nodded to assure her.

As soon as their tea had been poured and cakes served on their elegant plates, the duke leaned forward to engage Cammy in conversation. "Your husband told me about Lord Milkwood. Are you certain he was the one who attacked you that day?"

Cammy gulped her tea and coughed. "Yes, Your Grace. Quite certain. One does not ever forget the face of the angel of death."

He patted her hand. "We have men on him now. You are not the only young woman unfortunate enough to have encountered him. However, you are one of the lucky ones. You escaped with your life."

"Your Grace. My wife knows this. Do not unsettle her further."

Lorcan wanted to reach across the table and draw her into his arms. She had been all smiles a moment ago, and now he could see the strain in her eyes and tension in the tight set of her lips.

"I am all right," she hurried to assure him, although he knew that she was not.

He turned to the duke and tossed him a warning glance.

The man sighed. "Your husband is irritated with me. But I

need to be sure you've told us all there is to know."

Lorcan growled low in his throat. "I gave you his name, practically served him up to you on a silver platter. Leave my wife alone."

The duke held up his hands in supplication, which was laughable because this man was not the sort who gave in to anyone. "Very well. Let us have some dull conversation about the weather and accomplish nothing."

Cammy glanced questioningly from one to the other. "Your Grace, is there a reason why you are asking me about Lord Milkwood's attack when my husband has told you all there is to know?"

"Yes, there is. You see, I am of the opinion that he needs to be drawn out immediately."

Lorcan wanted to pound his fist into the man's face. "And I've told you that my wife will not serve as your bait."

"And I've told you that Milkwood does not leave his victims in any state to identify him. He will recognize your wife eventually and come after her whether you allow her to help us out or not. Look at her. Do you think any man forgets such beauty? Set aside your pride, Lorcan. It is safest if we are all watching over her while he makes his play."

Cammy turned ashen. "You think he will come after me?"

"No," Lorcan said. "We will grab him long before that. We already have men on him, shadowing his every move."

"We are on him, Lady Camellia. But such a man is unpredictable. What if he does not set off to kill again right away? Who knows when he may decide to act? Tomorrow? In one week? In a month? A year? We cannot allow him time to formulate a plan."

"So you propose to let him see me right away? You believe he will recognize me as the one who got away and can identify him?"

He nodded. "Yes. This is the only way to stay a step ahead of him."

She began to nibble her lip. "Lor?"

"It is all right, love. I will never agree to such a plan. You are not to be served up as bait. He won't have the chance to come after you because we will stop him before he gets within a hundred yards of you. We have female agents who are trained to serve as lures. They are at work attempting to draw him out as we speak. There is no need for you to get involved, and His Grace knows it."

"Anyone you put out there would only be second best," she mused. "He knows who I am. You would nab him for certain if I helped you out."

The duke's eyes widened in surprise. "Lorcan, indeed. You have found yourself a gem of a wife."

Lorcan's throat constricted as he stared at Cammy. "It is out of the question. I will not have you involved."

The duke regarded Cammy solemnly. "Lady Camellia, perhaps your husband is right. You are not trained for this sort of work."

"But I would have both of you guarding me. Lorcan loves me, so he will make all sorts of excuses as to why I must not be involved. I want to hear it from you. Do you truly believe Milkwood can be caught without using me as your lure?"

The duke sighed. "Probably, but not for some time yet. And the longer we watch him, the greater the risk of his catching on and eluding us. This is why I would like to use you as soon as possible. But I will never do so without your husband's permission."

Lorcan wanted to leap out of his seat and pound his fist into something. He was in a rage, but not so stupid as to pound the duke's face, especially not in front of a tearoom full of well-heeled patrons. He would end up in prison and not able to protect Cammy. "The answer is no. She will not do it. Ask her again, and I will shove my fist down your throat."

Cammy gasped. "Lor…"

The duke patted her hand. "Do not fret. It is merely an idle threat. He knows what will happen if he dares strike me. He is angry with me for encouraging you and with just cause, since he had my promise on the matter."

"But is it not worth breaking a promise to save my life?"

"Cammy!"

"Lor, I want you both to give it serious thought. I am bound to encounter Lord Milkwood at some point over these next few months. Worse, what if he has already spotted me and plans to…I don't know what he plans. This is why it is important for us to control the time and place of my meeting him again."

"Cammy, no," he said with an aching groan. "I promised I would keep you safe, and this is what I intend to do. We will put out lures for him. It does not need to involve you."

"Lor, I can do it. I know you will protect me."

His heart felt as though it was shredding. He had feared this would happen, so why had he not left Cammy behind in Taunton or Barnstaple? It was his fault for bringing her to London. His selfish fault, for he wanted it all. Her. The job. The happy home life. So he'd convinced himself this was an important part of her healing. Worse, he deluded himself into thinking Milkwood could be kept away.

He now had a wife ready to take on the role of agent of the Crown, and as angry as he was about it, he also admired her bravery. But it destroyed him to think she might be caught up in their operation and possibly be injured.

Everything she had said was right.

Milkwood, that piece of refuse, would soon have her in his sights. Wooton would be pleased, for this is how he liked to operate. Set up the target. Move in quickly. Clean up the loose ends. Move on to the next operation. This is how the man had earned his reputation as the Ice Duke.

But Lorcan had ice in his veins as well. "Your Grace…" He did not need to express the threat. The duke knew Lorcan would come after him if any harm came to Cammy.

"Stop glowering at me, Lorcan. Let's hope he selects another victim soon. Then we will have no need of your wife's involvement. Indeed, I will give it a month since you will be by her side during that time, and I will have agents on him as well. But once the month is up, if Milkwood has not acted, then we must force his hand. You know I am right. You will be back at work, and your wife will be alone. It is the only way to ensure she is protected. Do not make it difficult for her. She is a brave lass. Smart, too. She sees the situation realistically and wishes to do what is best to protect herself."

He saw by the look in Cammy's eyes that the duke had swayed her. She was nodding and agreeing with everything he'd said. "What will I have to do when the time comes?"

"Nothing, Lady Camellia," the duke said. "You only need to be seen by him. Make eye contact. That is all. Better if you pretend confusion, as though he looks familiar, but you cannot quite recall where you'd met him before. When he approaches you—"

"I am not letting him anywhere near Cammy." Lorcan was still fuming.

"You are right. It is more effective if you only look at him from a distance. I will have word spread that you are from Barnstaple and now in town. I have only to mention it to Lady Withnall, London's biggest gossip, and everyone will know of your arrival within the hour. Milkwood will make the connection and try to eliminate you before you recognize him as your assailant. That's when we'll have him."

Cammy was nibbling her lip again. "Do you not think word has already spread? My family is quite friendly with Lady Withnall. They were excited to have me and my sisters come to London. I'm sure they spoke of it to her. What if he already has me targeted? Have either of you considered this?"

In truth, they had.

Lorcan hadn't wanted to let on and unsettle her further. But she was clever and had an agile mind. He did not think another young woman in her position would be as clear thinking as she was turning out to be. "Yes, Cammy. We did think of it. That's why we've had agents following him since last night…and another two watching you."

She smiled and placed her hand over his. "I knew you would protect me."

It humbled him to know how much she trusted him.

"But I have one modification to insist upon," she said, suddenly looking toward a newly arrived gentleman being seated across the room. "That is Lord Milkwood, is it not?"

The duke paled but did not turn around. "Jesus, Joseph, and Mary! Lor, I give you my oath, I did not plan this. Has he noticed you, Lady Camellia?"

She smiled at the duke. "Yes."

"We're leaving. Now." Lorcan started to rise, but she kicked his shin, actually kicked it, and glowered at him to sit down.

"It is done, my love. Let it play out while you and the duke are here to protect me."

"Not to mention the other three agents assigned to shadow him," the duke added as a reminder.

"And the two you've assigned to guard me," she added. "Are they not here as well?"

Lorcan nodded reluctantly. "I see Fielding. And Campbell. Ah, there's Browning. Now Milkwood is motioning to one of the stewards. Our steward. What is he up to?"

The duke did not turn around, instead, he kept his intense gaze on Lorcan, who had the best vantage point to watch Milkwood without being noticed in return. "What is he asking the man?"

"I cannot tell. No…it is only meant as a distraction. He's just slipped something into the cup of tea the man is carrying on his tray. Blessed saints. The fresh cup meant for you, Cammy."

The duke did not react in the slightest. "What of our glasses of port?"

"He's slipped nothing into our glasses. It's Cammy he is after. Our steward is coming toward us now. Damn, Milkwood is leaving." He caught Fielding's attention and signaled for him and the other two agents to stop their quarry at the door.

They all watched in silence as the steward set the cup in question in front of Cammy. Her eyes rounded in surprise.

Lorcan took hold of her hand. "Don't drink it, love. Don't even touch it. The game is now at an end."

The duke rose casually and took the cup with him toward the men who had discreetly surrounded Lord Milkwood at the door. "Milkwood, I believe there's been a mistake made. This is your cup of tea, is it not?"

"Mine? Surely you are mistaken." He looked around in panic and then turned in rage toward Cammy. "What has the bitch told you?"

He'd said it loud enough for everyone in the tearoom to hear.

Lorcan was still holding Cammy's hand and felt a shudder course through her. "Lor, I feel ill."

"Look at me, love. Don't look at Milkwood."

"Why?"

"Because he's cornered, and he knows it."

She tore her gaze away from the tearoom's entry and stared at him in confusion. "Lor, he already knew I was here. We only arrived in town yesterday. He thought he was a step ahead of us. He meant to kill me today."

"But we were prepared, Cammy." He covered her hand with both of his own. "Although I did not expect he would move so quickly."

"Do you think he has been watching Chipping Way all the while? Lor," she said with a shudder, "what if I had not delayed my arrival by running away? What if I had not married you? Or told you of the attack? You wouldn't have known to stop him. I would have died of poison, and he would have gotten away with murder."

These same thoughts had been running through his mind, but he hadn't dared reveal them. They horrified him. He could not imagine what Cammy had to be feeling. "But you did tell me, love. I did know and alerted the duke. Milkwood will never hurt you again."

"Lor, I cannot look. What is happening now?"

He was silent for a long moment, just keeping hold of her hand as he waited for the final outcome.

"Lor?"

"He won't be bothering you, Cammy."

"Why?"

"He just drank the contents of your cup."

She gasped and turned toward the entry as Milkwood began to stagger. "Did the duke make him drink it?"

"No, he grabbed the cup before anyone could stop him. Not that His Grace would have any intention of stopping him. But Milkwood had to know it was his only recourse. He'd poisoned the tea, intending to kill you before you could identify him. Now he's taken it. He knew it was over for him, that he would now be connected to the other killings. He would never be a free man again if he remained alive. He would be locked away in an asylum for the rest of his days. Even if he were to inherit the dukedom, he would never be released."

The room was now abuzz.

He doubted anyone realized what was really happening, for the duke had approached Milkwood as though he was an old friend.

Lorcan strained his ears to hear what others were saying.

"A heart attack," someone muttered.

"Poor man. He did look ill as he rose to leave," an older woman said. "But calling his dear mother a bitch for worrying about him is inexcusable."

"They don't realize he was talking about me," Cammy said with a flood of relief.

"No, love. And we will see to it that no one ever makes the connection."

They sat quietly and listened to more comments.

"Pity, there is nothing anyone can do," their steward said, shaking his head as he came to stand beside them, having no notion of what had really happened or his involvement in delivering the poisoned cup to Cammy. "Not even the Ice Duke can save him."

"Fatal," said another of the passing stewards. "But that's what happens. The heart just bursts, and you are gone in a trice. The widowmaker, they call this sort of massive attack. And he was a young man, too."

Cammy kept her head bowed and her eyes closed.

"Love, it is over. We can leave. The duke will not return. He'll make sure the body is…"

"Truly dead?"

He groaned. "Something like that."

"Oh, Lor. I don't want to know any more."

"I know, love. Just remember, he got what he deserved. Shall we go back to Chipping Way? Or do you need to walk around for a bit?"

"I don't know. It feels so very odd, as though I am walking through a bad dream. I should feel sorry for him, but all I feel is relief."

He nodded. "There is no need to pity him, for he is another such as Lord Belfy. Born in privilege. Given all the advantages in life. But these men appreciated none of it. Instead, they resented everyone who stood in their way. Belfy would have killed his own brother to gain the Monkton earldom. Milkwood would have done the same to inherit his dukedom. Why wait when he could have it all now with careful plotting? He may have intended to act on his plan as soon as he was rid of you."

"My head feels as though it is going to explode. I think I do need to walk around for a bit."

"All right, love." He helped her out of her chair. "Let's go out this side door." He wanted to avoid having to pass the duke and his fellow agents as they disposed of Milkwood. It was a nasty business, but he did not give a rat's arse about Milkwood's fate.

He got what he deserved.

Lorcan's gut was still churning, for he hadn't wanted Cammy

involved at all. But Milkwood's actions had taken the matter out of their hands. He was relieved that it was over but not pleased with himself for failing to shield Cammy completely.

The duke would now wrap up matters in a neat bow, and no one would suspect anything.

This is how Wooton had trained them to handle situations. The newspapers would report the tragic death of Lord Milkwood at the King's Arms tearoom. Attack of the heart. Immediate death. How tragic for the young lord. Did he suspect he had a weak heart?

But the duke was right about his stubbornness in wanting to keep Cammy out of it. Love blinded a man. Had the woman in question been anyone other than Cammy, he would have considered all possible outcomes with the same frigid analysis used by the duke. Ironically, Milkwood's forcing their hand had led to the best possible outcome. But he was not so much pleased as repulsed by the incident.

His concern was entirely for Cammy now.

They stepped outside and were immediately struck by a blast of cool air. London air was nothing like the truly fresh air one found in the countryside. Cammy needed to take several deep breaths to calm herself.

"Love, look at me. Tell me what you are feeling."

"Not yet, Lor. Let's just walk slowly. But I am all right. Well, I will be all right. It happened so quickly, so effortlessly. He was there, and now he is gone. No fight. No chase." She stopped and looked up at him. "I survived his beating. I survived being taken hostage by Ezekiel and having a pistol put to my head. Yet, I felt sorry for Ezekiel. I don't know if he really had it in him to hurt me."

"I was not about to wait to find out."

She smiled shakily. "You saved me from him. And you saved me from Lord Milkwood."

"Bah! I did not. You noticed him first."

"But you noticed what he did to my cup."

"He should never have gotten into the tearoom."

She shook her head. "How were your agents to stop him without giving themselves away? You and the duke were on alert the moment we arrived in London. You had men shadowing him. And no one will ever know that Milkwood poisoned himself or what brought it about. It was an extremely smooth operation. Lor, is this not what you do day in and day out? Protect us from these bad men?"

He gave a curt nod. "Usually with more finesse."

"Stop berating yourself. You had me protected from the first moment. How could you know what Milkwood had planned? How could you control his thoughts and actions? But you were prepared for him, and this is what matters." She took a deep breath. "You were prepared, and now we have our lives ahead of us. Our happy lives. I am unharmed, and London is safer for his demise."

He listened as she spoke.

She was healing herself and him, he realized, for he could not be happy until he knew she was well and truly free of the torments of the past and of today's occurrence. He would watch her these next few days to see if there was any delayed shock.

He hoped there would not be. Cammy, despite being kind and gentle, was strong in spirit, as all these Farthingale women were.

They walked slowly to her uncle's carriage, which was stationed just around the corner. Mr. Mayhew was perched atop it in the driver's seat and greeted them jovially as they climbed in. "The tearoom is lovely, is it not Lady Camellia? Did you enjoy your tea?"

CHAPTER SIXTEEN

LORCAN HELD CAMMY in his arms that night and every night in the two weeks since the Milkwood incident had occurred. He saw that she was healing nicely and had settled into a pleasant routine of visiting Violet and Hyacinth each morning, then having lunch with her cousins. These were working lunches where they discussed setting up their Explorers Society and publishing articles for the club's new journal.

He had fallen into the daily routine of riding to the ministry to meet with the Duke of Wooton. So much for his desired time off. Still, he was not complaining. He enjoyed the work, and since he was still on holiday, these meetings rarely took up more than the morning.

Cammy was usually back at Number 3 Chipping Way by the time he returned, so they often took a stroll, and he would tell her whatever he was at liberty to reveal about his day. In turn, she would tell him of the new members who had joined her club and the progress of her publication.

They also talked in the privacy of their bedchamber in the evenings. Sometimes they would make love afterward.

Sometimes they would simply fall asleep, Cammy curled like a contented kitten against his body.

Last night, they had made love.

He smiled at Cammy as they sat around the breakfast table the following morning with her relatives; her aunt, uncle, and a few he had never seen before mingled with those who were familiar. Sophie and John always had a full house.

Cammy was casting him dreamy-eyed looks, and everyone around the table was grinning and snickering because they knew what a young couple in love did to occupy their nights, and Cammy's expression…blessed saints…revealed everything.

Fortunately, everyone's attention turned to Pruitt, the family butler, as he marched in carrying a stack of invitations on a silver salver.

"The Duke and Duchess of Edgeware are throwing a ball in our honor," Cammy read aloud as she opened theirs. "That is so nice of Dillie and Ian."

"Delightful," he muttered, trying to appear enthusiastic. In truth, he detested these society affairs. He maintained his smile because the Duchess of Edgeware was Cammy's cousin, Daffodil. She was also John and Sophie's daughter, and after the kindness they had shown him and Cammy all these weeks, he was not going to say or do anything to disappoint them.

Daffodil was better known as Dillie to her friends and family. In addition, the female cousins often met at her grand home to hold meetings of their newly established Explorers' Club. She had generously opened her palatial house to them and their growing membership. "Lor, it is a magnificent place. I cannot wait to see how they decorate it."

"I'm sure it will be quite splendid," Sophie said with obvious pride in her daughter.

Cammy's eyes were now sparkling. "I've never had a party held in my honor before. Have you, Lor?"

"Honestly, Cammy," Hortensia intoned. "Does he look like the dandified sort people throw parties for?"

She laughed and grinned at him. "I suppose not. But he is devilishly handsome, don't you think? Lor, I cannot wait to see you in your formal attire. You will look splendid. I shall have to borrow another of Violet's gowns for the occasion."

"You shall do no such thing," Hortensia intoned, the comment immediately seconded by Charlotte. "Sophie, you must take the girl to Madame de Bressard's shop immediately. Borrowed gown, indeed. I've never heard such utter tripe."

"I think our Cammy will look stunning no matter what she wears," her Uncle Rupert commented, setting aside his cup of coffee and pushing away from the table. "Madame de Bressard has all our best silks in her shop. Let her choose one of them for you, Cammy. She has an excellent eye and will design something lovely for the occasion."

"But can she finish it within the week?" Sophie said, opening her own envelope. "Everyone will be running to the shop as soon as they receive their invitations."

Theirs had been delivered to Number 3 Chipping Way where he and Cammy were still residing while their new purchase, a lovely townhouse just around the corner, was being refurbished. He had retained his Bloomsbury residence but chose not to move them in there since he intended to give it up as soon as their new home was ready.

He wanted Cammy to remain close to family.

In truth, she seemed to be thriving around them.

She cast him a smile that shot straight to his heart.

She was truly happy.

This is all he'd wanted, all he'd hoped for.

"Aunt Sophie, does it not feel odd to address your daughter as Your Grace?" Cammy asked, obviously feeling right at home among her family.

"Yes, but we only do so when in public. It still grates on Dillie's nerves when we do. She hates to think of herself as above her parents."

"Which she is not," Hortensia intoned. "She is still that impertinent child who abetted her twin, Lily, in her misadventures. But that is good, I think. To keep true to the person you truly are. This is why Edgeware fell in love with her and still adores her. I have never seen a bigger, more doting fool than that man. Although..." She stared at Lorcan.

He burst out laughing. "Should we not be doting fools over our wives? And are they not worthy of our love and attention?"

Cammy blushed as he cast her a look of admiration and took her hand in his. He still worried about her because of the Milkwood incident at the tearoom. One did not forget such things, especially when not hardened against it from experience.

But that devil no longer controlled her life or the happiness to be made of it.

Lorcan wanted her to be happy and carefree. Of course, she would always be careful when going around London, for there were cutpurses, petty thieves, and wicked rogues in abundance.

Last night she'd told him that he had given her the courage to discard her protective shell and regain her true self. The old Cammy, the fearful one who was willing to hide from love and life, was no more, she had declared. "It is all because of you, Lor."

"No, love," he'd said. "You accomplished this for yourself."

He was proud of her, adored the way she was now grabbing life and blossoming into the woman she was meant to be.

John, the patriarch of the family, glanced at his wife, Sophie. "Indeed, our wives are worthy of our hearts, of everything we are because of their love and support."

Cammy sighed and smiled at her aunt and uncle. "Beautifully said, Uncle John. After all these years, you and Aunt Sophie are still so much in love. This is what I hope for Lorcan and myself as we embark on life's journey together."

"A journey of love," Lorcan said, leaning over to kiss her on the cheek. "Speaking of which, I must get going. Wooton is expecting me."

"Ah, yes." She escorted him to the door as had become her habit. She saw him off each morning, kissing him sweetly before he rode off to meet the duke.

He liked that the duke relied on him and respected his opinions. "His summons did not sound urgent, love. Shouldn't take me long. I'll walk you over to our new house when I return."

She laughed lightly. "He is as bad as a jealous wife, I think."

Lorcan nodded. "That is exactly what he is. He does not like to share me with anyone, although he will grudgingly allow me to spend time with you. He thinks he is being on his best behavior. In truth, he is trying hard because he likes you and does not wish to get on your bad side."

"Oh, I doubt that. He demands your attention every day."

"Just for a few hours. Hardly anything. He has kept his promise not to send me off on any new assignments. It is killing him that he has to hold to his word for another two weeks. You've been an angel about his constant intrusions."

She reached up and kissed him on the lips. "I am happy, Lor. I never thought I would experience such joy. We will be in our new home soon and truly on our own as husband and wife. I love you so much."

He planted a scorching kiss on her lips.

She smiled up at him. "You called it a journey of love. There is no one I'd rather have with me than you."

He scooped her into his arms and twirled her. "It could only ever be you for me"

"Lor! I've just realized something important."

He arched an eyebrow. "What?"

"I never thought to ask you, but can you dance?"

"Can I dance?"

Her eyes sparkled. "Yes, that is what I asked. You seem more comfortable on a horse than in a ballroom."

He gave her another scorching kiss that left them both breathless and aching. "You'll have to wait and find out."

"Now you are just being wicked," she said with mirth. "Tell me. I have to know."

"Why?"

"Well, no reason other than I am curious. You are perfect in every other way. It is quite frustrating that I cannot find a single flaw in you."

"Flattery will get you everywhere, my lady. But I am still not going to tell you. However, I will claim the opening waltz, and we shall see how I do."

"Ugh, that means you know how to dance. Is there anything you cannot do to perfection?"

"Lots, Cammy. Have you forgotten everything we learned in *The Book of Love*? To see each other clearly for what we are and not what we want each other to be?"

"I remember every chapter and verse. Fine, I'll stop. You shall never hear another flattering word out of me even though you are the smartest man of my acquaintance. Handsomest, too. But you are a mediocre cards player, and I shall hold on tightly to that flaw. I think we must play again soon. Do you think you can beat me?"

"Not a chance. You will win every hand." He set her down and ever so gently caressed her cheek. "Love you," he said in a whisper and left the house.

Cammy leaned against the entry door as she watched him stride away.

Actions did not have to be dramatic to be effective.

That light caress.

His seductive smile.

The silvery glint in his eyes that held promise of the happy years to come.

What more did she need to be this exquisitely happy?

She was still standing by the door, staring at the front gate even though he had long since disappeared down Chipping Way, when her Aunt Sophie came up beside her. "Everything all right, Cammy?"

"Yes. Just missing Lorcan already." She smiled at her aunt. "How do you manage to run this busy household and appear to do it with such ease? Have you ever had a moment to yourself, just you and Uncle John? How can you possibly, when you've taken in every stray Farthingale from here to Scotland?"

"Oh, my. We haven't been alone in the house in ages. But we do love having family around us. All the family. You enrich our lives." She leaned in and whispered. "Even Hortensia, who can be the most crotchety old woman at times."

Cammy laughed. "She does know how to toss her barbs."

"But she is a darling at heart, and we enjoy having her with us. As for John and me, we always manage an hour or two at night to chat quietly in the privacy of our bedchamber. That is important, being able to share the events of the day with each other and work through any concerns."

"Uncle John adores you."

She shook her head. "We have had our fights. But yes, love is a wonderful thing. We can never stay angry with each other for very long. It hurts too much. We just want to be together."

"This is how I feel about Lorcan. But speaking of love, now that I am married, it is time for me to pass the book along."

"Do you have someone in mind?"

Cammy nodded. "Yes, Lorcan's brother, Donal. Is it permitted to pass it on to a man?"

"I don't see why not."

"I didn't think there would be any harm in it either. I've told him that he is to have it next, but he must return it to you once he is done with it. Do you mind being keeper of *The Book of Love*, Aunt Sophie? It seems fitting that you should be the one to hold it."

"I don't mind at all. When do you plan to give it to Donal? Hortensia and I will enjoy watching him fight the inevitable. Those Brayden men are particularly fun to watch as they take the fall."

"Oh, my. Yes. You should have seen Lorcan's brother, Shayne, and Willow together. I thought they wanted to kill each other. But all the while, they were desperately in love and just too stubborn to admit it. I thought I would hand the book off to Donal shortly before Dillie's ball. He'll be back in London by then, and Lor said he would be in attendance."

"We shall see if the course of true love runs smoother for him than it did for his brothers." She patted Cammy's hand and returned to the others in the breakfast room.

Cammy was about to do the same when Violet bolted through the front gate. "Pruitt!" she shouted to the Farthingale butler, "don't close that door."

Pruitt was a stoic Scott who had been in service with the family longer than anyone could remember. "Wouldn't dream of it, Miss Violet."

She was all smiles and animated chatter as she asked about his gout, gave him a hug, and then turned to Cammy. "Romulus is spending time with our Hyacinth this morning. She has grown so much, and he is going to leave us soon to return to his ship. I thought I'd give them time alone to get to know each other. Is that coffee I smell? And honey cake? Yum, I'm hungry." She locked her arm in Cammy's and drew her toward the food. "Good morning, everyone. Isn't it a lovely day?"

John and Rupert bussed her cheek as they took themselves off to work.

Cammy settled into a seat beside her cousin and cut a slice of honey cake for each of them.

"Cammy, do you have a gown for Dillie's ball? Because you can borrow one of mine. I do have several that are not purple. Although you'd look beautiful in any color. I'm sure Lorcan has told you that. He cannot take his eyes off you. But that is as it should be. He isn't much of a talker around others, is he? He grunts a lot, doesn't he?"

"She is not wearing a borrowed gown," Hortensia and Charlotte insisted.

Violet grinned at her. "Of course, what was I thinking? The party is in her honor. She must have a new one. Cammy, I'll have my carriage brought around at once. We must dash off to Madame de Bressard's and be there when her shop opens, or we shall be forced to fight our way through those marriage-minded mamas who will already be circling like vultures. She'll hardly have the chance to open her doors before they swoop in and pick off all the best fabrics."

"But what about Hyacinth? And Romulus? Do you dare leave

them for so long?"

"Romulus will manage. Besides, James and his Sophie will be with him," she said, referring to his brother, the Earl of Exmoor, and his charming wife. "They plan on strolling through the park and afterward visiting his Aunt Miranda. You met her last night. Is she not something…well, she's memorable, isn't she? They won't notice me gone since they will be occupied for hours yet. Let's pass by Daisy's and pick her up along the way. Do you want to stop by your new house first to look in on the workmen?"

"No, Dahlia has it all under control. She has done wonders decorating it. Lorcan doesn't care what I do, so long as I do not put up flowered wallpaper or frilly drapes in his study."

"Romulus was the same. Men like dark wood and leather. I think it is bred in them from the time they lived in caves and hunted bears and wolves. Nothing light or frivolous. Just dark. With a few animal skins tossed around for good measure."

"Why do you think that is?" Cammy asked, unable to stifle her grin.

"They like to think of themselves as forever wild and un-tamed. But they are quite domesticated, whether they will admit it or not. Romulus especially. You can see the joy in his eyes as soon as he steps foot inside our home. There is nowhere else he would rather be. While he is here, these are our days of heaven. Lorcan will be the same with you."

She nodded. "I hope so."

Violet rolled her eyes. "There isn't a doubt. It is so obvious he loves you. But this is how these Braydens are, faithful and loyal forever. However, if he gives you a hard time about his study, threaten to put up butterfly wallpaper. That will shut him up."

Cammy laughed. "I could never do that to him."

"Although…you could put up several of your bird drawings. They would look beautiful amid the oiled wood and yards of dark leather. Have you spoken to Dahlia about it? I think we must. If they are good enough to be included in Rose's chinaware collection, they are good enough for Lorcan's study. Speaking of which, have you seen Viscount Montague yet?"

"No," she said with a light frown. "I think he is avoiding me."

"Probably terrified of what Lorcan will do to him for cheating you out of the credit for your illustrations," Violet said with a snort. "I think we must ride past his house and toss eggs at it."

Cammy burst out laughing. "Violet, that is a wonderful idea."

"Really? You would do this?"

Cammy cast her a wicked grin.

Violet shot out of her seat. "Let's go raid Mrs. Mayhew's larder. But we must pick up Daisy first. She will not want to miss out on the fun. Plus, her aim is dead on."

Yes, it was going to be a lovely day.

CHAPTER SEVENTEEN

CAMMY STARED AT herself in the mirror, hardly believing her eyes at the transformation from pretty country girl to elegant Lady Camellia, wife of a knight. Her gown was an ice-blue silk confection, simple but elegant, that brought out the blue in her eyes and pink of her cheeks.

"Oh, my lady. You look stunning," said her newly acquired lady's maid.

"Thank you, Sarah." She and Lorcan were now settled in their new home, which happened to be around the corner from Chipping Way. It was a beautiful house on Merriweather Square that had a whitewashed facade, nautical blue shutters and door, and red roses along the ornate, black iron rail fence. It was not as large as the homes on Chipping Way, but it had a lovely garden and was more than adequate for their needs.

The interior was beautiful, for Dahlia had transformed the overly gilded rooms preferred by the former owner into a charming, more welcoming home that was designed for comfort rather than as a museum piece. Lorcan had not a single unkind word to say about his study, quite liking it, especially her drawings of birds in the wild. Dahlia had even put up a series of her sketches of cliffside caves near Barnstaple that Lorcan had particularly admired.

"See," Dahlia had whispered to her when showing her the finished interior. "It is just as Violet said. Men like their caves.

Toss in some raw meat from time to time, and he will never want to leave."

"What is that smirk on your lips about, love?" Lorcan asked, striding into their bedchamber.

She shook out of her thoughts. "Oh, Lor, hurry up and get ready, or we'll be late to the party. What happened to delay you?"

"I'll tell you while I undress. I sent word to your Uncle John to pick you up along the way." He glanced down at himself. "I am an utter mess."

"I can see that." She frowned as she took in his appearance, realizing something serious must have taken place. But it was Lor's way to make light of anything that had to do with his work. She quickly dismissed Sarah, feigning calm until the door closed and they were alone. "What happened? Weren't you and His Grace merely going over documents today? You look as though you were rolling around in a coal bin."

He nodded. "Something like it…well, nothing like it. I suppose I must tell you since you'll hear the gossip from some loudmouth lord talking about it tonight. Some arse tried to blow up the duke's office."

"With both of you in it? Lor! Are you all right? And the duke?" She started toward him, wanting to run her hands along his body to make certain he was unharmed, but he motioned her back.

"Love, I am full of soot. The ladies in your family will chase me out of town if you appear at Dillie's ball with your gown all smudged." He lightly patted his chest, sending a layer of dark powder and ash into the air. "See? But I am fine. So is His Grace. Most of the rebels we deal with are flaming idiots. And I do mean flaming. This particular fool set himself on fire when his gunpowder ignited before he'd tossed his explosive device."

Cammy's heart was in her throat. "He might have killed you!"

"No, love. Not even close." He tossed off his clothes as he spoke, dropping them on the slate in front of the hearth so as not to dirty their elegant carpet. "But we did try to save the undeserving wretch. I don't think he'll survive. The duke remained behind to question him."

The party seemed trivial compared to the safety of the country. Her heart was still in her throat as she noted a few rips to his jacket and the grime on his discarded shirt. Yet, Lorcan seemed so casual about this close encounter. "Do you think he will give up the names of his fellow conspirators?"

"Maybe." He tugged off his boots, tossing her another caution to stay back when she tried to approach. He casually began to unbutton the fall of his trousers. Her knees went weak, but she ignored her body's rapturous response and forced herself to listen as he continued. "I've ordered water and a tub to be brought up. That soot found its way into every crevice of my body."

She studied him intently, not because he had the finest body—which he did—but because she wanted to be sure he truly was unharmed. "I don't see any blood on you. Not even a new scratch."

He grinned wickedly. "The only scratches I have on me are the ones you put on my back as I made love to you last night. Lord, you're a wanton vixen."

Her face turned to fire. "Lor!"

"What? Should a husband not be pleased that he can make his wife wild in bed?"

She gave up and laughingly groaned. "You needn't be so smug about it. But tell me truly, is this a potential new threat against the country?"

"Oddly, I think it is a personal vendetta against the duke. The man we caught was a hired assassin, thankfully an incompetent one."

"Did he say anything to make you think his target was the duke specifically?"

Lorcan shook his head. "No, but I sensed it from Wooton's reaction. Something is going on that he has not seen fit to tell anyone about. It has to be something personal, or he would have confided in me by now."

They spoke no more as Jarvis and two footmen brought up the tub and buckets of steaming water. Then they heard her uncle in the downstairs entry hall. "Go off with him, love. I won't be far behind you."

She nodded and left without protest.

Had he wanted her to go ahead because he did not want both of them arriving late to the ball? Or was he worried that assassins would make an attempt on his life, and he did not want her anywhere close to him when it happened?

She wanted to run back to him but knew this was the worst thing she could do. Worrying for her safety would distract him.

She greeted her aunts, allowed her uncle to help her into his carriage, and feigned excitement to be attending her first ball ever. She smiled and nodded, but her thoughts were on Lorcan and his near escape.

To her relief, Lorcan arrived not far behind them. No more than a quarter-hour had passed before he entered the Duke and Duchess of Edgeware's grand home and turned every young woman's head.

He looked so handsome in his formal evening wear.

He had eyes only for her as he strode confidently toward the receiving line where she stood beside Dillie and her duke. Apparently, the two men were friends. "You're late, you arse," Edgeware muttered, tossing him a mirthful but questioning look as he took his spot beside them.

"Wooton had a little mishap."

Edgeware's eyebrows shot up in question. "Come into my study, we can—"

Dillie cast the men a frown. "Do not dare leave your wives alone to face this massive horde. You two can talk later."

Edgeware grinned. "Wouldn't dream of abandoning you."

Dillie cast him another warning glance, kissed his cheek, then leaned over and whispered in Cammy's ear. "Your husband and mine often work together. Ian hasn't let go of that part of his life, even though he is a duke with responsibilities to his estate and family.”

“And you are all right with it, Dillie?”

“I worry, of course. And I’ve even saved his sorry backside a time or two,” she said with obvious pride. “But this is what defines them as men. Their home life is important, of course. They love us to the depths of their souls. But they are not gentlemen farmers or elegant dandies. They are fighters. Hunters. Predators, when necessary. We cannot tame this out of them. So we must accept it. After all, we love them for who they are.”

Cammy nodded. “It is a constant tug of war, isn’t it? Wanting them to be safe, but also loving the fierceness and valor that forges their character.”

They said no more and returned their attention to the guests now gathered in a mad crush at the door. Then it was time to officially start the ball. Edgeware led his wife onto the dance floor. Lorcan did the same with her. “Moment of truth,” he said, tossing her a rakish grin.

The Edgeware gardens had been transformed to resemble a fairy glen, complete with a small waterfall descending into a torch-lit pool. The magic had been carried throughout the ballroom as well. It now resembled a fairy palace surrounded by bluebells and lavender and lush ferns.

“You should have worn your fairy wings,” he teased. “I will never forget the sight of you at the Ashcott Inn in Taunton. It was Midsummer’s Eve. You and your sisters were dressed as fairy princesses, your hair long and loose, masks covering your faces, gowns of shimmering silk, and fairy wings clipped to your back. I almost believed you came from another world. You looked ethereal, caught as you were in the glow of torchlight and fairy lanterns. You stole my breath away.”

“You never said a word to me that night. Augustus danced with June. I was hoping you would ask me. But you left so soon after you arrived.”

“I couldn’t stay. I had to help Shayne keep the peace in Taunton, particularly on this night of revels. But we shall have our dance now." He glanced toward the orchestra as they struck up the strains of a waltz.

Cammy closed her eyes and followed his lead.

He was an excellent dancer.

Was there any doubt?

She felt the warmth of his palm against her spine and the caress of his hand as he guided her in spin after spin in time to the music. Then others joined in, and the dance floor became a crush as couples twirled around them.

Lorcan maneuvered them onto the balcony, still waltzing but slowing his steps as he led her deeper into the garden and away from the crowd. "That's much better," he said, no longer dancing but simply holding her in his arms.

"Are you trying to compromise me, Sir Lorcan?" she teased, opening her eyes to find themselves alone beside the illuminated waterfall.

"Absolutely, Lady Camellia. Care to remove your clothes and have a dip?"

"Lor!"

He grinned. "Didn't think so."

She laughed. "You may have your way with me once we are back home and in our bed. It seems I am quite wanton when it comes to you. But it is nice, isn't it, Lor?"

"You and me?" He nodded. "Very nice."

They stood in silence, merely looking at each other.

The moon was a glowing, silver ball in the sky.

A thousand stars glittered overhead.

The strains of the waltz and laughter of animated guests carried on the breeze. Those faint sounds mingled with the soft *whoosh* of water cascading down the waterfall.

Stray droplets tickled her bare arms, frothing and spraying as they landed in the fairy pool.

Lor was watching her, his eyes as silver as the moon. "What are you thinking, love?"

She smiled up at him. "That we've been on quite a journey, haven't we?"

He nodded. "I would follow you to the edge of the world if that is where you wished to go."

"I am content to stay right here, beside you. For always, Lor."

"For always, love. Your happiness means more to me than anything."

"I am happy. Love's journey is a marvelous thing. The miles I've traveled between here and Barnstaple are nothing to the miles I've traveled from scared girl to confident young woman. The importance of that journey is immeasurable. I'm proud of who I've become."

"So am I." He cleared his throat. "Speaking of travels...you haven't been anywhere near Viscount Montague's home lately, have you? Someone egged it."

She blushed. "Did they?"

He laughed. "Actually, reports spoke of three young culprits."

"How awful."

"Three adorable looking little boys." He kissed her on the nose. "Glad you weren't caught, love. Where did you get the clothes?"

"Borrowed from your Aunt Miranda. She has trunks full of them from when your cousins were children."

"So, Miranda abetted your criminal enterprise? Why am I not surprised? Who were your accomplices? Violet, I'm sure. Who was the third?"

"Aunt Sophie's daughter, Daisy."

His eyes widened. "Gabriel Dayne's wife? An *earl's* wife?"

She nodded. "Are you angry?"

"No, love." It was all he could do to keep from laughing. "I intended to do far worse to the man. But I think I will let the egging be his lesson since he has lost enough."

"What has he lost besides a little inconvenience in having his staff clean up those broken eggs?"

Lorcan drew her up against him and kissed her with possessive longing. "He lost you."

She put her arms around him and gave herself over to the magic of the night and his intoxicating kisses.

CHAPTER EIGHTEEN

DONAL CAME UP to Cammy as she and Lorcan were returning to the ballroom after taking some air on the balcony several hours later. "All right, where is it?"

Lorcan smirked. "Nice to see you, too. Where is what?"

"You are asking about *The Book of Love?*" Cammy said with a knowing nod. "I left it on the desk in Edgeware's library. Just remember to take it with you when you leave."

He groaned. "Lor, I am going to punch you if you do not stop smirking."

"Can't help it. I know what is going to happen now that you have possession of that book."

Donal snorted. "We'll see who has the last laugh. I am not letting a musty, old book control my life. Have you seen Wooton? I was supposed to meet him here tonight."

Lorcan cleared his throat. "I'm sure he'll arrive soon. There was an incident at the ministry a short while ago. Some idiot tried to blow him up while he was in his office."

Cammy frowned. "Lor was there, too."

Donal arched an eyebrow. "You arse. Why are you so glib about it? You might have been killed."

"No, the assailant would not have gotten close enough to harm us. But he tried and accidentally set himself on fire."

"Did Wooton say anything else to you?"

"Such as what?"

Donal glanced around. "Have you seen Luciana Lessing?"

Cammy did not know who that was until Lorcan mentioned she was the Earl of Monkton's sister-in-law. "Oh."

Donal must have gotten to know her when they were all in Taunton dealing with Lord Belfy's threats. While Lorcan and Shayne had remained in town to protect the citizens, Donal had taken responsibility for protecting the Earl of Monkton and his family at the earl's nearby estate.

"Are you hoping to dance with her?" Cammy asked, her brain already hatching matchmaking plans, for why would Donal be asking about this Luciana Lessing otherwise? He must have taken a fancy to her while he was guarding her family.

Donal and Lorcan exchanged looks.

Cammy sighed. "What am I missing?"

"He doesn't want to dance with her," Lor said, also appearing not quite certain what was going on. "I think he needs to guard her. Am I right, Donal?"

He nodded.

Cammy was intrigued. One could easily get caught up in this agent of the Crown business. "Why must she be protected? Lord Belfy is dead. Is the danger not passed?"

Donal was still scanning the crowded ballroom as he spoke. "This has nothing to do with Lord Belfy. I am not at liberty to say more."

Cammy was even more curious now. "If the Duke of Wooton wants Miss Lessing guarded, obviously she is in danger. Is it related to today's failed attack on him?"

"Damn it," Donal muttered, ignoring her question. "I don't see her in here."

"She isn't in the garden either," Lorcan said. "Cammy and I were the only ones out there. Nor was she among the guests on the balcony."

Cammy turned to him. "Goodness, Lor. Are you sure?"

"Part of the training, love. I make it a point to notice every-thing. It becomes second nature. She must be somewhere in the house."

"I'll check the ladies' retiring room," she offered.

"Would you?" Donal smiled in relief.

But Miss Lessing wasn't there. She reported the news to Donal, who now looked seriously worried.

"Perhaps she is dancing, and you've simply overlooked her among the crowd on the dance floor," she suggested.

He shook his head. "I also make it a point to notice everything. Besides, she's a wallflower. Pretty enough, but very shy. When I was guarding her sister, Lady Monkton, and the earl, she hardly said two words to me. Spent most of her time quietly reading" He slapped his hand to his forehead. "I'm an idiot. Of course, she must be in Edgeware's library."

Cammy's eyes widened. "Oh, but *The Book of Love* is in there."

Donal tossed back his head and groaned. "Of course, it is. And she's probably reading it as we speak."

The three of them hurried down the hall to the library.

Cammy's heart was in a rampant beat as they approached the closed door. Lorcan held her back while Donal carefully opened it and peered in. "Damn it," he muttered under his breath, obviously tense, for he was doing a lot of swearing, mostly under his breath, but she could still hear him. "She's here. She's fine. She has that bloody book in her hands."

Miss Lessing looked up from her reading and quickly shut it. "Good evening, Mr. Brayden. Did you want the library? I shall leave you to it."

"No, Miss Lessing. I want you."

Her eyes widened. "You want me? For what possible reason?"

"I mean to say, I am taking you into my custody."

She gazed at him as though he had grown a third eyeball in the center of his forehead. "You are arresting me for reading a book?"

Donal stepped into the room and crossed to the window to peer out of it. "No, you are not under arrest. I am to guard you."

She shook her head in dismissal. "Whatever for? Good evening," she said, her gaze now fixed on Cammy and Lorcan as they stood in doorway. Cammy thought she was quite pretty in a quiet way. She had auburn hair with overtones of red, or perhaps it was merely the glow of candlelight that gave it the tinge of fire. She also had intelligent green eyes. "I am Miss Lessing. Luciana Lessing, but my friends call me Lucy."

Cammy smiled. "I am Lady Camellia Brayden. My friends call me Cammy. Delighted to make your acquaintance. This is my husband, Sir Lorcan Brayden. You may have guessed by the striking resemblance that he and Donal are brothers."

"Delightful," Donal said wryly. "Now that we are all bosom friends, grab that book, Miss Lessing, and let's go."

"Oh, but it is not mine. I saw it just sitting there on His Grace's desk, and it caught my interest. Oddest book," she muttered. "That faded, red leather binding seemed to call to me. But as I said, it isn't mine, and I cannot take it."

"You can," he said gruffly. "It's mine."

She laughed and shook her head. "Yours? Are you jesting? Do you know what this book is about?"

"I have a pretty good idea," Donal grumbled, casting a scowl at Cammy.

She was not in the least intimidated.

Lorcan was chuckling, but he sobered a moment later. "Go with him, Miss Lessing. My brother's orders came directly from the Duke of Wooton. I do not wish to alarm you, but he does not issue directives lightly. It must be for an important reason. Donal, what do you need me to do?"

"Just get word to His Grace that I have Miss Lessing and will take her out of London tonight."

"Where will you go?" Cammy asked.

He shrugged. "I don't know yet. Nor am I at liberty to tell you even if I did. Lor, post an ad in the *London Times* once it is safe to bring her back. I'll be sure to read it every day."

Miss Lessing resisted when Donal took her arm. "What makes you think I am willing to go with you?"

"I don't care if you are willing or not. You are in danger, and I am tasked with keeping you safe."

She glanced around as though searching for something or someone. "So you are determined to keep up this nonsense. I? In danger? Really, Mr. Brayden. I do not appreciate your jest at my expense."

"The danger is quite real, Miss Lessing," said the Duke of Edgeware as he joined them. "Bloody hell, Donal. Get her out now. I've just gotten word. Wooton's been shot."

Cammy gasped. "Is he alive?"

"Yes, supposedly it is merely a flesh wound. But any wound is serious if not properly treated. He is being tended by a doctor right now." He strode to his desk and unlocked a hidden drawer. "Here are some forged papers that might come in handy. And you will need funds." He handed Donal a thick envelope. "Get her hidden, and do it fast. Whoever is after you, Lucy," he said gently, "cannot be far behind."

"Please do as they ask, Miss Lessing. This is not a jest," Cammy said.

"Why would anyone want to hurt me? This must be a mistake. I am important to no one." But the young woman finally allowed Donal to lead her away.

They slipped out through the servants' entrance.

Lorcan raked a hand through his hair. "Ian, do you know what is going on?"

He shook his head. "I have no idea. Fielding came running over here to make certain Donal would get her away as soon as possible. That's all I know."

"I'm the duke's best tracker. Perhaps I had better return to the ministry with Fielding and question Wooton for myself. I'm sorry, Ian. I know this ball is being held in our honor, but the investigation has to start right away. We've already lost precious time."

"I don't think you'll get anything out of him. Stubborn man. Campbell and Fielding already tried to question him, but he won't talk. He wants to go after the culprit himself."

Lor's mouth fell open. "That is idiotic. Why will he not allow us to help? Is he certain there is only one person involved? Seems to me his nemesis has any number of underlings doing his bidding. We need to find those underlings before their trail grows cold."

Ian shook his head. "He won't allow it, Lor. Leave it alone for now."

"How can I? He is doing exactly what he accused me of doing when dealing with Milkwood. He cannot be objective about this matter. I have to go to him." He turned to Cammy. "Love…"

"I'm going with you. I can help." Cammy's head was spinning. She could not imagine what was going through Miss Lessing's mind. What possible connection would she have to the Ice Duke? Suddenly, she knew. "Lor, is she his daughter? I noticed a resemblance in their eyes and the shape of their mouths."

He and Edgeware exchanged looks. "Cammy, love. You cannot repeat this to anyone."

"So, I'm right? This is their connection?"

"I don't know, but I expect you are right. We truly did not put it together until you mentioned it just now."

Edgeware nodded. "Miss Lessing obviously hasn't figured it out, yet. But I think Wooton must have confided in your brother, Lor. I suppose Donal will tell her when the time is right."

"Or she will eventually figure it out herself," Cammy added.

Edgeware turned to Cammy, his expression one of admiration. "Seems all you Farthingale women are exceptionally clever. This investigation might require a woman's intuition. Not to participate in the actual legwork, of course. But to keep us from overlooking any angles."

She expected Lorcan to grumble that it was out of the question but was surprised when he did not. Instead, he included her in the conversation as he began to puzzle it out. "We know someone is out to kill Wooton, and it has nothing to do with any rebel plot or foreign intrigue. He obviously fears someone knows

Miss Lessing is his secret daughter…thank you, Cammy, for pointing it out. So, who would want to hurt them both?"

"The cuckholded husband?" Cammy offered.

"Yes, he is the logical suspect. But the man Miss Lessing's mother was married to died ten years ago. And His Grace is not married, so it cannot be his wronged wife."

"Are you sure he was never married?" Cammy asked.

Edgeware laughed. "No, not certain of it at all."

"Or perhaps she is adopted, and these are not her natural parents?"

Lorcan took her hand. "Come along with me, love."

Her breath caught. "You are taking me with you?"

"Yes, unless you would rather remain at the ball."

She glanced apologetically at their host. "Your Grace, I am so sorry. It is unpardonably rude of us to walk out on you. Dillie will never forgive me, and rightfully so. But…"

"The chance to assist in an active Crown investigation is irresistible, is it not?" He cast her a wry smile. "Dillie will understand once I explain it to her. Besides, you were here for the important part."

She cast him a bright smile. "Thank you."

"Cammy, one more thing."

"Yes?"

Edgeware grinned at her. "Try not to egg any houses along the way."

She left with Lorcan in one of Edgeware's carriages since she had come to the ball with her aunt and uncle, and Lorcan had grabbed a ride with Romulus and Violet. She leaned back against the elegant squabs the moment they were underway. "Lor," she said with a groan, "does everyone know what I did to Lord Montague?"

He cast her an affectionate smile. "Only the elite agents of the Crown. Wooton couldn't stop laughing when he heard. He admires you all the more for it."

"I like him, too. He is a most interesting man. Do you think he will be able to describe his assailant to me? I could draw a sketch of him. Shayne was able to do this for the arsonist Willow saw setting fire to the Ashcott Inn's carriage house. It would be helpful, don't you think?"

He wrapped his hands around her waist and lifted her onto his lap. "It would. But you are not to involve yourself beyond this. Do not encourage him. He is already eager to make an agent out of you. I will never allow it, Cammy."

She knew he meant it for her own protection. She did not have his fortitude or his predatory instincts. She could not even tell a fib without blushing. Nor could she ever be cold, calculating, or ruthless, or ever want to become that sort of person. "Then why are you allowing me to ride with you?"

"Because he will not listen to anything his agents have to say. But he might be swayed by you. Sometimes, it takes a woman's touch. Especially one he admires as much as he does you."

She shook her head to dismiss the notion.

"Cammy, what you survived…what you endured…and yet still maintained your beautiful soul, that takes enormous strength. You have no idea how proud I am of you. How much I admire and love you."

She wrapped her arms around him. "I do have an idea, Lor. You make me feel beautiful and happy every day. I am healing because of you. And you needn't worry that I might ever want to be an agent. I'd much rather be chairman of the Explorers' Club…and your wife, of course. These hands of mine were meant to hold a paintbrush, not a pistol."

He held her in his arms as their carriage continued along the busy London streets, past the Covent Garden hawkers and flower girls, past the well-dressed dandies on their way to the theaters and private clubs.

She rested her head against his shoulder. "Lor…"

"Yes, Cammy."

"I love you so much."

He tipped her chin up and lowered his mouth to hers, quietly absorbing her scent, the touch, and taste of her. She put great stock in *The Book of Love*, believing it had brought them together. Love was a miracle, with or without that book to help it along.

Love was a journey of the heart.

The carriage drew to a halt in front of the ministry.

He hopped out and held out his hand to assist her. "I love you, too."

No other words were necessary. She was the treasure of his heart, and he was glad she knew it. But he had learned something important from that book. Marriage to the right person was not a ball and chain, as some jokingly referred to it. Quite the opposite, it set you free to follow your dreams and become the person you wanted to be.

He was proud to be that husband for Cammy. She was blossoming into someone special, always loving, but now daring and confident of herself and her talents. He smiled as she cast him that dreamy-eyed look of love. "Come, love. Ready to save the world?"

Also by Meara Platt

FARTHINGALE SERIES
My Fair Lily
The Duke I'm Going To Marry
Rules For Reforming A Rake
A Midsummer's Kiss
The Viscount's Rose
Earl Of Hearts
The Viscount and the Vicar's Daughter
A Duke For Adela
If You Wished For Me
Never Dare A Duke
Capturing The Heart Of A Cameron

BOOK OF LOVE SERIES
The Look of Love
The Touch of Love
The Taste of Love
The Song of Love
The Scent of Love
The Kiss of Love
The Chance of Love
The Gift of Love
The Heart of Love
The Hope of Love (novella)
The Promise of Love
The Wonder of Love
The Journey of Love
The Treasure of Love
The Dance of Love
The Miracle of Love
The Dream of Love (novella)
The Remembrance of Love (novella)
All I Want For Christmas (novella)

MOONSTONE LANDING
Moonstone Landing (novella)
Moonstone Angel (novella)
The Moonstone Duke
The Moonstone Marquess
The Moonstone Major

DARK GARDENS SERIES
Garden of Shadows
Garden of Light
Garden of Dragons
Garden of Destiny
Garden of Angels

LYON'S DEN
The Lyon's Surprise
Kiss of the Lyon
Lyon in the Rough

THE BRAYDENS
A Match Made In Duty
Earl of Westcliff
Fortune's Dragon
Earl of Kinross
Earl of Alnwick
Aislin
Gennalyn
Pearls of Fire
A Rescued Heart
Tempting Taffy

DeWOLFE PACK ANGELS SERIES
Nobody's Angel
Kiss An Angel
Bhrodi's Angel

About the Author

Meara Platt is a *USA Today* bestselling author and an award winning, Amazon UK All-star. Her favorite place in all the world is England's Lake District, which may not come as a surprise, since many of her stories are set in that idyllic landscape, including her award-winning fantasy-romance Dark Gardens series. If you'd like to learn more about the ancient Fae prophecy that is about to unfold in the Dark Gardens series, as well as Meara's lighthearted, international bestselling Regency romances in the Farthingale series and Book of Love series, or her more emotional Braydens series, please visit her website at www.meara platt.com.

www.ingramcontent.com/pod-product-compliance
Lightning Source LLC
Chambersburg PA
CBHW071435200726
48294CB00002B/651